I0679646

THE WARLORD'S CONCUBINE

By

PAUL BLADES

Dark Visions Publications
darkvisionspub@gmail.com

Other books by Paul Blades:

Klitzman's Isle*
Klitzman's Empire*
Klitzman's Paradise*
The Taking of Cheryl Part One**
The Taking of Cheryl Part Two: Slaver's Bait**
Comfort Girl No. 4**
Sacrifice to the Emerald God**
The Blue Cantina: Anna's Surrender**

The Maddy Saga:

Vol. I	Maddy Become a Ponygirl*
Vol. II	The Training of a Ponygirl*
Vol. III	Ponygirl Champion*
Vol. IV	Ponygirl Summer*
Vol. V.	Ponygirl Love
Vol. VI	Ponygirl Season
Vol. VII	Ponygirl Gambit
Vol. VIII	Ponygirl Pleasures
Vol. IX	Ponygirl Peril
Vol. X	Ponygirl's Choice, Part One and Part Two

* Available as a paperback at Amazon.com and an ebook at bdsmbooks.com
** Available as a paperback and an ebook at pinkflamingo.com

军阀 外家

Chapter One

The Yangtze River runs from the port city of Shanghai to the foothills of the Tibetan Plateau, almost 4,000 miles. It has been called the 'main street' of China and divides the northern and southern regions of that ancient land. For centuries, the river has served as a lifeline for commerce between the eastern and western parts of that nation.

In April, 1922, the bend of the Yangtze at Junshan, about 350 miles, as the bird flies, from Shanghai, was controlled by the warlord Wang Ku. Wang was the absolute, brutal master of approximately 400 square miles of territory ranging from Chengshu in the west to Baling in the east. His writ ran about ten miles from each bank of the river, straddling the border between Hunan and Wuhan Provinces. It included the busy, port city of Yeuyang. His large, stone fortress, dating back to the 13th century, sat on a 500' high prominence in the middle of the Junshan peninsula, which, looking at a map of the river appears as a huge camel hump.

The river winds slowly here unlike its headwaters to the west where narrow gorges constrict its flow and make the river sometimes treacherous. From the upper reaches of Wang's fortress you can see for several miles in each direction, and the vista includes the town of Yeuyang and much of the river that stands within his domain.

Wang's army, on which his power rested, numbered about 350 men, more than enough to control the river traffic and to force the British trading companies in Shanghai to pay a small king's ransom to protect the shipments of opium and other goods on which much of their profits depended. That and the tolls that Wang extracted from each river traveler made Wang a very wealthy and powerful man.

On this date in April, 1922, Wang was getting ready to celebrate his fiftieth birthday. He had been the practical ruler of his domain for over twenty years. He was the proud owner of a British made, three decker, paddle wheeled steamboat and he was making ready to begin his spring visit to the great metropolis of Shanghai. It took four days to navigate the Yangtze by steamboat from Yeuyang, where his boat was docked, to Shanghai. He would stay there for the better part of two weeks and then return. He had business interests in the sinful city and liked to make the trip at least four times a year to check up on them. There were certain arrangements he had to make before he left, cargo that had to be gathered and loaded, and instructions to his underlings and retainers to be left. As we find him on the 7th day of April, 1922, he is about to perform a ritual that he engages in on every occasion that he spends any considerable time from his castle.

He is in the well appointed, sumptuous quarters that serve as home to his three concubines. Concubinage is an ancient custom in China and the three women that currently serve him as virtual sexual slaves are kneeling before him, foreheads to the floor, their exquisite silken gowns pulled up around their waists, their delicate, porcelain hindquarters presented for their master's whip. He will be away from them for more than three weeks and it is important for him to give them all a reminder of their duties to him and the consequences of disobedience.

Wang customarily uses a three foot long, thin, bamboo rod to discipline his women. It is thick enough so that the blows he lands do not normally result in lacerations and consequential scarring, and thin enough so that the rod remains flexible and so gives added emphasis to each blow.

The three women are delightfully beautiful. Two of them are Chinese, daughters of local merchants granted to him in exchange for certain economic concessions. They have served him since their eighteenth birthdays, having been especially schooled in the arts of love and culture for that purpose. When he tires of them, he will marry them off to one of his officers or to one of the other social climbing merchants within his domain. The two graceful, exquisitely thin, young women, Me Ling and Pu Wei, are 19 and 21 years old, respectively, have long, shimmering, black hair and faces that compare to summer flowers in their delicacy and serenity. Their breasts are small, firm, ripe apples to delight a man's lips; their hips are narrow and their feet are small.

The third indentured female is not Chinese, but Occidental. She has long, blond hair the color of butter which she keeps in a braid down her back. Her breasts are full and heavy, her hips wide and yet curvaceous. Her face is angelic, with a slim, perfectly proportioned nose, delicate lips and eyes of sapphire blue.

Where Me Ling and Pu Wei have round, exquisitely demure rear cheeks, the blond woman's are full and bold and yet enticingly firm. Her name is Tatiana and she is Russian. She is 22 years old. Her family fled the Bolsheviks in 1920, near the conclusion of the Russian civil war. They had gathered up what remained of their portable wealth and made their way south and east, hoping to reach Shanghai where relatives and friends awaited them. Their boat was intercepted by a river patrol of Wang's men. They had been traveling on a junk they hired in Chengdu, having crossed the border at Bakhty in eastern Kazakhstan and traveled by cart over the desert and mountains and down to the Yangtze. The overland trip had taken them almost two months.

Everything probably would have been all right. The boat master had made ready the toll to be paid. However, Lieutenant Yin decided to make an inspection to see if there was anything of value aboard from which an additional fee could be extorted. Hidden inside the lid of an old, battered trunk, he discovered the Lamitovs' treasure of golden, Russian Double Eagles. The specially minted, one ounce, czarist coins numbered close to a hundred.

Now, Yin was smart enough to know that there was no way he could make off with the Lamitovs' fortune. His master, Wang, or as he called himself, General Wang, would certainly learn of it and there would be no place in China small or remote enough for Yin to hide in. His men would certainly talk. At the least, his family would be massacred. And so Yin commandeered the boat and brought it into port in Yueyang. Wang was appropriately grateful for the lieutenant's discovery, rewarding him with three of the valuable coins, a veritable fortune to the young lieutenant, and gifting him a peasant's daughter who had been taken by Wang in lieu of taxes from a local farmer.

All of the male members of the Lamitov party were beheaded in the courtyard of Wang's fortress along with the boat's master and his crew of four. Tatiana's mother and two older sisters, Marina and Adriana, were sold to a whorehouse in Nanking, after witnessing their husbands' and brothers' demise, and having spent some time entertaining Wang and his officers. The beautiful, virginal Tatiana he kept for himself. The boat and its cargo, and the rest of the Lamitovs' belongings, were sold and the proceeds were split, 70/30, between Wang and the men of Yin's patrol.

Wang took a moment to appreciate the rearward pointing charms of his three concubines. Their rear cheeks curved gracefully, their pouty, little love lips, devoid of all hair, peeked out from under them. It was an inspiring sight. Last night, knowing that he would be away for three weeks or so, he had spent a lustful evening with his female property. The tincture of rhinoceros horn and certain local herbs had filled his prick with steel and given him five extraordinary climaxes. He had used all of their portals at one time or another. The exposure of the women's twin lower gates of pleasure now made his cock stiffen.

Wang was eminently grateful for the munificence of fate. He endowed a local monastery to officially record his gratitude and to ensure continued good fortune.

Me Ling, as the number one concubine, would go first. He stepped behind her and gave the bamboo cane a practice swing, producing a satisfying and pleasant 'whoosh!' as it cut through the air. Me Ling gave out a little sob.

Without further warning, Wang reared his hand back and brought the cane down on the almost snow white posterior of the trembling girl. The 'crack!' resounded through the well appointed room and Me Ling gave out an anguished cry.

"Oooooooohhhhhhh!" she yelled. Her little hands were balled up into tight fists and tears started to flow from her pretty, jewel like eyes. Wang reared his hand back again and delivered the second of the five blows that the slave would receive.

"Ahhhhhhhh! Ahhhhhhhh!" the slender, shapely girl gave out as the pain of the impact coursed through her. Her tears increased their volume, streaming down her pretty face and onto the soft, thick rug that lay underneath her. Two long, red lines marred the pristine flesh of her buttocks.

By the time that the fifth blow had been landed, Me Ling was sobbing woefully. The angry red lines across her rear cheeks were evenly spaced, expertly laid down, and looked like a tiger had drawn its paw across them from right to left.

Pu Wei had started crying silently when the first blow had landed on Me Ling's rear. As Wang prepared to give her her due, she started to sob and whine. Wang watched her dainty rear entrance contract in fear. He had spent twenty minutes plowing that hole last night. He recalled its tightness on his sturdy pole and the warmth of her bowel's murky depths. The young lady had never really become acclimated to ass fucking and he enjoyed the humiliated look she always gave him when he ordered her to present her rear to him, in much the same position she was in now.

Pu's piteous wails echoed through the room as he slowly, forcefully and methodically applied the five strokes to her bottom.   At the fourth stroke, she flinched and, as a consequence, he gave her one extra.

Now, it was Tatiana's turn. Wang had not used the full extent of his strength on Me Ling's and Pu's hindquarters. The flesh there was just a little too thin and delicate for that. With Tatiana, he need have no qualms about going all out. Her rear flesh was suitably padded to accept the full force of his blows.

The unhappy Russian girl was well aware that she always received the worst of Wang's attentions when it came to a whipping. Life was hard for the blond strumpet. When her family was obliterated, she cried for days and days, weeks. She had no idea where she was. Somewhere in China was all she knew.   She had only now, after two years as one of Wang's whores, begun to understand some elementary Chinese other then the one or two word commands her master gave her to suck his cock or spread her legs. Having no prospect of rescue, she awoke daily with a heavy heart. Me Ling and Pu were kind to her, at least they tried to be, but Wang's two wives were cruel and rapacious. Wang, as was his habit, was taking his number one wife, Li Hua, with him on his trip. His number two wife, Yu Jie, had to stay behind. There was no doubt that she would take out her anger on the three concubines, especially Tatiana, who she liked to torment with her seven tasseled whip and often forced to service her insatiable quim.

Tatiana's teeth were clenched tightly and her muscles tensed as she awaited her turn at torment. Every time that she was whipped, and it seemed to be very often, she was filled with self pity and remorse for the loss of her loved ones and her future. Muri, her fiancé, had preceded the Lamitov family to Shanghai and he had been awaiting her there.

Instead of the full, happy life that she anticipated with him, she now faced only a dark, dismal future. She spent all of her days and nights in the castle but for the occasional sojourn to a lake or into the mountains with her master. While he spent his days hunting or boating, he spent his nights abusing her or whichever of the other concubines he brought with him. Twice, she had snuck out of the seraglio and reached the outer walls of the fortress. Twice she had been caught and punished severely. She often thought of throwing herself out of the window of the concubines' dormitory to the cobblestones some 50' below, but her faith in an everlasting paradise deterred her. It was enough that she had to spend her life in hell; she didn't want to spend eternity there too. Besides, unless she did a header into the ground, the fall would probably not kill her, but would maim her for life instead.

The bamboo cane gave a vicious whistle as it tore through the air towards Tatiana's defenseless rear cheeks. When it struck her, it depressed the flesh where it landed. Tatiana emitted a woeful howl. Her ass burned as if a fiery torch had been dragged across it. The pain filled her whole being. Her stomach quailed and her heart pounded. She knew that she had four to go and that she dared not move an inch or she would receive more.

A few, seemingly everlasting seconds later, the second stroke descended. This one struck her rear on the curve of her buttocks, near the tops of her thighs. She howled again. Her body shook. Her chest was wracked with sobs. She clenched her fists tightly until her knuckles were a stark white. Her long, tapered fingernails, covered with red, shiny lacquer, dug deeply into her palms. Her mouth was dry as the desert that she and her family had had to cross in their ill fated flight from the communists.

The third blow produced an anguished scream from the young woman as did the fourth. She fruitlessly tried to prepare herself for the last, the one that she dreaded the most. Wang always put special effort into the final stroke.

The jaded, brutal warlord paused before delivering the last blow. His cock was as hard as a rifle barrel. If he were not beginning his voyage to the city of sin, he would surely take the time to have one of his whores satisfy him with her mouth. But it was almost eight o'clock in the morning and he wanted to travel as far as he could today.

Wang counted to three in his mind, the infernal instrument poised behind him. It made an evil 'whoosh!' as it sailed forward. The force of the blow lifted him slightly off of his feet.

The hysterical, blond concubine howled as she felt the impact of the cane. It was as if her master had taken a knife and scoured her skin with it, digging a deep channel across her rear. Her howl turned into a scream and then back into a howl again. Her face was awash with tears. When her howling ceased, her heavy, deep sobs resumed. She desperately tried to stop them, knowing that her master had his limits as to how much expression of anguish he would tolerate. As soon as she could, she closed her widespread, painted lips tightly and held them in.

Wang was immensely satisfied with the early morning session. He was sure that his whores would remember well the lesson he had taught them. The Russian would probably not be able to sit down for a week.

The cruel bandit, for that's what he really was, turned and handed the whip to his eunuch, Li Pao. Li would rule all of his women while the master was gone. He would make sure that they were bathed and painted daily as if their overlord was there.   He would, thrice daily, manipulate them to orgasm to ensure that they stayed sufficiently passionate. There was always the chance that a local or foreign dignitary or two would stop by while Wang was away and the enslaved beauties needed to be ready to service them.   Wang was generous with his whores and often, at dinner parties, he would have them whipped for the amusement of his guests and permit them to select one for use for the night. And it was a matter of principle. The women should know that even though his physical presence was hundreds of miles away, his will and his spirit still inhabited his fortress and dominated their lives.

Wang paused once more to take in the vision of the lovely, bare posteriors all lined with long, red marks. He took in the sight of their soft, hairless pussies, peaking out from under their marred buttocks like cute, little creatures wanting to come out and play. How long would it really take to satisfy his raging hard on, he asked himself. He could be quick about it.

Having decided to relieve himself in the body of one of his sexual servants, he had to decide which one. His thinking had already gone from the possibility of receiving oral delight to piercing one of their hairless honey pots.

It was the vision of Tatiana that was the most compelling this morning. While the lash marks on the two Chinese sluts were narrow and flat, the harsher impact of the cane on the Russian girl's ass had left a wider, almost purple imprint. The flesh was slightly raised on the places where she had been wounded.

Wang had decided. And when Wang decided something, the next phase was always action. He unhooked the buttons to the fly of his crisply pressed, elegantly tailored, red striped, olive brown, uniform pants and produced his manly weapon.

He uttered four words in Chinese roughly translated as, "Whore Number Three, ready yourself."

Tatiana had a clear understanding of the gist of the words if not their literal meaning. She quickly spread her knees, raised her rump and snuck her hand between her thighs, taking possession of her soft, tender, denuded crevasse. Immediately, her mind shifted from bemoaning her cruel fate to the necessity of flooding her quim with her juices to ease the passage of the heartless warlord.

Frantically, she began to rub at her unusually large button of love. She had not known it was unusually large until she had an opportunity to view the pussies of her two co-prisoners close up while she pleasured them for the amusement of her master or his guests. Her sisters had never fully undressed before her and sex was something just not talked about in her refined home. It explained a lot of things to her, such as why she had been tormented with longing for physical love ever since puberty, a longing that produced a guilt so strong that she actually confessed it to her priest. He had told her that God had sent her a trial to bear and the fate of her soul depended on her ability to resist the urge to pleasure herself or to seek relief outside of marriage. Ignoring her bulging clit was useless, however; her mind remained focused on it almost all the time. In the winter, she had to forgo underwear since the coldness when she went outside made the organ stiffen and rub against it.

Now, Tatiana considered her former trial as a gift. Wang was always severely displeased when one of his whores failed to lubricate herself satisfactorily for him. But it took only five or ten seconds of rubbing for Tatiana to begin to produce the discharge that would moisten her canal and insure her master an easy, comfortable time of it.

True to her nature, the Russian girl's twat was soon ready for fucking. Wang had watched the girl's delicate fingers as they snaked underneath her and addressed her wonderful, appealing entrance. He saw the red capped fingers slide into her quim and begin a thrusting motion, indicating that she was well ready for him.

Lowering himself to his knees, the warlord crept up to Tatiana's beckoning love hole. He presented his sleek, uncut cock to the entrance and pressed forward and up. His piece slid right in.

Wang gave an appreciative moan as he felt the warm, soft tissue of Tatiana's cunt's walls. He was tempted to linger inside her for a while, but he knew that he had to make quick work of it. He grabbed the girl's wide, graceful hips and began to thrust himself back and forth. His narrow eyes rolled backwards, his jaw slackened, his mouth opened as he absorbed the delights of Tatiana's pussy.

The girl, herself, was experiencing her normal, ecstatic pleasure at having her tunnel traversed by a hot, thick cock. Especially at this angle, her master's cock dragged across her engorged love bud enthrallingly. Momentarily, the pain she had just suffered was forgotten, the fact that she was a forlorn whore, a prisoner among strangers whose customs and language were foreign to her own, ran right out of her mind. Later, she would rue her bout of passion. She knew that God had his reasons for permitting the big Chinese man to capture and enslave her. Her thinking had brought herself to the point where she came to believe that it was a punishment for her heightened sexual drive, a drive that she had given into many, guilt ridden times by the use of her fingers back in Moscow when alone in her soft, comforting bed. And every time the callous, Asian man, his guests, his wives or her fellow prisoners drove her to passion, she knew that her tormented existence would be extended by the divine power just that much more as punishment.

Tatiana began to moan with pleasure as Wang's cock continued its sawing motions back and forth in her vagina. She clenched her fists and tightened her body, much like she had done when she was beaten, in order to try and fight off the completion of her passion. But it was no use. By the twentieth stroke of Wang's thick rod, her crescendo had started to build. By the twenty fifth, it was ready to burst. Before the thirtieth, her crises resolved itself by sending wave after wave of excruciating pleasure through her body. Her innards shook and her pussy throbbed.

Wang's cock took this as the signal to burst into rapid action. The warlord groaned as he felt his cock pulse and spurt inside the former Russian maiden. His hands gripped tighter on her hips, his eyes closed, his lips trembled. "Aaaaaaaarrrrrgh! Aaaarrrrrrrrgh! Aaaarrrrrrrrgh!" he shouted at each convulsion of his meat, each exclamation of his pleasure growing louder and louder.

When his cock's delivery of his seed to the pale, voluptuous concubine relented, he bent over her prone body and took a deep breath. Each time that he came inside the bodies of one of his indentured females, or any other one of the various sluts he fucked on his trips around his duchy, he made a little prayer of thanks to his ancestors and their family gods for choosing him to raise the family to such enviable heights and to provide him with so much delectable flesh to enjoy.

It was an immensely satisfied Wang that walked down to the dock to board his steamboat about twenty minutes later. It was his birthday in seven days and he planned a huge celebration in Shanghai at having achieved a half a century of life. Standing by the quay were seven, young, peasant girls. They had stripped off their peasant's garb, and their clothes were sitting in little piles in front of them. Wang gave the young women a cursory inspection. Major Won, as usual, had done a good job at selecting them. Considered virtually useless mouths at home, their fathers were glad to receive the small recompense for the transfer of their ownership to the great General Wang.

They were destined for the whorehouses of Shanghai. He ran a very elegant one himself and would pick the best of the lot before retailing the rest out. He would make a tidy profit and receive the gratitude of the owners and operators of the houses of delight which received them. They were all pretty and all virgins, something that had been checked personally by Major Won. They, or most of them at least, would remain virgins in a technical sense until they reached their destinations. He would, of course, sample the mouths and rear entrances of them all during the four day journey. He made a vow to limit himself to two vaginal deflowerings. After all, he was only human.

Wang nodded to the soldiers who were guarding the unhappy, young women and they began to hustle them on board. They would travel naked, in a large cage on the rear deck of the first level of the ship. There was ample room for them in the hold, but having them above decks made it easier to retrieve them when needed and simpler to feed them, clean them with a hose or to remove their wastes. As they ran fearfully onto the ship, encouraged by three foot long whippy sticks wielded by the soldiers, they left behind seven little piles of clothes, which looked like seven peasant women had disappeared into thin air leaving only their coarse raiment behind.

The living area for Wang and his party were on the upper level of the ship. He was greeted by the captain as he boarded the vessel and he had advised him that he was free to shove off. The powerful engines had been idling in a low rumble. His first wife and all his attendees were already aboard. Almost coincidental to Wang's arrival on the upper deck, the engine's grumble became a roar and the big wheel behind the ship started to slowly turn. It eased away from the dock and pointed itself downstream.

On the third level of the fortress, high on the hill that dominated the Junshan peninsula, three pairs of feminine eyes watched from the balcony to their abode as the large, bulky steamboat made its way to the center of the broad, muddy river. Each of them had different thoughts as they watched it go away. Me Ling was relieved that the man was gone since she would not have to service his thick cock with her mouth, something she was loath to do, until he returned in about a month. Pu Wei was relieved that her delicate little bung hole would be undisturbed for the time the master was away. Both forecasts were dependant on no VIP's showing up, of course.

Tatiana's thoughts were different. She watched the large boat drift away down the river with sadness. It was the route to her freedom, she knew that at least, and a trip she would almost certainly never make. She was no fool and knew that some day the master would tire of her. She had no idea what would happen to her then, but she couldn't imagine that it would result in her freedom or be better than her life here where, under usual circumstances, she only had to service her lord every three days.

A pit opened in her stomach as she watched the ship navigate the bend in the river. From her perch on the third floor of the fortress, she would be able to watch it wind its way downriver for another half hour or so. She had watched it disappear thusly many times. She knew she was torturing herself by watching it. She couldn't help it. Her longing for freedom was a heartache that permeated her entire being. As the ship got smaller and smaller, she wiped away her tears.

军阀 外家

CHAPTER TWO

Later, that same day, Violet Howard, a tall, lanky, stylish, 27 year old Englishwoman, with shoulder length, chestnut colored hair was looking out from the sixth floor veranda of the Sterling Hotel at the ragged, unfathomable skyline that was the native portion of Shanghai. She too had reason to be sad.

Violet had arrived in Shanghai just yesterday. She had traveled by ocean liner from Plymouth, through the Mediterranean and the Suez Canal, across the Indian Ocean into the South China Sea. Having caught unusually favorable currents, the ship arrived one day early. Right now, she wished that it hadn't.

She had come to China to marry Robert Preston, a 40ish trader for the firm of Babcock and Witherspoon. The firm was an old line Shanghai firm and obtained silks, jade, teakwood, silver, rice and a dozen other commodities from the Chinese hinterland. In exchange, it sent up river a plenitude of manufactured goods and, some people alleged, opium.

Opium had been the key to unlocking the vast China market to the British almost a hundred years ago in the first Opium War. At the point of British bayonets, the Chinese were forced, among other things, to permit the free trading of opium throughout the country. The proved to be an immense cash crop for the British who would import the product from its colony in India and sell it to the Chinese. The drug proved devastating to China, creating millions of addicts, destabilizing the central government and becoming a huge net economic drain in trade with the British. Although formally outlawed by the British in 1917, Shanghai remained an important port of entry for the drug for many years afterwards, cloaked under the vast volume of trade that passed through that port.

Violet, had heard many evil things about the opium trade from her father, who had help spearhead the drive in Britain to outlaw it. She knew that Robert's firm had a long history of importing opium to China, but he swore in his letters that they had nothing to do with it any more.

Violet was considered virtually an old maid by her family. Even though she was pretty, shapely, although a tad on the thin side, and amiable, she had had no offers. This was fine with Violet who studied the piano for many years. It was her passion even though she never attained concert hall quality. She had a small salary from teaching piano in a Devonshire private school, but lived mostly off of the income of her father. She loved the theater, poetry, good books, tennis and her coterie of female friends. There had been rumors about her sexual orientation due to her preference to spend her time with women, but they were not true.

Lord Howard was three degrees of relation away from the Royal Family. Lady Howard had passed many years before and Lord Howard lived as a bachelor for fifteen years. Unfortunately, he had developed quite ravenous gambling and drinking habits. He had died about a year before Violet's departure from England, having, in a drunken stupor, stepped from the front door of one of his favorite gambling haunts directly into the path of a speeding newspaper delivery van. Violet was his only child and heir.

Uncle Neddie, Lord Howard's younger brother, inherited the title. There was little else to pass on. The family estate was heavily mortgaged and Lord Howard had been deeply in debt. There had been a little cash, maybe three hundred pounds, in an account dedicated to Violet, and she had been able to live off of it for about a year. At the end of the year, there was some of the money left but it was clear that Violet would have to do something soon.

Violet was not a snob, although she had no desire to marry out of her social ranking. She found, however, the men of her social set vain, irresponsible, venal and shallow. All of the good ones, it seemed, had given their lives in the Great War or were so damaged by the experience that they were not husband material. These were the two principal reasons that she never married. After a long talk with Aunt Lillian, Uncle Neddie's wife, Violet agreed that she would have to marry or sink into the lower classes.

It just so happened that Aunt Lillian's cousin was great friends with the Earl of Wilford. His oldest son, Robert, was working in Shanghai and had been a bachelor all his life. The family had gotten together and demanded that he marry and produce an heir. Aunt Lillian called Lady Preston and they both agreed that Violet and Robert should marry. It was a wonderful opportunity for Violet to come into vast wealth and a chance for Robert to wed a solid, sensible woman of his own class.

Pictures and letters had been exchanged. Violet liked Robert's tone in his letters. And he was handsome. From everything the family and his friends told her, he was kind and considerate. He was Oxford educated, of course, and alleged to be abstemious when it came to alcohol. After a brief correspondence she agreed to marry him, recalling the phrase, "Close your eyes, spread your legs and think of England."

She was not without experience in matters of physical love. There had been a boy once, when she was nearly twenty. He was sandy haired, athletic, charming. One summer he had swept Violet off of her feet and they had done the deed. Many times, actually, throughout the entire summer. Violet had liked it. She had liked it a lot. In

September, the boy's fiancé came back from Southern France and that was that. Later, he was killed in France too.

Violet had had no knowledge of the existence of the fiancé and her heart was broken. She vowed never to fall in love again. That was why, when a union based not on love but rather on mutual convenience was suggested, she acquiesced.

Since the boat had arrived in Shanghai one day early, there was no one to meet Violet at the dock. The wireless had been out of order on board and she was not able to send a message in advance of her early arrival. She didn't have the telephone number of Robert's office or its address. She did have Robert's address in the International Settlement and she climbed into a taxi and gave it to the driver.

It took two hours to go the maybe five miles between the dock and Robert's house. The narrow streets were clogged with all kinds of humanity and the taxi had to edge forward slowly the whole time. It was not until they reached the International Settlement, that part of Shanghai in which the writ of the Chinese government did not run, that they were finally able to make some time. Robert's house was a mansion located near the edge of the Settlement on Hungkow Road. When she arrived, there seemed to be a storm brewing in the house. There was a panel truck in the large courtyard and some Chinese workers were loading suitcases and trunks into it. From the house was coming a god awful screaming, a woman's voice, like someone had violated someone's most tender sensibilities.

Violet climbed the four steps up to the porch of the mansion nervously. The door was open and she peered in. Seeing no one, she let herself in and called, "Robert! Robert! I'm here!"

The voices were coming from upstairs. Another Chinese worker began to descend the stairs carrying one more trunk.

Behind him came Robert and the source of the aural discord, a thin, well dressed, shapely, young Chinese girl. Her hair was cut into a fashionable bob and she was wearing a flowery, silk blouse. Her black skirt was tight and a little above her knees. She was wearing black, 4" high heels and sheer, silk stockings. She was still yelling as she came down the stairs. Violet understood why the words she was speaking were indecipherable to her. She was speaking Chinese.

It was then that Robert saw her. His face went white as a ghost's. His jaw dropped open and he started to stammer, reaching out for the arm of his companion.

The woman, who looked like she was maybe 22 or 23 years old, was looking down at her feet as she navigated the stairs and did not see Violet until Robert pulled at her arm. She stopped screaming.

"V,violet, what are you doing here?" Robert stammered.

"My boat arrived early," she told him. Her eyes were wide open in disbelief. From everything that she could tell, Robert had been living with a native tart. He was rushing to get all traces of her out of the house before Violet arrived.

Violet was shocked. She understood that men normally have more experience than women when they marry, especially a man creeping up on middle age. And she understood that sometimes they paid for their pleasures and even used native women to allay their passions. But to actually live with one bespoke a lack of social sense that cast great doubt on everything that she had been told about Robert. And he didn't even have the intelligence, or discretion, to move the girl out of the house a week early so that there would be no possibility of Violet being confronted with evidence of her in the very home in which she was to commence her married life. Violet realized that if she married Robert she would be the scandal of the whole International Settlement. Clearly, Robert had made no effort to disguise his relationship with the strumpet. She wondered if he was really breaking it off with her or just moving her to a new location, maybe not as convenient, but accessible readily nonetheless.

"I,I'm sorry, Robert," she said. "My taxi is waiting outside. I'm going to a hotel. If my things are delivered here, please arrange to forward them. I don't know where I'll be staying, but I'll get the number from the concierge and phone your office to let you know."

"I've reserved a suite for you at the Sterling," Robert said. "It wouldn't be proper for you to stay here with me until we are actually married."

Violet laughed bitterly. "You have an awfully warped sense of propriety, Robert," she said. "I had no intention of staying here. No one met me at the boat. I didn't know what hotel to go to and so I came here instead. I cannot pay for a ticket back to England and I don't know when the next boat will be leaving. I would ask if you would do me the courtesy of booking me a passage. I will endeavor to pay you back later, a bit at a time, after I get home."

"Please, Violet, let me explain," Robert entreated her.

Violet took another look at the floozy. "I don't think that there's anything to explain. Please send me a note as soon as you can as to when I will be sailing."

At that, Violet turned and walked out of the house. A she strode towards the door, the young girl resumed her screeching.

As she stood now, gazing over the mysterious, hyperactive city, Violet tried to hold back her tears. All of her struggles to accept this arranged marriage had been for nothing. She felt so alone in the world. She was sorry that her father had pissed the family fortune away, not that there had been all that much to piss away to begin with, but she did not hate him for what he did. Violet had a strong streak of fatalism in her. What is, is what's meant to be.

Robert called on her later that afternoon, around six. He begged her to meet him for a drink so that he could make things right with her. She had come all this way and had such high hopes that her marriage with Robert would work out that she decided that she should at least talk to him.

She drank a gin and tonic, Robert had a brandy. "So much for being abstemious," she thought. Robert begged her to forgive him. He explained that he had been living as a bachelor for over twenty years and that he had developed some very bad habits. He swore that his wild oats had all been sewn. He had been trying to break it off with the girl for weeks, but he couldn't get her to move out. He had hired the movers and had them do all her packing on the day that Violet arrived. That's why the girl had been so upset.

"Give me one week, please," he asked her desperately. He would be the laughingstock of the Settlement if she went back to England. He couldn't stand it. It would be humiliating. And what would his father say? The title that he held did not require it to be descended on his eldest son. His father could pick his younger brother, Lawrence, instead.

"I've bought you the ticket. You leave in seven days. Please let me show you who I really am before you reject me. Give me those seven days, please."

Violet gave it some thought. What would her life be like if she returned to England? How would she earn her keep? Giving piano lessons? And would she die an old maid? Maybe it was better if she could get a sense if Robert was sincere when he said that he would change. She could live with the scandal of him having lived with a native girl in their marital domicile if it brought her a lifetime of, if not happiness, at least contentment. The money didn't mean that much to her beyond what was absolutely necessary for her to live on. And then there was the issue of children.

Ever since her pathetic affair with Mr. Sandy Hair, Violet had convinced herself that having children was not important to her. However, when the issue was raised in the midst of the discussions with Robert's family, it seemed paramount to them. It had caused her to reassess her thinking. When she thought about it, she didn't want to spend a lifetime with no children to raise, no babies to hold close, no little girls or little boys to help grow up, no one to comfort her in her old age. She thought of that now.

"Okay," she said. "One week. But we'll start tomorrow. I'm too tired to do anything tonight and I've had quite a shock."

"I understand fully," Robert replied. "I'll come around at 10 tomorrow morning. We can have breakfast together and then I'll start to show you the sights."

The next morning, true to his word, Robert appeared at ten and they had breakfast together in her suite. He was bright and chipper, considerate of her opinions and feelings as she expressed them and, all around, just awfully nice. After breakfast he took her to the docks in the Chinese section of the city. There she saw the vast navy of junks and sampans that plied the bay, the lifeblood of Shanghai. They had lunch at the golf club and she met some of his friends. They had dinner at a Chinese restaurant where Robert was well known and he ordered everything in Chinese. They danced in the hotel ballroom until the early hours. The next day and the next and the next were all the same, except different. Robert had an activity for every day, tennis, horseracing, swimming. She even allowed him to convince her to play a round of golf with him. It was all she could do to hit the tiny, white ball. The Chinese caddy had to run into the woods many times to try and find it. She had fun nonetheless.

It was on the evening of the fifth day that she made her decision. Robert was nice, but she didn't believe for a minute he was sincere in his representation that he would not stray from the marriage. There was nothing to the man, no true sincerity. It had all been a foolish dream anyway. Something would happen when she got back to England. Violet had a strong faith and believed that God would reveal his plan to her in time.

The next morning, she had breakfast with Robert as she had every day. After they had eaten, she announced her decision to him. He was downcast.

"I am so sorry to have made you come all the way out here for this," he said.

"That's okay, Robert," Violet replied. "I've never had the chance to travel and now I've seen all kinds of exotic places. I've had fun here in the last few days and I can see why you prefer living here. I just think that the right thing for me to do is go home."

"But," Robert protested, "I still have one more day. You agreed to seven days and its not seven days until tomorrow. Let's pretend that you haven't made up your mind and we'll do the things I planned for us anyway. I think I owe you at least that. I'll hold on to the boat ticket and make all the necessary arrangements for your luggage."

Violet smiled. Robert seemed nice, but he was essentially a charmer. She could tell by how he looked at other women that he was a wanderer. In the long run, if it was kept under control, it might not be a fatal problem. They could reach an arrangement about things. But he lacked discretion and would get caught again and again and again. That she couldn't stand. She did enjoy his company, though and another day of sightseeing would help her put off the dismal feeling he knew she was going to have when the reality of what had happened hit her.

They spent the day touring some Chinese shrines outside the city. Robert called them gates. They were constructed to provide passages for the spirits, to grant good luck and good fortune.

"You have to leave an offering," he told Violet at their third one.

"What shall I offer?" she asked.

"A coin, perhaps," he said. He fished into his pocket and pulled out a large, silver coin and handed it to Violet. She placed it in the middle of the gate and closed her eyes, wishing for contentment. She felt Robert come up behind her and place his hand on her shoulder. He turned her body slightly and then he kissed her. Violet placed her hand on his chest and gently pushed him back.

"Please don't, Robert," she said sadly.

"You can't blame a guy for trying," he said.

"No, I don't blame you, Robert. You're just who you are and that is that," she told him.

They both got into the car that Robert's firm had provided and the Chinese driver took them back to the city. They were silent all during the ride. When they entered the city proper, Robert turned to Violet and said, "We can't have you sitting all alone and forlorn on your last night in Shanghai. Let me take you out to dinner and we'll go to a couple of nightclubs that I sometimes go to. You need to see a little of the wild side of Shanghai before you go."

Violet jumped at the suggestion. She promised herself that she would drink herself into near oblivion.

They had dinner at Club 42 in the Settlement and then they went to paint the town red. They went from nightclub to nightclub, dancing and drinking. In some of the nightclubs they had floorshows. Violet was shocked at the ludeness of the pretty, Chinese girls, but she did not object to it. She kind of enjoyed it.

Then they hit a couple of gambling establishments. Gambling was anathema to Violet because of what it did to her father. She was never going to see Robert again in her life and so she didn't object when he put down a few bets. He lost rather more than she thought reasonable at baccarat in several clubs. Finally, Violet told him that she wanted to go home.

"One last place," Robert begged. "Please, it'll top off your night."

Violet acceded to the request. The club was in the basement of a factory building on the outskirts of the city. There was a little peephole at the door. Robert showed his face and he was granted admission.

The floor of the club was crowded with people. The atmosphere was smoky and redolent of cheap perfume and spilt booze. A jazz band was playing. Robert brought her directly through the tables and chairs to the back of the club. There was another door there and another peephole. Robert knocked, an eye appeared in the door and then it was opened.

It opened to a large room full of gambling tables. Violet didn't know all of the games. From the number of people there, from all walks of life, she began to think that everyone in Shanghai had money to burn. There were Chinese men dressed in those silken gowns the men wear and little, round hats with tassels, there were younger, more modern dressed Chinese men who looked like gangsters. Violet recognized some of the people as Robert's friends and there were other obviously wealthy people there. Most of the women were dressed in high style, but a few looked as if they had seen better days. Some of the people didn't look like they came from money. They had desperate looks on their faces as they took their chances at the tables.

There were also Chinese girls serving liquor to anyone who asked for it. They wore short, little skirts that came down to their mid-thighs, high heel shoes, stockings and nothing else. They received generous tips from the gamblers and she saw one or two walk up the stairs to the upper floors hand in hand with a customer, their little, naked breasts shimmering.

It was thrilling for Violet to be there. Here was a life she had no inkling of. Her life had been protected, safe. Danger seemed to ooze out of the walls. It was fascinating.

Robert sat down at the baccarat table again and started to play. He lost about 200 pounds right away. You needed hard currency to gamble at this establishment.

Violet stood behind him for about twenty minutes and then, bored by the passing back and forth of currency and chips, not knowing what the game was really about, she looked around the room. She saw a roulette table. Now, that she understood.

Robert had finally had enough. He pushed back his chair and downed his drink.

"Let's go, Violet," he said, "before I lose my shirt."

"Okay," she answered him. "But I want to play roulette just once. Please,"

"Sure," Robert said. "How much do you want to bet?"

"What's the minimum bet," she asked.

"Five pounds," he replied.

"That'll do," she said. She reached into her purse. She withdrew a five pound note. "Please buy me a chip, Robert," she asked him.

"Let me pay for it," Robert responded.

"No, I want to pay," she said.

Robert dutifully went over the cashier's window and purchased a single red chip from the attractive, young, Chinese woman behind the cage.

When he returned, he gave the chip to Violet.

* * * * * * * * * * * * * *

Wang was preparing himself for a wonderful day. It was his birthday as of midnight that night and he had gone out with a few of his cronies to test his luck. Money had no meaning to Wang other than what he could get with it. His whorehouses were doing fine and the two factories he had invested in were paying off. His number one son was handling the loan-sharking end of the business in cooperation with one of the local triad gangs. His number two son directed a network of opium dealers in the city and he was also prospering. Of course, Wang was the senior partner in both enterprises.

Wang was not so sure of his position out in his remote fortress in Junshan that he couldn't use some insurance by having some going enterprises in the biggest city in China. Who knows, he might someday be forced out by the growing Kuomintang Nationalist Army. There were rival warlords who could start a war with him and snap up his territory.

The Blue Cantina was one of his favorite gambling houses. He had a couple of his own, but mostly for the common folk, nickel and dime action. They may be nickel and dime, but those nickels and dimes added up. As a culture, the Chinese were addicted to gambling and there was always plenty of money in it.

Wang was standing at the very same roulette table that Violet and Robert were approaching. Robert, recognizing the general even in his finely tailored evening wear, pulled back for a moment. He knew the general rather well and didn't want to get involved with him tonight. It was too late as Violet blithely approached the table.

Wang was on his best behavior. "Good evening, miss," he said to her when she approached. He was immediately attracted to her. She had a noble carriage and fine lines. She wore a long, slinky gown of russet colored silk. It clung to her torso in an alluring way. He could see that her hips were somewhat narrow, but not enough to call her skinny. She wore a string of pearls around her neck. Her chestnut colored hair was cut just below her shoulders and she had a habit of shaking her head to prevent strands of it from getting in front of her face. Her breasts, even though hidden behind her silk bodice, which was cut low in a deep 'v' so that the cleavage between them was exposed, looked succulent and full. In the smoky, dim light of the casino, he could not discern whether her eyes were a pale blue or slate green. In any case, she had a piercing gaze. He was about to compliment her on her beauty when he saw Robert.

"Mr. Preston, so good to see you," he said.

"And you, General Wang," Robert returned. "Here on your quarterly visit?" he asked.

"Yes, and today is my fiftieth birthday, as of one hour ago."

"Happy birthday, General," Robert congratulated him. "And many more," he added.

"Are you a real general?" Violet asked. "You're not in uniform." She was more than a little intoxicated.

"Yes, as you say," Wang replied. His voice was firm, but polite. He spoke English very well, having been sent to the British school in Shanghai by his father when he was a young man. It was during this time that he made all of his Shanghai contacts. "I am on vacation from my duties and dressed as a civilian so that I can relax and be with the people."

"That's very egalitarian of you, General," Violet said sardonically.

"General Wang commands a contingent in northern Hunan Province," Robert told Violet. "He is a very powerful man."

"I've heard that all the Chinese generals deal in opium," Violet said. "Do you deal in opium, General?"

Wang smiled. "I am a general of an army, Miss...." He hesitated.

"Oh, my fault," Robert said. "General Wang, I'd like you to meet my friend, Violet Howard. Violet, the General." He was astounded at the rudeness of Violet's question. Confronting someone directly in China was considered very bad taste. And Wang was definitely not someone to provoke.

Violet reached out her hand and proffered it to the handsome, older man. He had a definite aura of strength about him, was in excellent physical shape. He hardly looked 50, although she was not adept at guessing the ages of European men, never mind Orientals. He was tall, Violet thought, for a Chinaman. He shook her hand gracefully. She shuddered at the contact.

Wang had placed a large pile of chips on the table and was about to sit down. There were three other people already there, one, a man who looked like he had gambled away his life's savings, and two, a woman who sat peering intently at the carpet of numbers where you placed your bet as if it would speak to her if she looked at it long and hard enough. The third was another man, obviously the woman's companion. He looked tired and irritated and kept looking at his pocket watch.

"To answer your question, Miss Howard," the general said to pick up the discussion where it had been interrupted, "I am a servant of the people. My army guards an important trade route. Our government has signed a treaty with your government to forbid the sale of opium. I do my duty to enforce that ban and protect legitimate shipments. That is all." His eyes drank in Violet's whole body as if he had a right to possess it. Violet found it unsettling.

"A very clever response, General," Violet shot back. "I think that the trade in opium is a disgrace. Anyone who peddles it or supports it in any way should be ashamed of themselves." She then paused, realizing that she had launched a very impolite polemic. "But I'm sure that you're not here to discuss politics with me," she continued, trying to correct her social gaffe. "I'm sorry if I interrupted your play."

"Not all, Miss Howard," the general replied in his smooth, deep, slightly accented voice. "And how long will you be staying with us?" he asked politely. Inside, he was raging at this slut's impertinence.

"She's leaving tomorrow," Robert interjected, "on the evening tide, although I wish she wouldn't."

"You should stay, Miss Howard. I'm sure that you would love China if you got to know it," Wang told her. He had a place where she could stay almost indefinitely, for free, he thought. And she would have the opportunity to learn better manners.

"I'm sorry, but I can't," Violet said with a tone of sorrow in her voice. "It's a very beautiful country, what little I've seen of it, and the people are all so polite."

"Yes," Wang agreed. "We are a very ancient culture and learned long ago that politeness should be the basis of all human relations."

"Please don't mind me. Take your seat, General," Violet instructed him. The general nodded and sat down. There was a coterie of men standing behind him, his fellow criminals, men who were present out of respect for the warlord, and three of his best bodyguards. There was not an English speaker among them and Wang didn't bother to introduce them.

"What are you betting on?" Violet asked him as she stood next to him languidly, one hand on the table, her sole, red chip in the other.

"I feel very lucky tonight," Wang answered. "I'm putting it all on black." He pushed what looked like five thousand pounds in black and gold chips onto the square for black.

"And what are you playing, Miss Howard?" he returned.

"I'm not sure," she said. "My birthday is the 24th, maybe I'll play that. Or maybe 15, it was my father's birthday and he was a great gambler."

"So he has passed on?" Wang asked. The two other players placed chips down on the table, the man covering 7, 8, 9 and 10, and the woman placing two 25 pound chips on 17.

"Yes, about a year ago. I'm an orphan now."

"My condolences, Ms. Howard. Losing a mother and father is a hard thing."

"Yes," Violet answered, but her mind was on the question of the moment: which number should she put her chip on?

The croupier, a short haired, youthful, Chinese man wearing black pants, a white shirt and a bow tie, announced in clipped English, "Ladies and gentlemen, please place your bets."

"Oh, well," Violet said. "Since you're betting on black, I'll bet on red." She placed her chip down on the red marker.

Robert looked down, aghast. She was betting directly against Wang, and on his birthday! Wang was known as being notoriously superstitious and if he lost the first bet on his auspicious day, the most auspicious of the year, he would blame it on Violet. Robert was about to tell Violet to change her bet, but it was too late. The croupier set the little ball in motion.

Wang looked down at the red chip with intense anger. "This arrogant, English bitch has bet against me!" he thought to himself. He couldn't believe it.

Violet, completely ignorant of her faux pas, watched the steel ball make its circuits around the wheel. The question of going or staying kept nagging at her. She had told Robert that she would go, but, now she wasn't sure. Was she just being too sensitive about Robert's behavior? And after all, if it didn't work out, they could get divorced. She was sure that she would never have a problem proving Robert's infidelities. To have a home, not to worry any more about money, to raise a family, that was what had become suddenly important to her.

The wavering young woman made a decision. Sometimes, things had to be left to fate. If the ball landed in a red slot, she would believe that her decision was the right one and she should go. If black, she would stay.

The ball sailed round and round making a scraping sound. The background noise of the other gambling tables seemed to fade away. All eyes at the roulette table were on the little ball. After about six turns, it began to slow. It rolled down onto the edge of the wheel where the numbers are and bounced three times, skipping over 7 to 16. It rolled onwards and landed with a little clatter into number 19, red.

"Oh, my gosh," Violet exclaimed. "I've won!" She was so excited, she gave Robert a little hug. Then she looked down at Wang. His face appeared impassive, but there was just a little flickering of his right eyelid that any of his servants or followers knew usually portended disaster for someone.

"Congratulations," Wang told her, without a hint of anger in his voice. "You should go home now, while a winner."

"Oh, I intend to," Violet replied.

"Robert," she said as the croupier distributed another red chip to match the one that she bet and then swept General Wang's stacks of black and gold ones away, "will you cash in my chips for me?"

Robert, concerned at what Wang's reaction might be, eagerly agreed. Men had died in Shanghai for much less than what Violet did tonight. Wang probably had five hundred murders on his hands. He would not be too squeamish to take the life of a silly British girl. He wouldn't do it now, but later. His men would do it, several of the dozens of gangsters that owed loyalty to him.

It wasn't the money that concerned Wang. Now he had bad joss, bad luck, on his birthday, a very important birthday. And he had lost to the English bitch in front of men whose respect he needed. He would have to give this great thought. Clearly the stupid English woman had no idea what she had done. But she had caused him bad joss nonetheless and he had lost much face.

"Where are you staying," Wang asked Violet politely.

"The Sterling," she answered him nonchalantly.

"A very good hotel," he replied. He got up from the table. "I am finished here, Miss Howard," he told her. "Have a good voyage back to England. I'm sorry I can't convince you to stay."

"Thank you," Violet returned. "It's been a pleasure meeting you."

Robert hurried Violet to the car. "Violet," he started out when they got inside, "I have to tell you, talking to General Wang the way that you did was a very dangerous thing. He's one of the most brutal warlords in Southern China. He's connected to all kinds of illegal activities here in Shanghai. And then to bet against him! I'm worried about what he might do."

"Bet against him?" Violet asked.

"Yes," Robert replied. "He bet black, you bet red. That's betting against him."

"Oh, I really didn't think about it that way. I've never been to a casino before. I'm very sorry. And I didn't mean to speak to him so rudely. I guess that I had too much to drink. Will this make it difficult for you or your company to deal with him?"

"I don't know, Violet, but I'm sure that there will be repercussions."

"I'm so sorry, Robert. Should I write a note of apology to General Wang before I leave?"

"I don't think he would accept it," Robert told her.

They were silent the rest of the way to the hotel. She tried to put the issue of General Wang behind her. After all, tomorrow she was leaving. Violet was happy that the fates had confirmed her decision to return to England. It just felt like the right thing to do.

At the hotel, Violet went immediately to bed. Robert promised to see her in the morning.

He was there at ten o'clock sharp. Violet, a mite hung over, had already packed all of her things. Her trunks and suitcases were standing by the door waiting to be taken to the boat.

Breakfast was a solemn affair. Robert was committed to making one last attempt at getting Violet to stay. He just had to. Inside, he seethed with anger at the position the unreasonable young woman was putting him in.

"Violet, I know that it's just hours to when you have to leave and we've been over this again and again, but I would like to make one more appeal to you. I beg you to reconsider. I know that I could make you happy. I'll smother you with luxuries, make you the leading social light in Shanghai. I'll do anything you want. But, please, please say that you'll stay."

The determined young woman was sorry to see Robert in such a pitiable state. She couldn't think for a moment why her leaving should have this effect on him. They only knew each other for a few days. It couldn't be love, not real love, that is. He seemed awfully desperate to marry. That would be a mark against him all alone. Surely there must be someone out here he could wed.

"I'm sorry, Robert, I'm determined to leave," she told him.

"And that's your last statement on the subject?" Robert asked.

"My absolute last," Violet replied.

The air just seemed to go out of Robert. He looked down despondently at his plate. Then, after a few moments of heavy concentration, he looked back up at Violet.

"I'm sorry things didn't work out for us, Violet. I won't say another word on the subject." He smiled at her. "Some day, we will probably both remember this moment vividly and think about what might have been."

"I'm sure we will, Robert," Violet answered him.

"I've got an idea," Robert said. "I've got your ticket and I've taken care of the instructions for your luggage. Let me take you to Conchou Park. It's a beautiful place. Let it be your last memory of Shanghai. The cherry blossoms are in bloom and you can wile away the time before you have to board your boat. It's gorgeous. Please, let me show you this one, last thing in Shanghai. Technically, it's still the seventh day."

Violet thought about it for a moment. She didn't want to sit about the hotel all day. She worried for a moment that Robert might make a maudlin scene when she left for the boat. She looked at him carefully. He didn't seem the type. He would get over his disappointment quickly, probably already had. He was just a little boy who did not get what he wished for.

"Okay, Robert," she answered him. "That would be fine."

The park was crowded with people taking in the splendid view of the cherry trees in bloom. There seemed to be hundreds of them. It was a bright, clear day. The temperature was a very comfortable 75 degrees.

Robert and Violet walked side by side along the esplanade. She was wearing her off-white, pleated skirt that went down just below her knees and sported a narrow, black belt with a brass colored buckle. On top, she wore a brilliant, yellow blouse splashed with blue and purple flowers, pure cotton and crisply pressed. It had wide lapels and, with the three top buttons open, presented a modest portion of her breasts. She had bought it in the hotel shop yesterday. On her feet she wore a pair of white, high heeled sandals. On her left arm was a small, white hand bag.

Robert, as usual, was dressed in a well tailored suit. This one was grey with blue pin stripes.

Neither of them spoke. Robert seemed to be lost in some dark place. She was grateful for his silence. There was nothing more to say between them.

She looked around at the pretty, pink blossoms. Some wild geese were wandering over the grass looking for worms to eat. There was a delightful, light breeze. "What a wonderful place China is," Violet thought. "At least I'll have some fond memories of having been here."

They came upon a small square adjacent to a roadway. There were several souvenir and refreshment stands. People were crowding all around them. Violet had seen a few Europeans in their journey, but mostly there were Chinese men and women walking in the park, some of them with children.

"Let me get you something to remember Shanghai by," Robert said suddenly to Violet. "A little keepsake."

Violet smiled. Robert wasn't that bad a fellow. He just wasn't for her.

"Thank you, Robert," she said. "That's awfully nice of you."

"Stay right here. Don't go anywhere. I want it to be a surprise. Okay?"

"Sure," Violet answered.

She watched Robert disappear behind a souvenir stand. She had seen little, Chinese, good luck dolls and some inexpensive watercolors of the park. If she had a preference, she would take a watercolor, but, she thought, "I'll accept whatever comes my way." A wave of contentedness passed through her. The beauteous park had worked wonders for her disposition. Things would work out; she just knew that they would.

军阀 外家

CHAPTER THREE

Robert was taking longer than she had expected. Violet watched a large, black coupe with four doors pull up next to the park. It was facing to her left and about ten yards away. The driver, who was on the right side of the car, looked at her sullenly. It was disconcerting. The man in the front passenger seat got out and opened the door to the back. Then, in the blink of an eye, her whole world changed.

Vice-like grips took hold of her upper arms, swooped her up and hustled her toward the car. The man on her right, sliding over the back seat, dragged her in. The man on her left got in after and pushed her to the middle. The man outside pushed the door shut. A heavy cloth was pressed against her face, stifling her scream. The car sped away.

The whole thing took about five seconds.

A handful of people had seen the kidnapping. Most people knew to mind their own business in Shanghai. The men who had taken the white woman were easily identifiable as members of one of the local gangs. They wore dark suits, dark fedoras and had that certain look of resolution that a fearless criminal has. The dark coupe had gangster written all over it. Those who saw what had happened walked away as quickly as they could.

Robert rushed around the souvenir stand a moment later. He had purchased one of the good luck dolls. He had heard the car speed away, its tires squealing. Violet was nowhere to be seen. In her surprise, she had dropped her purse on the ground. He looked at it and then down the street. The car took a right hand turn about seven or eight blocks away and disappeared. He picked up the pocketbook and ran off to call the police, putting the little doll into his right hand, jacket pocket.

* * * * * * * * * * * * * *

Violet was fighting a losing battle with her captors. As the car careened away from the scene of her abduction, she struggled and screamed, writhing her body, pulling at her arms, trying to get the offensive, silencing cloth off of her face.

Before the car had moved more than a hundred feet, the man on her right placed his hand on the back of her neck and pushed her forward with great force until she was doubled over, her face between her knees. He leaned on top of her, securing her in place and took charge of her flailing hands. He brought them back behind her, crossing her wrists. He was strong, very strong, much stronger than she. She did not have the power to pull them away.

The man to her left let go of the cloth that covered her face and, going behind her, wrapped a length of leather cord around her immobile wrists several times, north and south, east and west. He tied it off three times. He was clearly practiced at this task because her wrists were firmly affixed very quickly. She tugged at them futilely. The fact of their confinement brought an intense feeling of sickness to her stomach and made her body shiver with fear.

The cloth had fallen from her face onto her lap. She took a deep breath so as to let out a mighty scream. Before she could let it out, her torso was pulled back up and shoved harshly against the seat behind her. The cloth was again pressed against her face.

Violet had never been so afraid. Her stomach was roiling and her heart was pounding. She wanted to beg the men to release her, to plead for her miserable life.

She pushed up with her legs and arched her back, trying vainly to escape the men's control of her body. A hand grabbed her throat and rudely pushed her down. The man to her left placed his left leg across her thighs, pinning her to the seat. The cloth was again pulled from her face. She opened her mouth to scream and something was jammed tightly inside it. It felt like a heavy, leather ball.

Her eyes took a quick snapshot of her surroundings. She saw her assailants in the back seat. They were Chinese, young, and had determined, cruel faces. The driver, the man who had stared at her with such evil intent, as she recognized now, back at the park, was an older man, heavyset, fat even, balding and hatless. He eyes were peeled towards the on-coming road. The man next to him, on his left, was thin, younger, and wore a black suit and a black fedora. He was turned, looking at Violet, and smiling. He said something to the men in the back seat in Chinese that he thought was very funny.

Violet shook her head as she tried to push the ball out of her mouth. One of the men pulled a wide, leather strap around her face and laid it between her lips. She felt the strap being pulled tight and tied off tightly behind her head, jamming the leather ball further into her oral cavity.

In delirious fear, Violet pushed down against the floor of the car with her feet in a vain attempt at frustrating the men's designs on her. She arched her back and shoved her shoulder against the man to her right. She kicked her foot against the front seat. She had no idea what she was doing, had no plan for escape. Her mind could only function on a very primitive level. She was doing anything she could think of to hinder their control of her body.

The car took a sharp, right turn and her body was forced to the left. A hand went around the back of her neck again, pushing it forward. When the blindfold went over her eyes, terror ran through her. She moaned and screamed, but the leather ball in her mouth allowed very little sound to emerge. She waived her head around desperately, attempting to foil their efforts to blind her. She failed. She felt them tie it off behind her.

Strong hands took hold of her ankles. She tried desperately to prevent the men from bringing them together. Her high heeled sandals were flipped off her feet. The men were too strong for her and they quickly had the ankles joined, crossing them. A strap was wrapped around them, crossed up and down and side to side several times, and then tied off. While one of the men, the man on her right, pressed his forearm down on her chest, pressing her back against the rear seat, the other man, despite her fierce resistance, was able to force her bound ankles down and tied them off to a ring on the floor.

Violet's window of opportunity to struggle against her captors had come to a close. She had lost all vision and speech. She could no longer use her arms. Her ankles had been captured and fixed in place. She continued to scream and writhe nonetheless.

Her dress was pulled up to her lap and a belt was wrapped around her thighs, forcing them tightly together. Another strap went around her neck and was tied off behind her. It was tight and she started to have difficulty breathing. She thought that the men were trying to strangle her and wondered, in her panic, why they had bothered to truss her up so securely if they were just going to kill her. She moaned and whined, little, truncated sounds emerging from behind her gag. One of the men must have figured out what she was so exercised about, because the strap around her neck was loosened.

The last touch was when one of the men put a hat on her head, tying its ribbon under her chin. It had a narrow, black brim with a long, black veil attached which covered her face and neck. Anyone looking into the back seat would see a cultivated lady sitting calmly between two men wearing suits.

Her struggles were over. She was sealed in darkness. Her body was completely confined. She could not arch her back without pulling the strap around her neck tighter. Essentially, all she could do was wriggle her fingers and toes and turn her head slightly from side to side.

The distraught woman's heart was still pounding away and she felt herself going into hyperventilation. Her whole body was shaking with fear. Her mind protested against her body's abuse. A needle pierced her upper right arm. She felt the drug being injected into her. It was done very quickly and expertly and was over before she even had a chance to react.

The men on either side of her sat back, their tasks performed. One of them lit a cigarette. There was the sound of masculine jocularity after a difficult job well done. It had taken less than a minute from when she was first dragged into the car to completely subdue her, although it seemed to Violet to be a whole lot longer. She was crying miserably. She made a useless attempt at pulling apart her bound hands and she jerked and pulled at her ankle tie. She screamed again, to little effect. Then, her mind became woozy and her body started to relax as the drug they had given her kicked in. Within three minutes after she had been kidnapped, she leaned back docilely and let the humming of the tires beneath the car lull her into passivity.

A hand straightened out her bunched up skirt so that it covered her again to her knees.

* * * * * * * * * * * * * *

Violet kept floating in and out of consciousness as the car sped along a road leading out of the city. Her shoulders were jammed against the arms of the men on either side of her and she cringed from the contact. Once, she felt a hand on her breast, squeezing it, and heard a man's voice laughing. Another voice, speaking harshly, intervened and the hand fell away.

After a while, the initial rush from the drug evened out and Violet began to regain some control over her thoughts. Her body still felt slothful and tired. It was hard for her to believe that what had happened to her. Just a few hours ago, she was sitting in her room in an elegant hotel having breakfast. It seemed so unreal now to be a trussed up prisoner in the power of ruthless, determined men, speeding to God only knew where, deep into the heart of China. The fact that she was blindfolded, could see only a black void before her eyes, accentuated the dismal turn in her fortunes and made her disquietude worse. Much worse.

Despite her sedation, from time to time, as they sped down the curvy, bumpy road, something would come over her, a wave of intense distress. She would moan a feeble plea to God and again try desperately to separate her captured wrists and pull her ankles free. Her efforts seemed to amuse the men, who all knew that she was irrevocably bound. After a few moments, she would give up and start to cry again.

She knew what was happening. It was General Wang. He had ordered her kidnapped. Robert had warned her. She figured that the men must have followed them from the hotel to the park and awaited their opportunity.

Violet rued the statements she had made to the barbarous warlord and her foolish bet against him. She hadn't known! Robert should have warned her! Was what she had done so bad that the evil man would have her murdered?

Her mind would drift to what he would do to her once he had full possession of her. Her imagination ran wild. She projected insufferable tortures, rapes, whippings, death. Just the thought of it made her whine and moan, her belly turn queasy and her body begin to sweat. She would tug at her confinements, and when that strategy failed once again, her crying would renew itself.

The leather ball in her mouth was invasive and offensive. Her tongue was pressed down hard against the floor of her mouth. Her cheeks bulged out slightly, her lips were spread wide. It tasted musty and dirty. She tried to push it from her mouth several times with her tongue, but then abandoned the effort. If she managed to get it out, the men would just put it back in.

It seemed to Violet that they had been traveling for a couple of hours. Each minute took her further and further away from rescue and closer and closer to her ultimate fate. She tried to fill herself with hope. Robert would alert the police, she told herself. He would tell them about the offense she had given to the general last night and they would round him up, force him to reveal where she had been taken and to arrange for her release. It had to happen. The alternative was just too horrible to think about. Then, she realized that her hopes were mere fantasy. The Shanghai police would do nothing. Wang was a powerful warlord. The police force was probably as corrupt as any in the world.

When the car slowed and made a turn to the right, rolling to a stop, Violet's heart began to beat heavily. She felt it thumping in her chest. Something was going to happen, something she wouldn't like, she was sure of it. She heard the car doors open and the men all got out. The doors closed again, leaving her alone. She heard the men walk away and then there was silence.

Here was her chance. She pulled and pulled and pulled at the bindings to her wrists, trying to get them to slip. She yanked and jerked on the binding that connected her ankles to the floor of the car. After about ten minutes, she gave it up as hopeless. She was totally immobilized. She issued a piteous wail of frustration.

The world around her was utterly dark and utterly silent. She wondered what time it was. It had been about eleven thirty when they got to the park. They had walked about for a good forty five minutes. It had been two, maybe three hours since she had been kidnapped. That made it about 3:30. Her ship sailed in less than four and a half hours. The thought of it sailing without her multiplied her misery. Why had she ever come to Shanghai, she thought. Why didn't she stay safe and secure in England? Why hadn't she told Robert that she didn't want to go out last night? Why didn't she keep her big, fat mouth shut when she was talking to General Wang? What had she ever done to justify this terrible thing that was happening to her?

She sat alone in the car for about an hour. Despite her terrorized state, the time passed slowly. She tried to stay calm, but every once in a while a wave of misery passed through her. Her body would tremble and a vast, sickening pit would open in her belly. Her total immobility magnified her distress. The men could do anything they wanted to her, take her anywhere they pleased. It was a disabling sensation. She wondered what they were waiting for. She speculated that maybe they were waiting for the general to show. How he would gloat over his prize, she thought miserably.

She didn't know if one of the men was keeping an eye on her, but she assumed that one was because it would be stupid not to. She was hungry, tired and she had to pee desperately. She didn't want the humiliation of peeing in the car, soiling her panties and skirt. The men would surely punish her for it.

Violet flinched when she heard the car door open. They untied the strap round her throat and then the one binding her ankles to the floor of the car and hauled her out. Someone removed her silly, black hat and threw it back into the car. Her ankles were still crossed so they had to drag her along by the arms to wherever they were taking her. They came to a stop. She hung limp in the men's hands. Their grip was hard and she moaned from the pain. She didn't know what the men were going to do to her, but she feared the worst. There was the unmistakable sound of flowing water. The air smelled damp and fecund. Someone said something in Chinese and the others laughed. The first voice was insistent.

The other voices turned compliant.

The men who were holding her stood her up straight so that her feet were off the ground. She felt hands lift her skirt and seize the waist band to her silken panties, pulling them down her thighs. She panicked, fearing that the men were about to rape her. Hands loosened the strap around her thighs and her panties were pulled to her ankles. Then her ankles were untied and they were pulled off of her feet.

She was wearing silk stockings and she knew that they had to be ruined by now. They were expensive and she rued their loss. While she still dangled a few inches off of the ground, hands disconnected her garter belt from the tops of her stockings and they were removed from her legs. Too afraid to resist them, she started to whine, believing that the men's assault on her sex was about to begin. She was pulled about fifteen feet from where she had been standing and strong hands pushed on her shoulders. They forced her body to a crouch. Hands spread her knees apart and lifted her skirt up around her waist. A foot kicked at her bare feet and, fearful of the price of disobedience, she spread them wider. When they were spread, the men just stood there like they were waiting for something. One lone hand was on her shoulder, steadying her. Then she realized what was happening. She was being given an opportunity to pee. With a sob of relief and complete disregard for the male eyes that surrounded her, she let her bladder open and released her water.

When she was done, the hand that was on her shoulder went under her arm, grasped it firmly and raised her to her feet. She was dragged forward. Her bare feet felt marshy grass, then some kind of board. They walked down the length of it and then she sensed that she was on the edge of something. She was pushed forward and fell. Strong arms caught her and brought her down to her feet. She was on something floating. A boat! One of those junks that Robert had shown her the other day!

She was dragged some distance from where she stood and guided down a ladder. When they reached the bottom, she was pulled to the middle of the room. One man held her bound arms behind her above the elbows while the other began to remove her skirt. She tried to resist by squirming her body and kicking her feet. The man behind her held her tightly. The man in front of her stopped what he was doing and slapped her viciously across the face. Her face stung fiercely where it had been struck. Her knees sagged and she screamed. He struck her again and bellowed a command to her in Chinese.

This took all of the fight out of the distraught young woman. Sobbing, fraught with terror, she ceased all resistance. Within a few moments her skirt was unhooked and it fell to the floor at her feet revealing her long, graceful thighs. Her pubic bush was full and fluffy; her belly sank to her loins sweetly.

Her garter belt dangled around her hips. The man quickly unhooked its ends and tossed it aside. Crouching down in front of her, he lifted one foot after the other, freed the skirt and tossed it, too, aside. She was naked from the waist down.

Violet's chest was heaving with sobs as he unbuttoned her blouse. When it was undone, he pulled it down over her shoulders and down her arms. She was wearing one of the fine, white, lacy bras that she had bought for her trip. It hooked in front between her breasts. The man undid the clasp and then drew the bra over her shoulders. Her pale, full breasts burst free.

The men took a few moments to admire her naked form. Her bare, feminine delights swung enticingly. They were pale white, even paler than the rest of her porcelain skin, with dark, almost red areolas and stiff, thick nipples. A hand slid over her ass and another groped a breast, squeezing it harshly. Violet whined a mute protest. The men exchanged comments and laughed.

Going back to work, the men pushed her down to the floor. Her breasts, belly and thighs scraped against the rough surface and Violet cried out in pain. Her bra and blouse were pulled down her arms to just above her bound hands. One of the men held her arms firmly just below the elbows while the other untied her wrists. When the strap was undone, he yanked the clothing past her hands and quickly bound her wrists back up again.

But for her gag and blindfold, Violet was now completely naked. Crying and sobbing, she turned to her side and tried to curl up into a little ball. The men had other ideas.

They worked quickly and efficiently, like it was something they had done a hundred times before. Her legs were pulled back and forced together and she was pushed back down on her belly. While one man held down her torso, the other quickly bound a leather strap tightly around her crossed ankles. He wound it around them three times one way, and then ran the strap the other several more. When done, he tied it off tightly. There was enough play left on one end for him to bend her legs back and connect her ankles to her bound wrists.

Realizing what had been done to her, Violet gave out a violent moan and tried to separate her hands and feet. She could feel the backs of her fingers jamming up against her heels. She tried to squirm her torso, but the man on top of her was too heavy. Her naked breasts were being mashed against the floor. She felt the hard, rough surface scraping her nipples and belly. It was far too late for protest or resistance.

They rolled her to her back, tied off another, shorter strap around and between her thighs just above her knees, and then rolled her back again.

Violet wailed and sobbed as she struggled futilely against her bonds. She tried to beg the men to release her, but her pleas emerged from her mouth as garbled murmurs. A spark of hope rose within her as he felt the strap that held her gag in place loosened. Fat fingers pried at her mouth and removed the leather ball that had been shoved in by the men in the car. Her hopes of being able to bargain with her captors was dashed when she felt a large, rough hand go under her chin and squeeze her cheeks harshly, forcing her mouth into an 'O'. She tried to beg and plead to be released. Her voice made a "Oooooouuuuuuuuuummmm!" sound, as a long, thick, leather plug was forced between her lips and pushed back until it filled her mouth, almost all the way to the back. It was attached to a leather shield that covered her lips and wrapped under her chin. Straps at the sides were pulled behind her head and buckled together tightly.

Violet pulled and tugged at her bonds in hysterical frustration. She screamed and yelled, producing noises that made the men laugh. She waived her head violently as if she could shake the gag out of her mouth. One of the men gathered up her clothes while the other tied a strap to the joinder of her ankles and wrists. He pulled it tight and then ran it through a ring embedded in a beam that ran across the overhead. He pulled on the end until Violet's wrists and ankles were hoisted high above her and then he tied it off. Violet moaned in pain as her shoulder and hip joints strained.

Dismally unhappy at her plight, Violet cried and sobbed. "Please don't leave me this way! Please!" she screamed uselessly. No actual words escaped her gag, just a series of high pitched sounds. For a few moments, she continued to struggle against her bindings. Then, realizing that it was hopeless, stopped. She let her forehead sink to the floor and moaned.

The men stood around for a few moments appreciating their handiwork. Violet could feel their eyes consuming her naked form. When she had been stripped, she had expected the men to rape her. She never expected this. Her predicament seemed unreal, like it had been dreamed up in some nightmare. Her mind refused to believe that it was actually happening to her.

She heard a cigarette being lit and smelled the smoke as it began to fill the small compartment. It seemed as if the men were waiting for something. She was self conscious of her nakedness. She had only ever been naked for one man and he had proved a bastard. Although the men had barely fondled her, she felt like she had been raped and violated.

The room, which had been filled with the sounds of her pathetic struggle and of the men's exertions, was now deathly quiet. Violet's heart was pumping wildly, her breath heavy. She could hear men's feet moving around above her, slapping the deck, the bare feet of sailors. They shouted and called to each other from time to time.

Being bound and immobile against one's will is one of the worst things that can be experienced short of actual, disabling violence. Everything that makes one a person has been taken away. This is precisely how Violet felt as she lay prostrate before the men. She looked peaceful and stationary, but inside, forces were whirling around as like to make her explode. As long as the men were still there with her, though, and the boat had not actually started on its journey, she still preserved the tiniest hope that she would not be left behind like this.

After about ten minutes, a time within which Violet's emotions ran from despondency to terror to anger and then back again, she heard heavy, male footsteps come down the ladder. They walked slowly, as if in no hurry. They had the sound of authority.

The man walked into the small room and stopped a few feet away from the distraught, young woman. Although she couldn't see him, she felt his eyes roaming her naked body, taking in her unhappiness. For a few moments, there was absolute silence and then Violet, her heart aching from fear and desperation, issued a forlorn whine and mewed a piteous plea. There was no response.

Someone called down into the hold in Chinese. One of the men who had trussed her up so cruelly returned an acknowledgment and the three men, one by one, stepped towards the ladder. As they stepped away, Violet began a frantic series of sounds, shouting and pleading desperately not to be left behind. Her body rocked and she strained at her bonds. The men, ignoring her, trudged up the ladder and the hatch was closed and locked behind them. Bare feet re-sounded on the deck above her, the sound of men running to their stations. A short while later, she felt the boat rock beneath her as it was poled away from the bank. It paused for a moment and then, as if the wind had picked up its sail, it jerked into motion. Her heart sank.

军阀 外家

CHAPTER FOUR

It took ten days for the junk to navigate the Yangtze from Shanghai to Junshan. For Violet, they were ten days of pain, suffering and misery.

Violet had no doubt where they were taking her. She had heard of Hunan Province, but she had no idea where it was. She had no idea of how far away it was from Shanghai, no idea how long it would take her to get there. No one told her anything. The men, there were five of them, operated the boat with cool efficiency. They never talked to her except to give her one or two word commands in Chinese, all of which she did not understand and had to learn.

She spent the first day of their trip, and all of that night, hogtied, gagged and blindfolded.

When the boat set sail, Violet cried and sobbed, her body shaking from fear. She whined, pulled at her hands and feet, shook her head, all out of a frantic feeling that she should be doing something to free herself, that once she stopped and accepted that there was, in fact, nothing she could do, her condition would enter a phase of permanency that was too awful to contemplate.

It only took about five minutes for her to surrender to the harsh reality of her bonds. All that was left for her to do was to cry and pray.

When she realized, after an hour or so, that no one was going to come and untie her to make her captivity more bearable, an intense depression settled over her. She lay there sadly, her forehead against the deck, thinking of all the things that were being taken away from her, trying to ignore the growing ache of her shoulders and thighs.

Being deprived of the use of her limbs, her voice and her sight was a strange and horrifying experience. She felt like some huge, evil spider had come upon her in her sleep and bound her with its web. Her body had betrayed her. When she thought of how easily the men in the car had captured and bound her wrists, she became nauseous. Her hands dangled above her, hidden from her sight. It was like they were no longer part of her or subject to her will. They had been useless to defend her. Her legs and thighs had also turned against her, their weight pulling viciously at her shoulder muscles. Her eyes, which had formerly brought her light and color and, at times, joy, brought her now only a suffocating darkness. Her mouth refused to close, refused to reject the soul steeling intruder that occupied it like a viscous leach.

She tried to fight off the feelings of terror and despondency, but she had little success.

Her predicament was so unreal that, at times, she felt that if she wished for it hard enough, her bonds would fall away, the men would all realize that they had made a terrible mistake and they would turn the boat around. That feeling passed very quickly as the cold reality of the tight straps around her ankles and wrists came back to her.

As the long, interminable, lonely day wore on, her moods and emotions swung back and forth. At times, an over-whelming sadness would pass through her and she would begin to cry again. She despised herself for doing so much crying. She hadn't cried in years. Not even when her false lover had betrayed her. She considered herself strong, self reliant, brave. But how could she be brave when the men had such total control over her and she faced such a terrible future? How could she be self reliant, when she couldn't even use her hands or legs? How could she be strong when the men, and there were so many of them, were so much stronger than she was? Even if she were to get herself free from her bonds, it would take a miracle for her to get away.

When her mind turned to rage, she would ask herself, what kind of men are these that would treat a person so? They had no right to treat her this way, no right to strip her of her humanity. After all, she was a British subject, not some cheap, Chinese whore who could disappear without a trace. She wanted to strike out at them, obliterate them, toss them into the fires of hell. They didn't have to treat her this way. If they wanted merely to prevent her escape, all they need do was keep the hatch to the hold closed and locked.

She realized that her treatment was almost certainly a result of General Wang's direct orders. She was being intentionally brutalized, being turned into a totally controlled being. She had sensed that it was him who had come down to the hold to look at her just before they sailed. It made her stomach turn to think of him gazing on her nakedness, of what he was going to do to her. She would rather die than submit to him.

And then her mind would turn to terror. Of all the emotions, that was the worst. Her stomach would fill up with bile, her heart would pound, her body would tremble. If this was the way she was being treated now, what would her treatment be like when she was fully and irrevocably delivered to his hands? Would he whip her? Torture her? Burn her with red hot irons? Give her to his men? Kill her? Fear would pierce her, an intense, fiery, disabling fear. A feeling of misery would come over her so intense that it seemed to seep out from every pore of her body. Her body would tremble, her insides quail. She would cry and cry and cry.

There was shame. She was ashamed that she had been so easily captured, ashamed at her powerlessness at resisting them, shame at her nakedness and her cowardice. Shame that she knew that if she was confronted with torture and pain she would surrender anything, everything to avoid it. She would cry and beg and plead for mercy. If one of the sailors came down and offered to free her, even for an hour, she would debase herself in any way that he demanded to obtain even temporary dispensation from her fate.

Finally, there was indifference. Her body would turn limp and her mind would cloud over. She would cease to care if she lived or died.

Time passed by slowly. She yearned for distraction from her plight. She listened to the feet of the men above as they moved about the boat, working it. She listened to the sounds of the river as it splashed past the advancing boat. She listened to the creaking of the boat as it rocked against the current. She listened to her own piteous whines and moans.

After a while, her mind started going in and out of a dream state. The gentle rocking of the boat made her weary. It felt good to empty her mind and let the motions of the boat soothe her. She would doze off and she would begin to dream. She dreamt of her father, her mother, who had died when she was quite young. In one dream, she was back at her small room in Devonshire where she lived while she taught the piano. She felt safe and secure. There was a piano there, although her real room was much too small to ever hold one. She sat down and played and played and played. She felt so free, so happy.

She awoke with a start. She panicked. She was awake, but not awake. Everything was completely dark. She tried to blink her eyes, but her eyelids wouldn't move. For a second, she thought that she had gone from her beautiful dream into some horrid nightmare. Then she tried to move her hands and feet and, when she could not, remembered exactly where she was and how she got there. She began to cry all over again.

Eventually, her concerns about her body began to take precedence. The temperature outside that day had been balmy, but, its continual battering of the boat made Violet's little chamber hot and stifling. She could feel sweat oozing out of her body. The air was stale. She was hungry. She had not eaten lunch that day. She and Robert were going to supp after their foolish stroll in the park. She had to pee again, even though she hadn't had anything to drink since breakfast. She was thirsty. Her shoulders and hips ached. Her inability to call out to anyone to assuage her physical torments, brought on a new cycle of dismal emotions.

It wasn't until what seemed like several terrible, heart wrenching hours had passed that someone came down to check up on her. She heard the hatch unlocked and opened and footsteps came slowly down the wooden ladder. At the sound of someone coming, a chill went through her and a pit opened up in her stomach. Was he here to hurt her or help her?

Whoever it was paused for a moment as if taking in the sight of her for the first time. Violet raised her head and mewed a plea. The man yelled something to her in Chinese, something very adamant. His voice was sharp, his tone deep. He crouched down in front of her and tapped several times harshly on the gag covering her mouth and repeated it twice. His quick, dramatic reaction to her plaintive entreaty sent a wave of terror through the bound and helpless woman. His meaning could not have been more clear: "No talking, or else!"

The man stepped to her side and she felt the strap that held her hands and feet aloft loosen. She gave a sigh of relief as her limbs lowered. His hands wandered over the knots that held her bound tightly as if checking them. Satisfied, he gently pushed her to her side and then her back. He freed the bond around her thighs and pulled her to her knees.

Despite her continued fear, Violet was grateful for the man's attentions. Perhaps her situation was about to change. They couldn't leave her that way, all trussed up like a goose, for long, could they?

She was conscious of the exposure of her bare breasts and the fulcrum of her thighs. The man paused as if taking them in. After a moment, he placed his hands on her knees and urged her to spread them apart, giving her a command in Chinese. His voice was stern, but not unkind. Violet knew that spreading her knees would bring her loins into full view, but she was too afraid to disobey. She moved them apart slightly, but the man kept up an insistent pressure on the inside of her thighs until she had separated them widely. She trembled as she expected to feel his hand grasp her vulnerable sex. Instead, she felt a bowl pressed under it. The man gave her a command. He wanted her to pee.

The unhappy woman cast aside her chagrin at her nudity and the intimacy of the function and, after a second or two, was able to force her bladder open. A stream of warm liquid poured into the bowl. The relief of the need to void her urine was almost pleasurable. When she finished, the man withdrew the bowl and wiped her sex with a rough rag.

Violet knelt there expectantly, hoping that the man would free her gag so that she could communicate with him. She heard him get to his feet and place the bowl she had filled some distance away from him. He then came forward and crouched in front of her again. He patted the outside of her thighs and gave her an order. She realized that he wanted her to put her thighs back together so that he could reapply the strap that had gone around them. She gave out a disappointed whine. She yearned to beg him not to make her lie down on the floor again. He repeated his command, harshly now, and slapped the outside of her knees forcefully. Violet knew that she had no choice but to obey him.

Her heart aching, she raised herself up and maneuvered her knees toward each other until they were close. The man wound the strap around her thighs several times, snaked it between them twice and then tied it off. She felt his rough hands on her shoulders. He tilted her forward and lowered her again to the floor. She whined with dismay. He ignored her and, once he had her back down, stood, took up the strap that he had loosened before and ran it again through the ring in the beam above her. She felt her hands and feet rise and she gave out a miserable moan. As he pulled them up high, she groaned in pain. Having finished, he picked up the bowl, turned away from her and walked up the ladder. The hatch closed behind him. She heard the latch being locked. To Violet, it had the sound of a nail being driven into a coffin.

The man's visit, in which his power over her was made so explicitly clear, launched a new round of misery for her. It was apparent that her abysmal, cruel confinement was not to be temporary. How long would they leave her like this, she asked herself despondently. It might be days and days and days. It was too horrible to think about.

"No talking!" the man had yelled. Although his words were in Chinese, there was no doubt of what he meant. Didn't a victim have the right to plead for mercy? How would she ever be able to communicate to the men any of her needs? And she was hungry and thirsty! Didn't they intend to give her any sustenance?

She was grateful for the relief to her bladder, but it felt like the man had raised her arms and feet higher than they did the first time. Her shoulders and hips screamed in pain. She struggled to keep from crying. She knew she needed to control herself or she would never last. And then the dam burst and she sobbed and sobbed and sobbed.

An eternity later, when the boat stopped moving, Violet assumed that they were anchoring for the night. She tried to remember what time sundown was yesterday. She believed that it had been about 6:30 or 7. "How far could a sail boat go in a day?" she wondered. "Did they stop exactly at sundown, or was there a moon to sail by? How far have they taken me?" She realized that she had no idea. It depended on the wind, the size of the boat, the strength of the current, the skill of the captain. She realized that whenever they got to their destination, there would be no way for her to know how far they had traveled.

About an hour after the boat stopped, the man came down the ladder again. Violet remained fearfully silent. He untied the strap above her, released her thighs, brought her to her knees and let her pee. When done, as before, he returned her to her abject state. Her heart nearly broke as she thought that he was going to leave again without giving her something to drink or eat but then he sat down in front of her, crossing his legs. He leaned over and unfastened the belt that held her gag in her mouth. Violet's lips trembled as he pulled it out. She had to force herself not to beg and plead with the man to be untied. When she felt her blindfold being removed, her heart leapt with joy.

The man sitting in front of her was dressed in khaki trousers and wore a loose fitting, grey, cotton, pullover shirt. He did not look like a peasant or a fisherman. His jet black hair was cut too well and his face had a sophisticated demeanor. He looked to be about 35 or so. His visage was stern, his posture stiff. The man had brought a lantern which was hanging from one of the rafters. It was swaying gently back and forth, causing the shadows on his face to keep shifting. It was hard to get a measure of his character since his expressions seemed to change depending on the light that was cast on it. One thing that she did know was that he was dedicated to enforcing General Wang's rules on her treatment. She could expect little mercy from him.

Violet's eyes misted and her lips trembled. She had to crane her neck to look up at him. He had a clay jug with a narrow spout. He brought it to her mouth and tipped it forward. Violet felt the cool liquid splash over her tongue and against her throat with joy. He let her drink her fill. He would pour some water in her mouth, let her swallow it and then make a motion with the jug as if asking her if she wanted more. When she finally shook her head 'no', he put the jar down and picked up a wooden bowl that was by his side.

Violet saw that it contained a mixture of rice and fish. Using a pair of chopsticks, the man proffered her a piece of fish. Violet was humiliated that she was to be to be fed this way, her naked breasts and belly on the floor, her hands and legs bound above her. Why hadn't he fed her when she was on her knees? She felt like she was being treated like a circus animal or a puppy. It was clearly intended to degrade her. She knew that she should refuse the food until they treated her with some dignity. But if she refused, the man would certainly go away for a long time. She had already been experiencing severe hunger pangs. Add to that the fact that she knew that eventually she would give in. She hadn't the courage or the fortitude to go days and days and days without eating. She would have starved for nothing and, having had her resistance broken, she would feel even worse.

So, humiliating or not, she ate. She had to keep her neck extended and her mouth wide open to ensure that she got every grain of rice or clump of fish that the man was giving her. Her useless hands squirmed above her back. Her eyes were filled with tears.

The food had a pleasant texture and its spices were redolent of ginger, lemon and pepper. The meal tasted heavenly to her. She quickly forgot her shame and took in each portion gratefully. After he decided that she had had enough, the man proffered her more water and she drank.

For the entire journey, this is how she was fed, on her belly, her arms and legs joined behind her, her neck straining to receive it. Each time, her lowly, degraded status was brought home to her. Afterwards, she would cry and berate herself for surrendering to this humiliation.

And the whole time that she was on the boat, this man's was the only face that she saw. It was as if the ship was crewed by ghosts. She heard the other men from time to time, especially later, when she was permitted on deck, but never saw them since each time that she went up she was blindfolded.

When the man started to retrieve her impedimenta, Violet felt a wave of sorrow. The experience of human contact had calmed her but had now come to an end. It had taken all of about 10 minutes; she had been alone, by her estimate for four or five hours. He restored her gag first. For a moment, Violet hesitated to open her mouth when he proffered it to her. His hand moved like lightning. She felt the blow before she saw it. The open palm slapped her face harshly as the man uttered an angry admonition to her in Chinese. Her cheek burned where it had been struck and Violet felt tears welling up inside her. She looked up at him dolefully. He proffered the gag to her again and she opened her frowning mouth at once.

When he buckled the gag off behind her head, he gave it an extra tug to insure its tightness. When he went to place the blindfold on her, two tears dripped from the corner of her eyes and down her cheeks. With a gentle gesture, he wiped them off with his finger and then covered up her eyes. She listened unhappily as she heard the man's footsteps go up the ladder. Then she was alone in the darkness again.

After the man left, Violet tearfully prepared herself for a long, lonely night. "How can people be so cruel?" she thought miserably. "Why do I have to be treated this way?" The man had looked stern, but not unkind. He had wiped the tears from her face almost like he was sorry for what he had to do. "Then why didn't he release me? Why did he leave me all alone?" She hung her head, resting her forehead on the floor.

She thought about her experience with her caretaker, the mixture of gentleness and harshness. His gentleness gave her hope that her conditions might improve. His harshness made her fear him and what punishments he might inflict on her if she disobeyed him or broke any more rules.

Although he was gone and probably would not come down until after the sun rose, just the fact that he had come at all gave her some minor comfort. She had been afraid that they would never feed her or give her something to drink. And the fact that she had seen a human face, the first one since her kidnapping many hours ago, gave her some relief. From now on, when the man came down, even if her blindfold was not removed, she would have a vision of him. She could think about his face, picture it in her mind. Even when she was lying down here alone she would know that he was not far away. He was a lifeline to the world. He was a human being just like she was. Maybe, eventually, he would see the human being in her?

But her conditions had not improved. For all she knew, she would be forced to lie like this interminably. She was still a dismal prisoner, bound into immobility, her life stolen from her. When he had reinstalled the strap that bound her to the beam above her, he had made it higher than before, causing her more agony. He had slapped her viciously. And then there was always the question of what was going to happen to her when they got to where they were going. She was General Wang's prisoner, no, more than that, she was his property.

The man undoubtedly knew that and knew, at least in a general way, what would happen to her when they reached

Wang's domain. He clearly didn't care. His duty to his warlord was more important than any of her sensibilities.

She slept fitfully through the night. It was strange to know that darkness was all around her when she couldn't see it with her eyes. She rested her forehead on the deck. It smelt of dirt and dampness. The gag in her mouth was an ever mindful presence. Her full breasts were crushed beneath her chest. She would fall asleep for ten or fifteen minutes and then, when she tried to move her body in her sleep, and could not, come back to awareness. The reality of where she was and what the men had done to her would hit her all at once and she would start crying all over again.

When she thought about the fact that a mere 24 hours ago she was a free woman with a plush hotel room and a comfortable bed to sleep in, it broke her heart. She thought of her room, her trunk and luggage, her home in Devonshire. The boat that she was supposed to be on was on its way back to England by now, a place that she would probably never see again. Although she hadn't made the boat, her luggage probably had, and it was sailing away from her, would arrive in England while she would not. She imagined herself laughing and dining with the other passengers, Shanghai and General Wang only an interesting anecdote to tell her friends. Then, she realized that she had to stop thinking like that. It would drive her mad.

She had not realized how much noise the boat made when it was in motion and how little it made now that it was at rest. It was like the world had retreated a hundred miles from her. She could hear the water lapping gently on its sides. The wood of the boat creaked lowly as it rolled ever so slightly back and forth.

She tried to let the relative silence of the night sooth her. It would last for a little while and then she would remember where she was. From time to time, she still struggled with her bonds and broke into tears when her efforts to free herself failed again. Feeling her hands bound behind her sickened her. The gag in her mouth was a vicious, invasive presence. Her inability to move virtually a single muscle made her feel like she was teetering on the edge of insanity. "This can't be happening to me!" she would protest in her mind. "It can't! It can't!"

Then she would remember that this was only the beginning of the misery she would have to suffer. At the end of this journey, regardless of how long it took, she would be faced with dire consequences. None of the possibilities that she could realistically think of looked good. For all practical purposes, her life was at an end. She would have no power to make her own decisions, no ability to determine her future. This was what her current treatment was all about. She realized that. From now on, assuming that Wang in fact would let her live, every iota of her life would be carefully controlled.

It was a long, terror filled night, the worst night by far in her entire life, the worst that she could imagine she would ever have.

When the noises above her resumed, she knew that it was dawn. The man came down the stairs after a while and released the strap that had kept her so cruelly confined to her belly. She sighed, thankful that the awful tension on her muscles had been relieved. He brought her to her knees. She was allowed to pee once more and, when she was done, the man lowered her back to her belly. Then, to her delight and amazement, he began to untie the strap that connected her feet and hands.

Once they were free, he slowly and gently let her lower her legs down until they were on the floor. He loosened the tie around her ankles. Violet rejoiced in the freeing of her limbs. He gave her a few moments to stretch them and then he took hold of her arm and gently and patiently brought her to her feet.

Violet swayed as she tried to make use of her legs. It felt so strange to be on them after so long. Her heart leapt when she felt herself being led to the ladder. He guided her up the stairs and out into open air of the deck.

Her consciousness of her nudity rose immediately. She knew that there were men out there. She could almost feel them raking her with their eyes.

She was led further down the deck. When she was brought to a standstill she felt her wrists being untied. Her hands were free for the first time since she had been kidnapped. Her joy was short lived as he refastened them together in front of her. They were lifted above her and tied off to a spar. She felt all the men's eyes on her naked form. She wondered whether she had been brought up here for their amusement. Her breasts swayed and she cringed in shame. Then someone poured a bucket of cool river water over her head. The act was repeated several times until her hair was soaked through and her body completely wet. Two hands started to scrub her body. She recoiled at the familiarity, but was happy that she was being bathed. She felt soap against her skin making it slick. She was joyful that she would soon be clean again. Under the circumstances, she didn't mind standing in front of the men naked, or to have this unknown man's hands range all over her, over her breasts and buttocks, her belly and up and down her legs and arms. He even delved between her thighs and in the divide between her rear cheeks, making them clean. When she was fully soaped, buckets of water were poured over her again and again until it was all washed away. When they were done, she was left there for a while so that the sun and wind could dry her. She could feel the warm breeze on her naked body. She reveled in it. It made her feel fleetingly free.

Before she was returned to the hold, her caretaker rebound her hands behind her back. When they had descended the short ladder, he ordered her to her belly on the floor. He retied her ankles and the strap around her thighs and then brought her legs up again and affixed them to her wrists. He did not connect her to the beam overhead. He left her there, as she was, for a few minutes, and then returned with her breakfast, a meal similar to the one she ate the night before. Before feeding her, he removed both her gag and her blindfold. This time, though, after she had eaten, he restored her gag but left the blindfold off. He gave her an inscrutable look and then left.

Violet was relieved to be able to see. It was her first chance to take stock of the room in which she was being held prisoner. It was about 20' long and 15' wide. The overhead was about 10' over the deck, with several beams crossing it. A small porthole was built into each side, high up. The glass on them seemed dirty since they only admitted a faint yellowish light. The hatchway had been left open and sunlight was pouring through it. She rolled to her side and dragged herself over to where it was coming in. She could see the sky. It was a deep blue, with occasional, small, fluffy clouds passing overhead. She lay there all morning, looking up, watching the clouds go by.

He came back to let her relieve herself and to give her lunch. When she was done, he put her blindfold back on, restored her gag and fastened the strap that led up to the beam above her, immobilizing her once more. Violet mourned the loss of light. Knowing that it shined all around her, even faintly, accentuated her deprivation. She stayed that way all through the afternoon and through the night. She was released just once, after dinner, when he brought her up to the deck and had her sit on the rail, her ass hanging over so that she could empty her bowels. When she was done, he cleaned her, returned her to the hold and her immobilizing tie.

Whenever the man left her free of the tie to the overhead beam, Violet felt that she had been granted a great boon. Just having the power to move to her side, either one, or to slide herself across the room, or, if her eyes were free, to look up at the sky through the hatch, was infinitely better than having no ability to move at all.

The second time that she was left free of the immobilizing strap, she managed to maneuver herself to her knees. Her knees and ankles being so closely bound together, she felt a little like she was kneeling at prayer. This was the best position. Since her legs rested on the deck, they were not a weight on her shoulders. It made her feel so much more like a human being to be off the dirty, dusty floor.

When the man saw her this way he yelled angrily at her in Chinese. He advanced to her swiftly and shoved her to the deck. She gave a whine of pain as her shoulder struck the hard surface. He flipped her to her back, grabbed her nipples between his thumbs and forefingers and pinched them severely, making her groan with pain. He held them while he repeated the words he had yelled at her when he saw her kneeling. She understood the message: English sluts lie on the floor.

To emphasize his instruction, he slapped her soft, tender breasts both harshly, twice. They stung fiercely where he struck them. Violet called out in pain through her gag each time. He brought her to the center of the room and fastened her limbs to the beam. It was lunch time, but she got no lunch that day. After he left, Violet sobbed in misery for half an hour, until, finally exhausted from her expressions of anguish, she fell asleep. She never got up on her knees without permission again.

That was her basic routine. She spent long, lonely hours in varying states of stultifying boredom and soul crushing dread. Compared to the times she spent alone, unable to make any volitional movement, times that crept by at a glacial pace, the times that she spent with her caretaker, or any of the other unknown men, went by in the blink of an eye. She spent, on average, 23 hours each day alone in her darkness. The times that she had even the briefest contact with another human being, were limited to maybe, when all put together, one hour per day.

On the third day, in the afternoon, she was allowed to walk the deck blindfolded and naked, the man at her arm, for five minutes, and then a little longer each day. Sometimes, when he brought her back below from her bucket shower or her walk, her blindfold was removed, sometimes not. On occasion, during the day, as she lay in the hold, he released her wrists from her ankles allowing her to ease the pain on her shoulders and to stretch her legs. On the other hand, he made her spend long, monotonous periods on her belly, blindfolded and gagged, with her ankles and wrists pulled high, her mobility reduced once more to zero. Whenever she felt that strap being affixed, knowing that long tortuous hours of immobility was facing her, she would whine and cry, her body would shiver, and despair riddled nausea would course through her.

Several times, the man left her blindfold off while she was affixed to the beam above her. At first, Violet was thankful to be able to see. After a while, though, she realized, to her dismay, that being able to see what was around her merely accentuated her helplessness. She could not turn her head to see what was behind her. What she saw in front of her remained the exact same for hours and hours. She knew that light shined on her distended arms and legs, but she could not see them. When she let her head down, she saw the same small, dirty patch of floor. Her nakedness seemed more shameful in the light. She was able to imagine what the men saw when they came down the ladder, a naked, grotesquely bound, helpless, foolish woman who had let herself be kidnapped in broad daylight; someone stupid enough to insult the great and powerful General Wang and who was paying the consequences.

Only once again did the man have to discipline her. It was in the afternoon of the fifth day. She had been left blindfolded and with the immobilizing tie on her wrists and ankles all morning after having spent the night that way. For some reason she could not fathom, that day she had not been taken for a bath. It had been a particularly difficult night. She had had terrible dreams of punishments and whippings. Having been kept in darkness and immobilized for almost 18 hours straight, she felt she was going to go mad. When he was done feeding her, he restored her gag and blindfolded her again. She whined with unhappiness at the prospect of many more hours in darkness. When he went to attach the immobilizing strap to her ankles and wrists, she lost control. "Please don't, please!" she yelled out miserably. Her voice was stifled by her gag, but the sound of attempted words was crystal clear.

The man stopped what he was doing. Dropping the strap to the floor, he walked purposefully back up to the main deck. He returned a few moments later.

Violet was beside herself with fear. She had broken a cardinal rule. When he returned, she was already sobbing. She felt him untying her wrists from her ankles. When he was done, he brought her to her knees and then pushed her torso down so that her forehead was on the deck and her ass was raised in the air. A moment later, Violet heard a vicious swishing sound and, almost contemporaneously, a line of fire broke out on her proffered rear. She screamed with pain.

Her body started to shake. She heard the sound again and another fierce blow landed on her rear cheeks. The pain reverberated throughout her body and she screamed again into her gag. He struck her a third time, this one harder than the first two. She was too overwhelmed with pain, at first, to even scream. When she recovered her senses, she let out a woeful howl.

She continued to whine and cry as the man retied her ankles to her hands and then both of them to the beam above her and left.

The wounds on her rear cheeks burned for at least a half hour. Violet cried and cried for the longest time. He did not return for dinner. He did not come at breakfast time. She could not hold her bladder any longer and so she released herself and was forced to lie in her own urine for hours.

He did not come back to her until after noon the next day. Violet cringed when she heard the sound of him coming. He gave her water and then took her outside for her bucket bath. Before tying her back up, he made her scrub the floor where she had soiled it. Only after he had retied her and fastened her to the beam above her once more, did he give her anything to eat. When he left, he left her blinded and gagged, as before.

On the morning of the next day, the seventh, her privileges returned.

The days and nights were long and it seemed as if the trip would last forever. Hour after hour, day after day, she lay in the hold confined to one degree or another. At times, she thought that she would go crazy. It was like being in a horrible nightmare that would never end. With nothing to do but think, she would go over and over again and again the events that led to her abduction. She would try and think of home and the pleasant life that she lived there. She would plead with God to help her bear her cruel captivity.

Knowing that above her were men, human beings, who, if they wanted to, could set her free, made her confinement more horrible

She had no doubt that the fact she was English made the men take more pleasure in causing her suffering. For her, she knew, despite her conscious efforts to rise above the prejudices of her race, the fact that the men were not white men made her shame and despair at their control of her more intense.

When she thought about it, and she had no time to do anything but think, she realized that the manner of her treatment was part of General Wang's revenge against her. It was like a window into his cruel mind. It made her shiver with fear each time she thought of it.

Likewise, the fact that the men on the boat had not touched her sexually was also unquestionably part of the warlord's instructions to them. There was no other way to explain it. She knew that she was attractive, or at least, not unattractive. They were men. She was naked and totally in their power. Although she had only seen the face of the one man, she knew that others of the men had come down to take care of her, help her relieve herself, give her a drink. She hadn't seen their faces, but she could tell from the cadence of their steps, the way they handled her body, the sound of their voices when they ordered her back to her belly, that they were not her caretaker.

When they were alone with her in the hold, who would ever know what they did to her? She would never be able to identify who did it. The fact that none of them had even attempted a small caress, a minor grope, was indicia of the fear that their leader instilled in them. And if these men had reason to fear General Wang to that extent, then her terror at the prospect of finally being delivered unto him was more than justified.

She devised various strategies to take her mind off of the fact that she was bound so cruelly. She would sing songs to herself, try to remember childhood rhymes. One of the best was when she played the piano in her mind. She only did this when she was blindfolded. She would create imaginary hands and watch them as they played the notes, the music ringing clearly in her mind.

At times, her wild imaginings approached delirium. She pretended she was precious cargo on a mystery ship and constructed a complex plot involving the clash of navies, heroism and redemption. Or she was a prisoner of pirates and her lover and his men boarded the ship to save her. Other times she repeated prayers that she knew over and over and over again in the hopes that God would hear her.

She would yearn for the sound of the hatch above her opening, imagining she heard it a thousand times. She tried to wish her caretaker to come down and spend some time with her, even if only to break her lonely, monotonous torment. It was heartbreaking to lie there for hours and hours on end without human contact, like some animal being transported to its slaughter.

Most of the time, though, she just lay there in lonely, abject misery, wishing to end the roiling of her mind and the torment of her body by sleep or death.

It was late in the afternoon on the tenth day when the junk docked in Yueyang. Violet's blindfold had been restored after lunch and she had spent the last few, unhappy hours hogtied and with her ankles and wrists connected to the beam above her. When she heard and felt the boat bump against the dock, she knew that they had arrived and that soon she would learn her fate.

She was overwhelmed by panic. Her whole body was consumed with fear. What would happen to her now, she asked herself miserably. She began to cry again, something that she had not done for several days. Her body trembled, her mouth went dry and her heart beat heavily. As she awaited her certain to be dire fate, she began to wish that her voyage could have gone on forever.

She lay there for several hours, her muscles aching, bemoaning the approach of her moment of truth. Each minute was like its own little hell. She must have imagined the sound of the hatch being opened a dozen times. Each time, her stomach turned over and her throat constricted.

What she didn't know was that they were waiting for dark to unload her. The abduction of an Englishwoman could produce difficulties, even for a warlord like Wang. The fewer people who knew she had been brought here, the better. There was no reason to invite problems.

Once darkness fell and the port area was relatively clear, she was finally released from her cruel confinement. When the hatch opened, she began to sob. She sobbed as she was untied from the beam, she sobbed when her feet were untied. She sobbed as she was led up the ladder. Still blindfolded and gagged, naked, stumbling, her hands bound behind her, she was whisked across the dock to an awaiting car. She was forced into the back and then driven through the town, across the broad tributary stream that separated it from the Junshan peninsula and up the steep hill on which Wang's fortress sat.

One of Wang's soldiers sat on either side of her. She could feel their rough uniforms on her naked arms and thighs. Her nudity made her cringe with shame. When they arrived at the fortress not more than fifteen minutes later, she was taken from the car and made to walk across the stone courtyard. Strong, male hands were holding onto her upper arms on either side of her, pulling her quickly on her way. She was taken through the interior gate, across the inner courtyard and into the fortress itself.

Violet's body was trembling. That terrible, queasy feeling had returned to her stomach. A fearful sweat had broken out all over her. Where were they taking her? What were they going to do? Was she going to be brought directly to General Wang? Would she be beaten, whipped, raped?

She was brought by Wang's soldiers directly to the fortress's medieval dungeon. She felt herself descending a long set of stone stairs that curved to the right. The air smelled musty to her. When they reached the bottom, she was brought down a hallway. She could hear the echo of the men's boots on the stone floor. There was a jumble of keys, the sound of a latch turning and the opening of a large, heavy door. She was escorted through the door and pulled into the little cell. The men pushed her down on her belly, onto a thin, dirty pallet. To Violet's extreme unhappiness, they retied her ankles together and connected them to her wrists. When they left, the heavy, wooden door, as it slammed shut, sounded like the knell of doom.

* * * * * * * * * * * * * *

Lieutenant Cheng watched the soldiers take the naked, beautiful, long legged Englishwoman away. He had been honored when the general had ordered him to take charge of his new concubine on her trip to the fortress. He had followed his instructions to the letter, down to his civilian garb. He had been told to keep her discipline and discomfort intense and he had done so. He had been awaiting a reason to beat her and had kept her in her harsh confinement for a long time, after getting her used to some freedom. He knew that it was just a matter of time that she would break, and she did. He was certain that when he whipped her she had learned something new about cruelty and discipline.

As he watched her go, he realized that he had fallen in love with the unfortunate woman. No one would know how much he longed to take her in his arms and comfort her, how much he desired her flesh.

Washing her naked body each day had been torture for him. His cock would grow rock hard as he used his hands to rub soap over her heavy, porcelain breasts, over her soft, round rear cheeks, let his fingers brush along the line of her love lips, his palms the length of her inner thighs. When she knelt before him, waiting for him to give her the bowl to relieve herself in, he yearned to put his lips on her luscious looking, fat nipples, to take possession of her fur covered loins, to bury his cock in her flesh.

He knew that he should put her out of his mind. She was the general's property. Men who coveted the general's property lived short lives. But could he? That was the question.

军阀 外家

CHAPTER FIVE

It was six days later that General Wang's steam boat pulled up to the dock at Yeuyang. It had been a marvelous trip. Li Hua, wife no. 1, had spent a mountain of money on fabrics, jewelry, perfumes, everything that she could think of. She had serviced him dutifully too, something that he didn't always get. Not that he needed the sexual outlet, as there were dozens of whores to fuck in his houses of delight and dozens more in the whorehouses of his friends.

Wang also had made some acquisitions. He had procured three, pretty graduates of the Golden Bough Orphanage. The girls had turned 18 and were about to be released to the world. Wang was a benefactor of the orphanage and used it primarily as a source for whores. He usually brought two or three of them back with him on every trip. It humored him that the foreign charities that supported the orphanage applauded him for his work in finding employment for their female graduates.

In reducing females to bondage, Wang had found it helpful that they receive a complete change in their environment. Thus, peasant girls went to the city and city girls came to the country. Miss Harris was a case in point. Altering her environment from a privileged member of Western Civilization to essentially a slave in the Eastern would make it easier to subdue her.

The real prize that he obtained in Shanghai, however, wasn't the virginal orphan girls. It was the French whore who was gifted to him by his sons as he was leaving.

It seems that the girl had been dumped in Shanghai by her lover several years before. He had moved on to better pastures with a blond, American actress, leaving Estelle high and dry. Well remunerated work for an unskilled, white female in Shanghai was limited. So she did what millions of other pretty, young women throughout history have done in such situations. She started to peddle her ass.

It was Estelle's goal to earn just enough to pay for a boat ticket back to France. She was pretty and a new face and so she started having a modicum of success. Money from wealthy traders and bankers, and their sons, started to pour in. Estelle decided that she would stay in Shanghai for a while and build up a nice bankroll for when she went back to Paris.

And then, she made a fatal mistake. A man came into her life. Paolo was a Eurasian, half Chinese and half Portuguese. He had grown up in Macao, and had run some whores there. He had gotten into a little trouble and had decided to move his operations to Shanghai. He had introductions to some of the local boys and it wasn't long before he was looking to do some recruiting. Estelle came right out of the pimp's handbook. He introduced himself to her, wined and dined her a few times, told her that he loved her. She fell for him like a ton of bricks. She was, at first, happy to share some of her earnings with him, he was a great lover and even whores need a good fuck now and again. One night, when she came home from a 'date', Paolo insisted that she hand the money over to him. She refused and threw him out.

The next night, as she was on her way to a local watering hole where she intended to troll for a scion of a banker or trader with the right amount of cash, a car stopped suddenly next to her. Within a few seconds, much like Violet, she was dragged into the car.

The men took her to a house in the Chinese district. They fucked her for hours. After a while, Paolo showed up. He took a whip and laced her naked body while she screamed in pain. By the next morning, Paolo and Estelle had an understanding. She was working for him and, in exchange, she would get whatever he wanted to give to her, if anything. Oh, and he took away her passport.

Over a three year period, Paolo had assembled a stable of four high priced tarts. They were all deathly afraid of him. On nights they came back short, he would beat them with a thick rubber hose, tie them up and throw them in a closet. He had all of their passports. One of the girls he had was new. He had had to replace a, long, lanky, Russian whore. She had tried to leave him. Some of the triad boys found her at the docks with a ticket for Hong Kong and a forged passport.

They brought her to a building that the triad owned and played with her while waiting for Paolo to arrive. He brought the three remaining girls with him. What they saw and heard that night revitalized their loyalty to him. He let the triad boys keep the Russian.

Paolo had his eyes on a 22 year old, buxom, Australian sheila. She was kept by one of the leading bankers in the city in her own penthouse apartment. He gave her plenty of spending cash, bought her fine furs and the like. She was a whore already and didn't know it. The banker had let certain persons know that he was desirous of moving on from the relationship and didn't want any problems with her. Paolo was scheduled to make the move on her in a week. Three days in the triad house and she would be a dedicated employee.

Paolo made it a firm rule never to have more than four girls working for him at a time. It was hard enough to keep track of them as it was. The Russian girl was a good example. Where did she get the money for a boat ticket and a forged passport? She had to be cheating him. When he took on a whore, her pussy belonged to him. So any whore of his that moonlighted was using his pussy. That wasn't fair was it?

So Estelle had to go. She was the oldest of the crew and had been, frankly, a little shopworn when he took her over. In Macao, he had just turned the girls whose bloom had faded over to somebody who didn't run a high style house and made a little money off of them right up to the last. He could do that with Estelle. He had a couple of offers. But when he heard that Wang's sons were looking for a special present for their father's fiftieth birthday, it was serendipity. He liked the boys and had some money out on the street with them. He was making a steady profit.

Estelle didn't know it was D-day for her, D for done, that is, when they went down to the docks. She was just told that she was going to be a birthday present for the general. The stupid whore hadn't caught on until she was in a little room way below decks, on a cot, hogtied and gagged, and the boat was pulling away from the pier.

Estelle was very nervous when she was brought up to Wang's bedroom late that afternoon. The boat was already 45 miles upstream from the city. The soldiers who escorted her tied her wrists off to a hook in the overhead before they left. She had been stripped. She still had a quite appealing shape and her tits were good. There was just a couple lines in her face that were tell tale of her age. Her chin sagged just a little bit. She was only 29, but a very hard 29.

Wang thought a little introduction was in order. He was dressed in a luxurious, silken robe with pretty, colorful, Chinese flowers printed on it over a background of blue.

"I assume that you speak English," he stated more as an inquiry.

"Y,yes," the girl stuttered out.

"Good, that will make this easier. I am General Wang," he said in his polite, Oxford accented English. "Since I now own you body and soul, you may, for the time being, call me 'master'. Is that agreeable to you?"

The girl squirmed. Her face was a mask of anguish. She had hoped and prayed that what she thought had happened when she found herself all tied up down in the bowels of the ship and the ship leaving the dock, had not happened. Well, what she had just learned was that the thing that she feared had happened, had happened. She was a long way from Paris now and getting further and further away by the second.

She hesitated. "Does he really want me to call him master?" she thought to herself, panic welling up in her belly. Working for Paolo was one thing. He owned her, but he really didn't own her. This guy was taking things to a whole new level.

Estelle knew that there was only one answer to the question. "Yes," she whimpered. Her uplifted hands were getting sweaty and the buttons on her well sized breasts were stiff from fear.

"Good," Wang said. "We should get along well then. It's my custom to give my new slaves a sound whipping first thing so that there are no misunderstandings later. And so, tonight, in a minute or so, I'm going to thrash you to within an inch of your life. I'm not going to gag you. You can yell and scream all you want. I'm used to it and it will be good for you."

Estelle was biting her lower lip and her body shuddered. She started to whine. "P,please, master," she managed to get out, "p,please don't whip me." She had already started to cry and he hadn't even picked up the whip yet.

She wondered who this guy was and where he was taking her. The name seemed kind of familiar. She didn't pay attention to politics and that stuff. She wondered for a second if this was a little game that Paolo was playing on her or something.

"Now, I said that you could yell and scream all you want, er,....What's your name again?"

"Estelle," she said softly. Her body was trembling, making her heavy breasts shudder, to the general's delight. Estelle had short, black hair with little ringlets that curled up on either side of her face. She had shaved her pubic region in deference to the preferences of her wealthy Asian clients. She was still wearing the deep purple fingernail polish she had been wearing when she came aboard, a perfect match for the sheer, flowing dress that was now down in the little cabin where she had been kept prisoner along with her silk panties and dark maroon high heels. She had not been wearing a bra.

"Yes, well, Estelle, as I was saying," Wang continued, "I said that you could yell and scream all you wanted. I didn't say that you could talk, did I?"

"N,no" she squeaked.

"Since it's your first day, I'm going to be light on you. I'll whip you for that tomorrow. I think that you'll have all that you can handle tonight anyway."

"Mmmmmmmmmmm!" Estelle emitted frantically, pushing her lips together. She knew better than to speak. Another whipping! Tomorrow! Her mouth was turned down in a frown. Perspiration covered her upper lip. She shifted on her bare feet. Her brow was wrinkled and her hands started to open and shut above her, as if testing to see if the bonds that forced them in the air were tight enough to hold them.

Wang went over to a closet on the side of the room and opened the door. Wang's room, the stateroom of the ship, was exceeded in size only by the engine and dining rooms. A large, ornate bed stood against one wall. Estelle was dangling from a hook in the open area just opposite the bed, somewhere Wang would have no trouble getting full use of a cane. He took one from the closet now.

It was a little sturdier than the bamboo one he had used on his sluts a couple of weeks ago. It would bruise heavily.

Tomorrow, the girl would not be able to move without pain all over her body.

"We'll start off with the cane, all right?" he asked her playfully.

Estelle was dying to speak again. She wanted to beg and plead to be spared, promise to always obey him in all things, tell him the pleasure that she could bring to him, that he could keep her naked and all tied up all the time when he wasn't using her. She would say or promise anything to avoid what was heading implacably towards her.

She couldn't answer the man. Her mouth was all dry and her heart was thumping. She didn't know what it was like to be whipped with a cane. Paolo had used the rubber hose mostly, since it didn't mark.

"I asked you a question, slave girl," he said. "Do you have an answer?"

"N,no," she said. Tears were streaming down her face.

"I thought I told you to call me master," he said calmly. "Didn't I?"

"Y,yes,'" she answered. Then, realizing her mistake, said, "Yes, master."

"That's much better," Wang said. "We can deal with that tomorrow as well."

Estelle issued a deep, fretful moan at this information.

"Let's get started, okay, Estelle?"

"No, master!" Estelle shouted. "Please, no, master, please!"

Wang ignored her response. He swung the cane forcefully at her body. It landed on her side, just over her rib. It made a loud, 'thump!'

"Ooooooooooooooh!" Estelle yelled. "Oh, god! Please don't! Please!"

Wang paid her no attention. His blood was up. He didn't have an army big enough to throw the foreigners out of

China, but he could capture, enslave and torment their women.

Wang worked the cane around the poor girl's body. He struck her across the back, on her thighs, front, sides and back, on her arms and across her breasts. At this one, the French girl wailed the loudest. The room was filled with her agonized pleas for mercy. After a while, she forgot to speak English and started to beg for surcease of her torments in French.

"Non! Non! Non!" she called out desperately. Wang had worked up quite a sweat. He looked at the swaying, moaning body of the French girl and wondered if there was any place on her that he had missed. He looked down and he saw the backs of her shins. He leaned over and swung the cane forward at the back of her left leg, smashing the cane into the muscle there. Estelle raised her leg, howling and shaking it as if it were afire. When Wang struck the other one, she lost her balance and was prevented from falling to the deck only because her hands were bound to the hook above her.

Wang felt refreshed. Now he knew that he would have an enjoyable voyage back to his fortress. He had three more days to play with her and the three new and, as yet, unused whores. Wang had plans for them. All of the operating bordellos in the town of Yeuyang were licensed or owned by him. He had been meaning to open a high class one. It was a busy town, busier since he had gotten his steamboat and started making regular runs to Shanghai. There were a good number of wealthy merchants in town now. They deserved a place that met their high standards of refinement. Estelle would run the place for him. She would still service the clients, those who could afford her, and she would also lend an air of sophistication to the place, train the girls to act gracefully and to fuck energetically. Once she got to know the power inherent in a whip, she would put it to good use, especially if the success of the whorehouse was directly related to whether she experienced torment at his hands. Tomorrow, he would use the narrow dressage whip on her. It would produce nice, long, thin lacerations, the kind that usually healed very well. It would be agonizing for her.

For now he was done. He had a raging hard-on that needed servicing. He reached above the still moaning woman and released her hands. She fell to the floor. He poked her with the cane.

"Estelle," he said. "You have a duty to perform. Get up or I'll whip you some more."

Estelle heard the general through her fog of pain and unhappiness. She struggled to her knees. Wang had opened his robe and had his long, thick cock out. She knew exactly what she had to do.

The naked, French whore rose up and subsumed Wang's prick into her mouth. Her body was a mass of painful sensations from her beating, but she knew that she had to do her best or suffer some more. She fought through the haze and fear. She slid her lips over Wang's cock slowly, holding them tight against his skin. She swirled her tongue around his meat. Her hand snuck inside his robe and she began to cup his balls. "I'll show him that I'm a good whore," she thought. "Maybe then he won't beat me."

She pleasured his tool assiduously for more than twenty minutes. Wang groaned his pleasure. Four times, she brought him to the brink of completion and four times she relented her efforts just in time. Finally she let him go over the top. He had his hands on her head. His knees sagged as he came. He groaned loudly as his juices ran down his throbbing cock. "Happy Birthday!" he said to himself.

* * * * * * * * * * * * * *

So, the trip upstream had been a great pleasure. Estelle taught the new girls how to suck cock. They must have sucked every cock on board before they were done. He resisted piercing their hymens. The merchants of the town would pay dearly for that right. He did introduce them to the whip, though. It was obligatory. He had Estelle whip them. She did it with alacrity while he watched. She was going to be a good madam. And she was, he had discovered, a good fuck too!

His thoughts often turned to Miss Harris. He realized that she would have probably reached the fortress about a week before he did. He had given the men in the boat a set of written instructions to Li Pao, his eunuch, about how she was to be treated. He had threatened the men on the boat with death if they committed a single sexual act on her body. Other than for purposes of hygiene, she was to remain untouched. She was to be bound continuously and never have the chance to see the shore. It would add to her sense of hopelessness not knowing anything about the trip to his fortress. Her confinements should begin as strict as possible and then gradually taper out to the more endurable. If a man was striking you with a club and then, instead, started hitting you with his hand, you would think that that was an improvement, something you could live with. If Miss Harris was to become a good and faithful concubine, she would have to be always aware that much more restrictive and harsh conditions could be arranged for her at any time.

As his servants began to unload the booty from his trip to Shanghai onto the dock, General Wang hurried ashore. His first task was to consult with the officer he left in charge, Major Won, to make sure that there had been no problems while he was away. Then he wanted to see his concubines and have a celebratory fuck with them all. After that, in a day or two, he would deal with Miss Harris. She had stewed in his dungeon for the better part of a week already. A few more days wouldn't hurt her.

军阀 外家

CHAPTER SIX

At the moment that General Wang's boat hit the dock, Miss Harris was in her cell in his dungeon being punished. Li Pao, who had been training her for the last six days, had decreed that she should 'ride the pony' for several hours today.

Violet did not know that her owner had arrived. Her cell had no window. In fact there was little about what was going on around her that she did know.

Li had served General Wang for the last eighteen years. He had broken in quite a number of concubines for him in that period. Most of them were silly girls like Me Ling and Pu Wei, his master's current Chinese concubines. While they had received schooling in the sexual arts, in a theoretical sense since General Wang would not have accepted them as his concubines had they not been untouched virgins, the general's ideas about discipline and the duties of a concubine needed to be instilled. That was Li's job.

After their ritual deflowering by their new master, the Chinese girls spent at least a week in the custody of Li. There they learned how to be sexually responsive for their new lord, how to manipulate the muscles of their honeypots for his pleasure, how to suck a cock with alacrity and most of all, how to obey, all from practical experience.

Since these pretty girls had already been aware of their principal duties before being officially accepted as one of the master's concubines, they were much more accepting of the need to hone their sexual skills. For what use was a concubine without sexual skills.

The foreign sluts that his master picked up from time to time were another story. Most of them did not appreciate the honor being given to them to serve as a sexual servant to a great man like General Wang. They were reticent to engage in all of the practices a lord like General Wang might demand. Some were horrified at the thought of placing the general's cock in their mouth. Others recoiled from the sexual use of their dainty, rear entrance. Most of them were, well, reticent is not strong enough of a word and reluctant just doesn't express it, let's say horrified at the idea of engaging in the physical act of love with another female. But enjoyment of the vision of two beautiful women ardently engaging in mutual pleasure had long been a means by which privileged men reignited desire. No concubine could deny that service to her lord.

What better place to convince these female, foreign devils of the importance of their new duties, and to motivate them to learn the skills that they would need, than in the general's dungeon. The instruments of persuasion were already there. They could be placed in spirit deadening isolation for long periods of time and the cries and scream of pain of the general's other prisoners, men and women who were paying the price of the general's displeasure, served as efficient motivators.

On the day of her arrival, Li had waited a little more than two hours before descending to the bowels of the fortress to greet her. It was important that there be some demarcation from her time on the boat, which, from Lieutenant Cheng's report, was appropriately arduous, and the next cycle of her transformation from a privileged, pampered European to a subservient sexual servant.

Violet was pretty much where she had been left by Wang's soldiers. She had spent the time mostly cowering in abject fear. She knew that she was in an underground prison of some kind. Descending the stone stairs, the echo of the men's boots, the jingle of keys, all told her that. What they didn't tell her was what was going to happen to her there.

No one had yet explained what General Wang's purposes were in kidnapping her. Robert had been so adamant about the general's murderous propensities, that Violet could not exclude the possibility that that was to be her fate. Perhaps, she worried frantically, the general wanted to inflict some prolonged, exquisitely painful process on her first, one that he would watch with bemused satisfaction. Maybe he was arranging a gang rape for her, making her service a long line of his soldiers time and again, until her body could accept no more.

Her most reasonable theory was, she thought, that she had been brought to his domain for his sexual use. At least initially. Her treatment on the boat seemed to presage this. Her mind revolted at the thought of being his slave. She remembered well the look of cold hearted lust he had given her in the casino. She had felt that he was imagining his mouth and hands on her breasts. But what choice did she have? She had already experienced a sample of his cruelty. It had nearly driven her mad.

She was actually of two minds about this. The first was that she was a subject of the British Empire and a white woman, within 3 degrees of relation to the King, and no tin pot Chinese general was going to force her to voluntarily engage in sexual relations with him. He could force her, she knew that. He had the power to bind her and render her open for him. The man on the boat had shown her that. But he could not force her to be an active participant in it, to collaborate in her own violation. She would never give him that satisfaction!

On the other hand, she lived in absolute terror of the things he might do to her to force her to yield to him. The three strokes she had received while on the boat had been excruciating. Everything he had done to her so far, or more properly, ordained to be done to her so far, had brutalized her almost beyond her power to bear it. If pleasuring him had been the price of her freedom on the boat, she would have paid it in an instant. She would have done anything he wanted.

She knew that at some point there would be the moment of truth, when one of these two competing thoughts would win. She feared it more than anything.

Violet was relieved that she did not have to spend her time awaiting the pleasure of her owner lying on the stone floor of her cell that she had felt under her bare feet. The pallet was thin and odiferous and greasy, but it was softer than the floor, softer than the deck of the hold where she had been kept prisoner for ten, or was it eleven, days. She wasn't really sure.

It felt strange that that travail was now over. It had seemed like it would never end. Her body still remembered the gentle sway of the boat. She was fully cognizant, though, that a new one was about to begin. Lying on her pallet, trussed, blinded and gagged, she wondered, sadly, how long she would have to wait until someone came to untie her and initiate it. She hoped and prayed that it would not be as long as her periods of isolation on the boat. The torture of not knowing her fate was excruciating.

Being locked in a dungeon cell was an experience of a far different quality than being a prisoner on the junk. Dungeons bespoke ancient, medieval tortures, long suffering, forgotten prisoners. On the boat, there had always been some sound to remind her that she had not been completely separated from the world. Her cell was as silent as the grave. The smell was of decay and rottenness. Who had been the last one to lie on the thin pallet on which she lay now, she wondered. What had happened to them? How long did they have to endure Wang's cruelty? Was it a woman, like her, destined for his bed? Or was it a man awaiting his sentence of death?

She tried to speculate on the size and configuration of her cell. Seeing only darkness, seemingly adrift in a void, it helped to anchor her to have an idea of what her surroundings were. From what she could tell, her pallet lay in the right corner. She didn't know how big her cell was, but she remembered walking four small steps before the soldiers had thrown her down. Adding the length of her pallet to her footsteps, it was probably ten feet long. Assuming it was square, it would be 10' by 10'. 100 feet square. She had moaned loudly several times to test her theory and the lack of a significant echo seemed adequate proof.

She jumped when she heard the key in the lock of the door to her cell. She was lying on her left side, facing the wall, her arms and legs connected behind her. Her heart began immediately to beat wildly, her stomach to twist and turn. She felt her body trembling. She heard the door swing open and what sounded like carpeted feet on the floor. There was a period of delay, as if whoever it was was doing something. Then a pair of hands, boney, strong, soft hands, began to untie her knots. A terrible chill went through her.

The miracle of modern electricity had not yet reached Junshan. There was talk of power lines being extended westward from Nanking. Wang knew that with power lines would come the national government and so he had done everything he could to resist it, no matter how nice it would be to sit under an electric light at night like he did in Shanghai. Kerosene was the fuel of choice in his mansion. Every room was equipped with lanterns that, when lit, provided a modicum of yellowish light. At night, when the men who had the task of caring for the prisoners, if that's the right word, were off duty, the lamps were extinguished. During the day, when the men needed lights, they were ignited.

Li had made special arrangements for the two guards to remain on duty until he had had the chance to deal with their new prisoner. The narrow stairway that led from the main floor had lanterns distributed strategically down it. Lanterns lit the guards' station and the hallway to the cells. There were no lanterns installed in the cells themselves. Why give the cells' inmates any resources to help promote an escape or to avoid their just deserts by setting themselves on fire? And why waste kerosene on prisoners? When one of the guards wanted to deal with a prisoner, he brought a lantern with him and hung it from a hook. When he left, he took it with him. Otherwise, the prisoners were kept in total darkness. It helped make them more docile. And, the hook could be used for other things.

When he entered Violet's cell, Li had brought a lantern with him. He hung it from the hook in the ceiling and turned the wick high for maximum illumination. He approached the naked woman. The fingers behind her back were fluttering nervously and she was making a little whining sound, reactions to his presence. He would give her something to worry about.

He released her feet from her hands and her ankles from each other. Then he stepped back. He had also brought along with him the 3' long whippy stick that was his standard tool of persuasion. He waited until the female foreign devil moved her legs and showed some sign of life. When she did, he raised his stick and delivered a fierce blow across the side of her right thigh.

"*Stand up! Stand up!*" he yelled at her in Chinese.

Violet felt a line of fire across her thigh. She screeched and tried to turn away from whoever was abusing her. She raised her knees to her chest and tried to curl up into a protective ball.

"*Stand up! Stand up!*" Li yelled again. His voice was high pitched, kind of like the yodel of a country singer. This time the whip landed across her right shoulder.

Violet screamed again. She heard the man's angry words in Chinese, but did not understand them. Was he ordering her to do something or just hurling imprecations of hatred at her? In her panic, she did not know.

For Li, the woman's reactions were typical. He really did not expect her to get right up. But the pain of the whip would be a great motivator for her to learn what the words meant.

Li reached out his hand and grabbed Violet's hair. He pulled it harshly. The woman's body followed it. She was whining and crying. He pulled her to her feet. Her body swayed as if unused to standing. He released her and stepped back again.

"*Spread legs! Spread legs!*" he yelled.

Violet had heard these words many times. Trying to suppress her sobs, she spread them instantly. Some demon had come into her cell!

Li took in the vision of his master's new slut. His interest in her was purely professional. Her gag and blindfold hid her face, but her frontal attributes were clearly visible. The yellowish light of the lantern made everything about her seem soft and warm. He took in her heavy, pale breasts, her long legs and narrow hips. He could see why the general was interested in her. He had seen him often play with the large breasts of the Russian girl. He liked to whip them too. This one's breasts were not as large, but they were much larger than what was traditional for classical notions of Chinese beauty. To Li, women with large breasts were more like cows. He had teased and stroked and suckled at the Russian slattern's breasts until they came into milk for just that reason. The general liked to drink from her at breakfast. Li made sure that the cow was milked regularly, at least twice a day, three times if the master was away, so that she would continue to lactate.

This one's breasts also seemed adequate for that purpose. Perhaps he would give the Russian's a rest.

He did admire her slender hips. That was appropriate for a woman of pleasure. Her legs were too long and she was too tall, taller than the Russian. Her thighs were appropriately graceful and toned. He looked at her sex. Her bush was wiry and full. These foreign women disgusted him. Was she a peasant? Peasant women didn't shave their pussies. They had hair under their arms and copulated in pig shit. And her feet were too big.

Her hair was too short, but that he could fix. In a few months she would sport long, languid hair as is appropriate for a concubine. How could she wash her master's body with hair like that?

Violet was trembling in terror as she awaited the man's next actions. Her shoulder and thigh still burned. What had he hit her with? It felt like a narrow stick of some sort. She readied herself for another blow.

He wanted to see her ass. "*Turn around!*" he yelled at her. He gave her a couple of seconds to comply and then he struck her across her belly with the whip.

"Eeeeeeeeeeeeeeee!" Violet screeched as she felt the fierce burning of the blow. "What does he want? What does he want!" she asked herself frantically.

Li took hold of her shoulders and spun her body around. "*Turn around!*" he yelled again as he did it.

Violet tried to listen carefully to the words so that she would know them if he called them out again. Did they mean turn around or show me your ass? She cringed fearfully as she expected another blow across her back.

"Ahhhh!" Li said to himself. "Her ass is perfect!" It was round and firm and yet small and graceful. It was pale white, having never seen the sun. And her fingers! What fingers! They were long and thin, delicate, like young branches of a tree in spring. They would flutter across his master's belly and thighs like butterflies as she serviced him with her mouth.

"The mouth! I need to see the mouth!" His mind exclaimed. He was getting excited. "And the eyes!"

Placing the whip under his arm, he stepped closer to Violet and unhooked the straps to her gag. The gag remained in place since it was lodged firmly in her mouth. He untied the blindfold. That fell away in his hands.

"*Turn around! Turn around!*" he screamed at her.

Despite her terror, Violet recognized these words. She had just heard them. She spun around as fast as she could, hoping to avoid another blow from the whip. She took in the form of her assailant. Her eyes were still trying to get used to the light. He stood about 5'8", a little taller than her 5'6". He had narrow shoulders and was thin with small hips. The light was above and behind him and she could not really see his face. It made him look like he was a figure who had sprung from a nightmare. He was dressed in a long sheath. The glimmer of the light off of it told her that it was silk. In the dim light it could have been either blue or silver.

The eunuch looked into Violet's eyes. "Wonderful!" he said to himself. In the soft light, it was hard to see if they were green or blue. They were piercing and frank and bespoke an innate intelligence. They were challenging too, not obsequious. Her nose was straight and maybe a trifle too long, but on her it looked good. He needed to see her mouth. He stepped forward and reached out to grab the gag so that it could be removed.

Violet saw the man's motion and flinched. It looked like he was going to strike her with his hand.

Li pulled his whip from under his arm and slashed her across the breasts. "*Stand till! Stand still!*" he barked.

"Oooooouuuuuummmm!" Violet called out. Her breasts burned like the blazes. She hunched her shoulders and bent her waist in a natural reaction to protect them from another assault. She saw his hand rear back and she ducked her head down.

"*Stand still! Stand still!*" Li screamed.

Another blow landed across her left upper arm. Violet felt like she had been stung by a hornet. She knew what the man wanted. She just didn't know if she could do it.

With supreme effort, she brought herself back to where she was standing when the man reached out to her. "If he's going to strike me with his hand, he's going to do it. It's better to get it over with than suffer more blows of his whip," she thought miserably.

"This one learns fast," Li thought. "And she has courage. The Russian girl had been a blubbering ball of absolute terror by now."

He reached forward again and took hold of the front of the gag. The girl stood her ground, although her body was shaking with fear. He eased it out slowly.

Her lips were pouty and full, like ripe cherries. They were trembling. Her face recorded her vulnerability but showed character. "She will be interesting to have around," he thought. "The general will love to slide his cock across those lips and to see them suckling the breasts of the Russian girl."

All in all, it appeared that the general had made a good acquisition. It was his duty to see that she reached her full potential. He owed it to his master and he owed it to her. Since she was a concubine now, and forever, she would learn to get pleasure from the fulfillment of her role. The better she fulfilled it, the better would be her pleasure. He couldn't wait to see that face in ecstasy, the eyes half closed, the lips parted and pursed as her orgasm coursed through her. "Tomorrow," he thought.

Now that he'd seen her, it was time to get down to business.

"You General Wang new whore!" he yelled at her in English. Before he came into the general's service, Li had worked in a whorehouse in Shanghai. His lot had fallen low after the Emperor had been forced to reduce his court for economic reasons and he was, as one of the younger eunuchs, dismissed. There had been many of them. Some of the dismissed eunuchs killed themselves rather than leave the Forbidden Palace. Others had done like he did and took employment in whorehouses. Regulating sluts was what he knew best, whether they belonged to the Emperor or to a whoremaster.

In the Shanghai whorehouse, Li had acquired the basics of Pigeon English. He had had to deal with many of the English devils. General Wang won the right to his services in a card game with the owner.

He didn't like to speak the foreigner's tongue. It was harsh and discordant. Not like Chinese, musical and harmonious. This one would learn to take her orders in Chinese or suffer the consequences. For now, she needed to know what her new in role in life would be so that she could adjust herself. He didn't know the English word for concubine and so it came out 'whore'.

Violet's heart skipped a beat. They were the words she had been afraid to hear. "Oh, God!" she exclaimed to herself. "Oh, God!"

"You learn fuckee, suckee good!" Li continued. "Tomorrow we begin."

That was all the slut needed to know.

He pointed to a spot on the floor to his left and yelled in Chinese, "*Kneel down! Kneel down!*"

Violet realized that he wanted her to move to that spot and she did so as quickly as she could, keeping an eye out for his cruel whip. She stood there awaiting further orders.

"*Kneel down!   Kneel down!*" Li yelled again.   He emphasized his command by giving the slut a harsh blow to her rear cheeks.

Violet's gag was off and her voice was unrestrained. "Ooooooooooooooh!" she yelled as the message of pain was received by her brain. "What does he want?" she asked herself frantically. "What does he want?" Her tears were flowing in a steady stream.

Li tapped the end of his stick on the floor in front of her several times. "*Kneel down!*" he shouted.

She got the message and hurriedly lowered herself to her knees. The floor was cool and rough. She hoped that she wouldn't have to kneel there long.

Li had brought a wicker basket with some supplies in it. From it he drew some ropes. He went behind the cowering female and attached a rope to her bound hands. There was a number of small iron bars embedded in the floor. Underneath them was a small gap so that you could pass something under them. The bars were just below floor level so that you could walk over them and not trip. Li ran the end of the rope to a bar just behind the woman and tied it off. He then took smaller ropes and attached them to Violet's ankles.

"*Spread legs!*" he yelled at her. "*Spread legs!*"

Moaning her fear, her lips jammed tightly against each other, Violet obediently spread her knees further apart.

The eunuch affixed the rope from each ankle to one of the embedded bars, fastening Violet's feet in place. He stepped over to her pallet and retrieved the gag he had tossed there. He came around to Violet's front and presented it to her. "*Open mouth!*" he ordered harshly.

Violet put two and two together and spread her lips. She moaned mournfully as the thick, fat wad of leather crossed her lips and filled her mouth. Li leaned over and buckled it behind her head. As he did so, she took in the smell of his perfumed body. The silk of his gown rubbed against her face. She cringed at the contact.

Li stepped back to look at her. Her brow was furrowed with unhappiness and fear. He reached out and took possession of one of her breasts and squeezed it with his fingers. The girl's eyes took on a troubled mien. He took no sexual pleasure from touching her. He had no sexual urges or needs. But he did appreciate the touch and feel of a woman's body from an esthetic point of view. Her breast was wonderfully firm and soft all at once. He cupped the breast and gently squeezed her thick nipple with his fingers. It was hard with her fear. "Yes," he thought. "Tomorrow I will give you an orgasm, maybe two or three. We'll proceed from there."

Violet's body tensed up at the contact with her breast. She, of course, did not know that Li was a eunuch. She only knew that she was vulnerable to whatever the harsh man in front of her wanted to do to her. She shivered in fear, but, yet, the fingers on her nipple had produced a tingle in her loins. It was unsettling.

Li went back to his basket and returned with a wide band of leather. He stepped behind the naked, kneeling woman and circled it around her neck, buckling it tightly. He came back around front with another rope.

The collar had a golden colored ring in the front and Li passed the rope through it and tied it off. He then brought the rope to the floor to a spot just past her spread knees. There was an embedded bar there and he passed the rope through it. He stood back and looked into Violet's troubled eyes. As he pulled the rope, Violet's neck began to be forced down. She mewed behind her gag as her head went lower and lower. When her chin was about 6 inches from the hard, stone floor, he ran the rope through a bar about three feet ahead of her and tied it off.

Violet's back strained as her torso was bent over to accommodate the pressure on her neck. She was bound as tightly, tighter even, than she had been bound on the boat during her ten days of hell. The rope on her hands was taut, immobilizing them. She couldn't move her head up or down. Her ankles were fastened in place. She sobbed as she realized what was in store for her. She assumed that it was night, based on a rough estimate of time since she had left the boat. No one would come to release her until the morning at the earliest! The man might leave her here even longer than that!

The distraught woman issued a mournful cry, muffled by her gag. Li picked up his basket and his whippy stick. Holding them in one hand, he reached up and, after lowering its wick, took the lantern from its hook. He glided to the door of the cell. He turned, put the lantern on the floor outside in the hall and, taking a last look at his bound and forlorn prisoner, swung the door shut.

Violet was immediately plunged into total darkness. She heard the jingle of the keys and the lock click. And that was all.

Anguish rose up in the poor woman like a flood. She emitted a long, loud, mournful wail. Her heart felt like it was going to break from sadness. "Oh, god! Oh, god! Oh, god!" she screamed in her mind.

Her body still burned where the cruel man had struck her. How was she supposed to know what he was ordering her to do? And he said that she was General Wang's whore! Her stomach flipped when she heard the confirmation of all of her fears. "I'm not a whore! I'm not a whore!" she tried to shout. "Please, God, please help me!" she prayed. "Pleeeeeeeease!"

She sobbed and wailed for a long time. Her back was aching terribly and her knees were being ground into the stone floor beneath her. Her shoulders were pulled back and strained by their fastening to her hands. "Why are they doing this to me? Why?" she cried out. Her muffled voice died in her lonely cell.

军阀 外家

CHAPTER SEVEN

It was a long, dolorously hard night for the young Englishwoman. She was locked in a tomb-like prison, deep in the heart of China. She had hoped and prayed that the torment she had suffered in her journey to this place had ended, only to discover that her plight had worsened. The darkness that closed all around her in her subterranean confinement was like an evil force stealing her soul.

After a while, Violet brought herself back under control. It was just a matter of time. She just had to wait, not panic, and eventually she would be released from her cruel tie. She did not know what she would face tomorrow, but she would bear up under it.

She tried to think of better times, her childhood growing up, her father who, with all of his faults, she had still loved. She had had friends back in England, good friends. She had been an active, educated, social person. Could she live on those memories?

She didn't think so. If they continued to treat her this way, she would die. That would be the best, she thought. All her fears, all her sorrow would be gone. There would be no more need to choose between complicity in her enslavement or resistance. No more whipping, no more harsh, angry men to torment her. Dying certainly couldn't be harder than this.

The jailers came on duty shortly after sunrise. Most of the people in Wang's domain did not live by clocks, they lived by the sun. When it was up, it was time to work. When it was down, it was time to stop.

They paid no notice to the door behind which Violet knelt so unhappily. And she took no notice, through the thick wooden door that kept her a prisoner, of them.

It was not until somewhat after ten that morning that Li came to relieve her from her cruel confinement. Violet's heart leapt when she heard the door opening. Light came pouring in. She prayed that it was for the purpose of releasing her and not for any other reason.

Li stepped in. He was holding a lantern. With him was a trembling maid, dressed in a light green cheongsam style blouse and a pair of white, pegged pants. She was wearing wooden sandals and was carrying a tray in front of her. Her long, black hair was tied off behind her head and the rest cascaded down her back. From the downward angle of Violet's head, all she could see were their feet.

The eunuch gave the girl an order and she acknowledged it readily. She put the tray down on the floor and removed the cloth covering. On one side was a wooden bowl containing a steaming porridge. In the other was a long, deep, thin, blue and white, porcelain bowl that was empty. In the middle was a small carafe. The girl took the long bowl off the tray, hustled around the bound woman and knelt behind her. She slid the bowl under Violet's sex and nodded to the eunuch.

"*Piss!*" Li ordered. Unlike yesterday, he did not shout his command. His voice was stern nonetheless. And he had his whippy stick in his hand.

Violet had been looking up at the man dolefully. She had struggled mightily during the night to hold herself in, knowing that he would certainly punish her for peeing on the floor. She felt the bowl slide under her and heard the instruction, one that she was very familiar with.

She sighed as her water released. When she had filed the bowl, the obsequious maid took it and placed it back on the tray. There was a matching porcelain top next to it and she used it to cover the bowl.

With that out of the way, Li untied the rope that held Violet's head down. She looked up at him uncertainly, not knowing whether this signaled that she should raise her head or not. He gave her a hand signal that permitted it and for the first time in about twelve hours, she was able to straighten her back.

The strain of straightening herself made her groan. A tear escaped her mist filled eyes and flowed down her cheek. Li went behind her and released the rope holding her hands to the iron bar in the floor. He signaled to the maid and she took the bowl of porridge off of the tray and placed in front of Violet.

Li came around front. He reached behind her and removed her gag. He then took his whippy stick and tapped the side of the bowl. "*Eat*," he said.

Violet looked down, appalled at the man's command. She didn't know the word, but she knew what he meant. She was ravenously hungry, not having eaten since noon the prior day. But to eat like an animal? She couldn't do that.

"Whack!" Li had delivered a blow of his whip to Violet's back. "Owwwww!" she cried. Her eyes flashed at the man.

"*Eat!*" he said again, this time with more insistence.

She decided that she had no choice. She certainly didn't want to give the man occasion to strike her again, or worse, to take the food away and rebind her. Tears in her eyes, she leaned her head down and started lapping at the bowl.

To her surprise, it was tasty. It was sweet. There were raisins in it and some spice that she couldn't place. She discarded her objections and began to eat the porridge with relish. When it was all gone, she licked the bowl clean. It was the best meal she had had since she was kidnapped. She looked up at the man, signaling that she was done.

The maid took the bowl away and brought to Violet the small carafe. She held it out and proffered it to Violet's lips.

Violet looked up at the man first. She didn't want to make any mistakes.

"*Drink!*" he said.

The maid tilted the carafe and a heavy, fruity liquid poured out onto Violet's tongue. It tasted like apricots and maybe oranges. It was so good that she tried to lick the lip of the carafe when the flow of juice had stopped.

The girl removed the carafe from her mouth and brought it around to her tray. She looked up at Li and he nodded to her again. She took a wet cloth off of the tray and returned to Violet. Smiling at her shyly, she wiped the bound woman's face until it was clean. She returned it to the tray and placed it in the wooden bowl. She put the cloth over the tray items and stepped back, waiting for Li's next command.

Li went over to the pallet where he had thrown Violet's blindfold and retrieved it. Coming from behind her, he circled her head with it and tied it off. He reinserted her gag. He then crouched down and untied both of her ankles. When he went around front, he commanded Violet to "*Stand up!*"

She knew this command from last night. She struggled to her feet. Li attached a lead to the ring of her collar and gave her a tug. He moved off and Violet followed him.

She rejoiced as she found herself going up the stairs. The stairway led to the main hall of the fortress. Violet felt the rough stone under her feet turn to smooth. She could hear the sounds of other people around her, but she put her concerns of modesty aide. What relevance did that have now?

They began to ascend a set of carpeted stairs and then another. Violet wondered where the man was taking her. Was she going to be greeted by General Wang? Should she be afraid? She was so happy to be out of the dungeon that she couldn't care less what they did to her.

Li pulled her to the left. She sensed the maid, who had been following them, go to the right. They walked down a long hallway, slowed and a door opened. They went through it. Violet had the impression that there was someone standing by it. There was more walking and then another door was opened. Violet heard the sound of water being poured. The room felt steamy and warm. There was tile under her feet. She heard the rustling of clothing being removed and the soft giggles of young girls. Li removed her blindfold.

She was in an ornate bathroom. The walls were covered with tiles with paintings of red, green and blue flowers. There was a tub in the middle of it. It looked to be about 10 feet on all sides, as big as her cell. A smell of scented oil was coming up from it. Young Chinese women, three of them, were standing around it. They all had long, black hair tied back into ponytails and bright, cheery faces. One of them had just tilted a large vat over and spilled its contents into the tub. There was a fire under the vat and the same woman pulled a lever and water poured into the vat to be heated. The other two had just doffed their green and white blouses and pants, presenting pretty, little breasts and hairless loins.

She felt her hands being loosened. Her gag was removed. She looked at Li. *"Take bath,"* he said roughly, pointing to the tub with his stick. He turned and left the room.

Violet didn't know what to do. Was this really a tub of steaming, hot water? Was she really going to get to take a bath? She was incapable of moving. It seemed so unreal to have come from a dungeon where she had been tied up like the lowest of all living things all through the interminable, dark night, and brought to this elegant room and told that she could enjoy one of the blessings of civilization, that she could make herself human again.

The two young, naked women came up to Violet and, taking her arms, urged her forward. The tub was about three feet deep and there was a ledge around the edges of it. Violet put her foot on the ledge and felt the hot water wash over it. She gave a little gasp. The young women hopped in past her and then, pulling on her arms, brought her in the rest of the way. The girl who had been at the vat tossed her clothes aside as well and joined them

For a moment, Violet had to do little jumps until her skin got used to the temperature. Slowly, she lowered her body down, covering herself, bit by bit until the water went over her shoulders. Then, laughing, she immersed herself in it completely.

It was heaven. Her body felt like it was being renewed. The water was slightly oily and she could feel it working on her skin. She brought her head up and let her hair wash back. For a moment, she was filled with joy. And then, where she was and what she was to become crossed over her. All the trials and tribulations since she last was a free person, standing in the park, looking forward to a journey home, ignorant of the terrible future that awaited, passed through her. She felt her sorrow bubbling up. She tried to hold it back, tried desperately. The Chinese girls, sensing her unhappiness, crowded around her. When she felt one of them put her arms around her, Violet started to sob uncontrollably.

The girls eased her over to the side of the tub and helped her take a seat on the ledge. She could hear them murmuring soft words of comfort. The sounds of their friendly, sweet voices made it even worse. She felt like she would never stop crying. Gentle hands rubbed over her shoulders and over her head. One of the girls clutched her to her body and hugged her closely. Violet hugged her back gratefully.

It took a while for Violet to calm herself down. The way that the men had been treating her, she didn't know how long this pleasant interlude would last. She decided that she would enjoy it while she could.

She pulled her head back from the girl who was hugging her and mouthed, "Thank you," to her softly. The girl put her fingers to her mouth and shook her head. Then she removed her fingers and gave Violet a kiss on her lips. She pulled her head back and smiled.

They pulled Violet to the middle and made her stand. One of the girls swam to the edge of the pool and returned with a jar of pink soap and some sponges. She dipped some of the soap onto each sponge and the girls started to wash her body. Violet closed her eyes and let them.

She had never had those tendencies, although some of the cruel men in her set had started rumors that she had. In England, one would not take a bath with three other naked women. Nor two, nor one. You certainly would not let them touch you, never mind let them rub their hands over your breasts while the others washed your back and neck. They led Violet to the shallow end of the tub where the water was only a few inches deep. She felt hands pulling at her thighs and then the sensation of the soft sponges running across her skin. One of them washed her rear cheeks and in between while another washed her loins. The girls seemed amused by her pronounced bush of brown, curly hair. When her bottom half had been fully soaped, they led her back into the deeper end and washed her off.

It was when they did her hair that she thought she had attained paradise. Her hair had not had a good wash for more than a week, almost two. On the boat they limited themselves to washing it with river water. It was oily and tangled and dirty. One of the girls jumped up from the pool and ran over to the large vat. There was a spigot on the side and she opened it and filled a ceramic jug with clean, hot water. She ran back and poured it over Violet's head. It was just the right temperature to make Violet moan with satisfaction. She ran off to get another pitcher full and, when she came back, she repeated the exercise.

One of the women poured a thick shampoo over her hair and then, pushing Violet's head back, squirted herself underneath her and let it come to rest on her lap. She placed her hands on Violet's head and began to massage her scalp.

The girl had strong, knowledgeable fingers. Violet was soon lost in a reverie as they brought her to a state of peace and calm. To her, it seemed to last for hours. It brought her to a timeless state. The other girls were huddled around her stroking her skin. Her hands rested on their shoulders. It felt so nice to have their soft bodies next to hers. One of them, emboldened, leaned forward and took one of her nipples in her mouth. She gave it a languorous kiss. Violet sighed as the pleasurable sensation ran through her. When she realized what had been done to her, she lifted her arm up and gently pushed the girl away.

This was, apparently, the signal that the bath was to come to an end. One of the girls went and got some more clean water and rinsed the soap out of her hair. She repeated the exercise two more times.

The girls brought Violet to the shallow end of the tub and walked her out. Two of them brought large, soft, fluffy towels and began to rub her body and head with it. When she was dry, they brought her to the edge of the pool, had her sit down and began to brush her hair. She felt some perfumed lotion being melded into it.

Violet felt like she had not for a long time. She was a woman again, not a mere prisoner. "Is this the life of General Wang's whores?" she asked herself. "Is that what I'm being shown?"

The door to the bathroom opened and Li stepped in. The girls all bowed their heads to him and slinked away from

Violet. Was she supposed to bow her head too? She bowed her head. All the joy of her bath washed away the moment she saw him and his three foot long whip. "*Stand up!*" he ordered her. Violet hesitated for a second.

The whip struck her back. "Ooooooooooouuuu!" she yelled. Her voice echoed through the room. Tears came to her eyes.

"*Stand up!*" he said again, louder now. Violet immediately rose to her feet.

"*Turn around!*" he ordered. Violet turned and she felt her hands being bound behind her once again. A feeling of deep sorrow came over her. During her bath, it was almost like she was not a prisoner, a slave, a whore. With her hands tied behind her, she resumed her status. Her blindfold was reapplied and then her leash. She felt a tug on the strap that led to her collar and she began to follow her keeper.

They exited the bathroom and Violet felt the soft rug on her bare feet again. They walked about fifty feet and stopped. She heard another door opening and she was pulled through it.

When the blindfold was removed, she saw that she was in a sumptuous bedroom. It had tall, wide, curtained, French style windows that went almost all the way up to the ceiling. It was a corner room. There was a large bed in it, larger than Violet had ever seen. The bed had four tall bedposts and was covered by green, satin sheets. She saw another door that looked to be a closet. There was no other furniture in the room.

"Oh, god!" Violet exclaimed to herself. "This is Wang's bedroom. He's going to fuck me! Oh my god!"

She looked at her keeper dolefully. His face was blank. "*Turn around!*" he ordered her sharply. Mechanically, Violet showed him her back. She had an empty feeling in her stomach. Was this the moment of truth?

When her hands were loosened, Li took his whippy stick and slapped it on the bed, saying, "*On bed! On bed!*"

For the second time in three minutes Violet hesitated. The whippy stick came flying across the back of her thighs. "Ohhhhhhh!" she yelled. She stepped away from Li. She turned to him and shouted, "No!" The whip shot out and struck her in the arm. She turned in reaction and it hit her other arm. When she tried to turn back, the whip struck across her breasts.

"Ooooooooou! Ohhhhhhhhh! Ahhhhhhhhhhhh!" she cried out at each blow. She turned to run and he caught her foot with the end of the whip. She fell to the floor. He whipped her once, twice, three times. He struck her back, her thigh, her rear.

Violet was screaming in pain. Then she felt the rain of blows stop and heard the man yell at her, "*On bed!*"

She was still trying to react to the order when another series of blows struck her. She was amazed at how quickly he could wield the whip. Her left shoulder was struck, then the middle of her back and then the upper part. Each blow sent a fierce message of pain to her. She screamed and screamed and fought herself to her feet. She jumped on the bed and the blows ceased.

Violet was sobbing. There were lines of fire all over her body. She looked at her keeper with hatred. Li pointed to the head of the bed and said, "*There!*"

She looked where he was pointing and with a deep sob retreated to it. He stepped over and climbed on the bed with her. He had the strap that had been used to tie her wrists in his hand. He made a gesture with wrists crossed and said, "*Hands in front!*"

With full realization of what it might mean, Violet obediently placed her hands in front of her and crossed her wrists. She watched unhappily as he tied them together. He pushed her to her back, saying, "*Lie down!*"

Sniffling and sobbing, Violet lowered her back to the bed. This wasn't how she expected her first violation to happen. She had thought that she would be braver and not give in. The pain of the whip was too much for her.

Li took her wrists in his hands and brought them up above her. He tied them to a ring in the center of the headboard. He got off the bed and brought back two long cords. He tied one to each of Violet's ankles. He then pulled one of the ropes to the side of the bed until Violet's leg was spread out. He tied it off to a ring. He repeated the exercise for the other ankle.

Violet now lay spread eagled on the huge bed. Her knees were slightly raised and her feet pointed more toward the side than to the corners. She watched him dolefully as he left the room.

She closed her eyes and cursed herself for her cowardice. She pulled on the rope that had her wrists captured, but to no avail. She tugged at her ankle bindings without result. She lay back, her stomach aflutter and her heart heavy. When the door opened again, it was not what she expected.

Li had come back. He was carrying a tray. On the tray was a bowl of hot water, a razor, a shaving brush, a cloth and some soap. He placed the tray on the bed and then got up himself. He took one of the pillows from the head of the bed and slid it underneath Violet's rear end, propping her sex upwards.

Violet looked on, astonished. Then she remembered the hairless sexes of the girls in the bathroom. She realized that she was to be rendered hairless as well. She didn't like it, but it was better than being raped.

Li shaved the pussies of all the concubines, every day. It was his way of being assured that they would be smooth as a baby's face down there for their master. Too many times he had to whip foolish girls who had done a poor job of it. Also, it emphasized that he was the ruler of the seraglio. Afterwards, he rewarded each one of them with a powerful orgasm with his hand or with his mouth.

After getting a good lather on his brush, Li applied it to the young woman's loins. When the hair was well soaped, he took the straight razor off of the tray and began to shave away the curly growth.

Violet had closed her eyes when he had started to lather her loins and kept then closed though the entire procedure. Tears flowed from her eyes as she felt the eunuch manhandle her private area with the insouciance of a barber. She saw in her mind the sexes of the girls in the bathroom, how smooth they were, how dramatically it displayed their lower lips, the divide between them. It was bad enough to be naked for these men, but now she was going to have to display herself as brazenly as a Turkish whore. She felt the man's hot hands push her love lips this way and that as he scraped their sides free of hair. No one had handled her there since she was a baby other than one man, whose face she would rather forget. When she felt the razor scrape away the hair on her perineum, close to her most secret place, she stiffened and issued a sob. She felt humiliated and defeated. It was clear that it was not her body any more. It belonged to the general and he would have it as he wanted it. She knew that soon, she didn't know when, but soon, he would cast his eyes upon it with salacious intent. It made her shudder to think about it.

When Li was done, he took the cloth and wiped the slut's pussy clean. Now it looked good, he thought. He took the tray off of the bed and out of the room. Violet awaited his pleasure, of course.

He returned quickly. He was carrying a jar. He climbed up on the bed with it and opened its lid. He took a scoop of the pasty liquid inside and dribbled it on the Englishwoman's pussy. "Now we will see," he thought.

Placing his hand on her loins, Li started to gently massage the paste into her skin. He knelt between her forcibly spread thighs. He took his time in making sure that the lotion penetrated deeply. He looked up to see what his efforts were producing.

Violet flinched when she felt the hand apply itself to her lower belly. She kept her eyes focused on the ceiling so she wouldn't have to watch the man take his liberties with her. His hand was hot. The lotion, she had to admit, felt good going in. She shifted her hips slightly as she felt her lower belly gain some warmth of its own. She shifted them again a few seconds later. When she felt a tingle in her sex, she pulled slightly on the ropes that bound her ankles. When it wouldn't go away, she closed her eyes and arched her back in frustration. When she felt the man's thumb carefully and gently part the lips that guarded her entranceway, she whined with dismay. When she felt her fluids being spread over her clitoris, she sighed and twisted her head.

The experienced eunuch was watching her carefully. The promise of her beauty was being fulfilled. He watched as the nascent signs of sexual pleasure developed. He saw that she had her eyes closed, but closing her eyes was not going to stop anything.

He took his time. He abandoned his assault on her fortress for a moment and was content to glide his fingers over the outer lips, rub the skin of her belly softly and then the insides of her thighs. He crawled up, closer to her and let his hand wander across her belly to her breasts. Lightly, he brushed their tips with his fingers. The points were stiff already. The woman gave a shudder when he touched them. Her hands, tied off above her, were clenched, her face was soft and her lips parted slightly. Her breathing was beginning to become slightly labored.

He brought his hand back to the center of her being and lovingly massaged her labia. They were infused with blood, dilated. He ran his finger up the moistened divide. The Englishwoman arched her back and sighed.

Violet was beside herself. Her body was betraying her. She knew that she should revolt against the man's assault, but she didn't want to, couldn't. His hands felt so good on her flesh. Her heat was up. She knew that she would be remorseful later, but that was later and this was now.

"This is the man who whipped me!" she thought. "This is the man who left me so cruelly tied in that dank and dingy cell for so many hours! This is the man who is making me into the general's whore! How can I let him make me feel like this?"

Li was rubbing Violet's button of pleasure softly. He was watching her lusts grow higher and higher. He felt no lust of his own, but it was a matter of pride that he could induce such reactions in his master's sluts. Their knowing that he had this power over them made them easier to handle. The ease with which he forced them to pleasure day after day, up to three times a day when they were not being used by their lord or one of his guests, shamed them, taught them their place. He ruled their cunts and so he ruled them.

The woman was approaching her crisis. He removed his hand and placed his lips upon her mons. Her legs tightened and she sighed. He let his tongue travel the length of her slice and she squirmed. When he placed his tongue on her clit, she groaned and arched her back. He let his tongue wash up and down on the hardened button. Violet was rocking her hips and issuing a long, seemingly agonized moan. Her breath became heavy, her thighs started to shudder, she ground her loins against his face.

Violet's mind was somewhere else. Her body had taken it away somewhere. She was one long, mass of electrified flesh. When the man put his tongue on her puss, a wave of intense pleasure flowed through her body. She knew she was lost. Her one lover had never done this. She had heard tell of women who let men do this to them, but she had always vowed that she never would. It was unclean and, if not perverted, abnormal. She had enjoyed sex, the regular kind, but never had been tempted to ask her lover to do this, just as she had never done the other thing that men like. That was for whores.

Her passions were growing higher and higher. Her whole being was concentrated on her pleasure, she felt her crescendo building. Sex had never been like this!

Li saw that the general's new whore was ready and he began to flick his tongue at the hard point of flesh. "Oooooooouuuuuu! Ohhhhhhhhhhh! Ooooooooooh!" the woman yelled as she came. Her hips bucked and her back arched. Her legs pulled hard against their bindings. Her hands twisted in their tie.

Violet groaned at each fierce contraction of her crevasse. Her heart was pounding, her breasts were tight, she was finding it hard to catch her breath. She screamed her pleasure.

When he saw that the slut had peaked, Li let her body wind down. He removed his tongue from her sex, caressed the insides of her thighs and ran his hands lightly over her pudendum to give her the full benefit of her aftershocks.

The eunuch rose from the bed and untied her. She had done well for her first day. Now that the ice was broken, she was lost. It was as it always was. Some of them took longer, some, like this one, shorter. They all ended up at the same place.

Li bound, gagged and blindfolded the woman. He re-attached her leash and led her from the room. His room, not his master's. He always broke them in on his bed and sometimes, later, made them come into his room so that he could service them there. It made it very piquant to have them exploding in lust in the bed of a man who felt no lust in return.

Violet was too overwhelmed by what had just happened to wonder what their destination was when they left the bedroom. After they had walked fifty or so steps, she was counting them, they stopped and she heard the man knock at a door. A panel slid open, a man grunted and the door opened.

She knew, however, where they were going when they started to go down the stairs. She whined a complaint and that empty, fearsome feeling came back to her stomach. She didn't want to go back to her cell. Hadn't she been good?

And then she remembered that she hadn't been good. She had run away, refused an order, spoken without permission. As they went lower and lower towards hell, her hands started to sweat, her mouth turned dry and her blood started rushing in her ears. "Oh, god, oh, god, please no, please," she repeated again and again. When she felt the rough stones against her feet, she almost collapsed.

Down, down, down they went. When they had reached the bottom level, she counted the steps as she had counted them on the way up. "Thirty one, thirty two, thirty three, thirty four...." At that she started to get nervous. She was sure that it had been thirty three steps from her cell to the stairs.

"Thirty nine, forty, forty one...." She stopped counting. Her blood had turned to ice. Where were they going?

They arrived at their destination about twenty steps later. The arrangement of the dungeon was that there was a guard's station when you fist came down the stairs. At night, there was a steel barred door that was locked to make it harder for anyone who had somehow escaped their cells to make it upstairs. There was a door at the top that was locked at night as well.

Ten cells lined up along the wall to the left. Ten cells were usually enough, except the one time that there had been a minor peasant revolt. Several landlords of large estates begged General Wang to put it down. It was easy. The peasants had broken onto the home of one landlord at night and slaughtered all the inhabitants. They had pitchforks and clubs. Wang had Mauser rifles, a machine gun and horses. The revolt died out quickly. Wang spent a week rounding up rebels and their families. At one time, they had two hundred souls down here, 20 to a cell. It got so they had to just bind their arms and legs and leave them lying in the hall. Once the executioner got busy, though, he made short work of them. 255 heads were mounted on poles around Wang's fiefdom. 125 females found themselves on their way to whorehouses and seraglios at an immense profit to the warlord. In payment of his services to the landlords, Wang took possession of the estate of the family that had been killed, was paid ten pounds of gold and secured a commitment to pay annual tribute from eight wealthy landlords. He expanded his territory by 50 square miles and incorporated 16 new villages. It was a good week's work.

At the end of the row of cells was the work area of the dungeon. It was here that thieves' hands were cut off, hot irons applied to the tongues of agitators and questions put in a not too delicate way to people with information that Wang desired. For Li's purposes, there was a whipping stand.

The stand was a gibbet from which dangled a chain for the confinement of the victim's hands. There was a ring in the floor so that his, or her, feet could be secured. At the end of the arm of the gibbet, a beam ran perpendicular to it so that, if it was desired, the victim's legs could be hoisted wide apart for access to the most delicate parts of their bodies.

The hook in Violet's cell was certainly adequate for the purposes of administering a few blows. But if you really wanted to get whaling, you needed the space afforded to you by the whipping stand.

Violet was brought to a halt just under the gibbet. Li untied her hands and then brought them around in front of her. He pulled down the chain and attached the bracelets to her wrists. Then he stepped over to the pole that support the overhead beam and pulled on the chain until Violet's feet were barely touching the ground. Stepping over to where the concubine dangled, he tied a strap around her ankles and then anchored them to the ring in the floor.

The young woman knew something was wrong when the bracelets were attached to her wrists. She groaned with fear when she was hauled into the air. Li removed first her gag and then her blindfold. When Violet saw where she was, saw the various implements of mayhem, she pissed herself. It happens.

The area was dimly lit. The kerosene lanterns cast a yellowish, eerie light on everything.

"Oh, god, no, please," Violet uttered meekly to her keeper, as she thought of him, her face a mask of frantic anxiety. When she saw him select a long, thin whip from the wall, she began to cry. "Please don't whip me," she squeaked piteously. "I'm sorry I disobeyed you. I won't do it again, I promise."

Li swung the whip through the air. It made a high pitched whirring sound. It was a very thin steel rod covered with leather. It would make long, thin lines of red on Violet's body, but, if handled expertly, would not break the skin. Li was an expert. The marks would fade in a few days.

When she saw that Li was not mindful of her timid entreaties, she tried a different tack.

"Please, no!" she shouted desperately. "Pleeeeease! Pleeeeease! I'll do anything you want! I'll be Wang's whore! I'll fuck him! I'll fuck you! Pleeeeeease! Pleeeeease don't whip me!"

Li chose the fine, round surface of Violet's rear cheeks for the first blow.

"Ooooooooooowwww! Ooooooooooowwww! Oh, god! Oh, god!" Violet yelled. If the whippy stick produced fire, this whip produced lava.

Li stepped around her. The second blow went across the front of her thighs.

"Ahhhhhhhhhhhhh! Ahhhhhhhhhh! Oh, god! Please stop! Please!" the frantic woman cried out.

The third went across the back of her thighs. The fourth across her belly, the fifth, and so on. The eunuch took his sweet time, letting the terrible effects of each stroke of the whip fully penetrate the slut's consciousness before delivering the next. Violet screamed until her voice was hoarse, "For the love of god, please stop! Pleeeeease! Pleeeeease! I'll be good! I'll be good! I promise! I promise! Ahhhhhhh! Ahhhhhhh!"

She reserved her loudest, most piteous scream for the blow that crossed her breasts.

Violet had not known that pain like this existed. She had led, not a sheltered life, but, as most people did in England, a life free from violence. She had fallen off of a horse when she was thirteen and broke her arm. That hurt a lot, but that was just a hairline fracture and did not compare to the agonizing pain she was experiencing now. She felt like her body had been dipped in flame, that a thousand wasps had attacked her, that a million, tiny, red hot irons had been applied to her body. Her tears had flowed down her cheeks and had been soaked up by the leather collar she wore around her neck and then passed on to her chest. Her whole body was shiny from sweat. Long, red lines had sprung up on her body like some strange form of rash, with only a spot of blood here and there.

Li had limited himself to ten strokes. Violet did not know right away, at first, that he had stopped. She continued to yell and scream hysterically for a good minute. When she saw that her ordeal was over, she just sagged in her bonds and sobbed.

There was a good reason that Li had removed her gag. He wanted her to, as she had, abase herself in her effort to avoid what she had earned. Later, when she should certainly know better than to engage in behavior like she did today, the gag would stay in, since Li usually did not like to be distracted from his pleasure.

Li waited twenty minutes or so to let the moaning, sobbing, young woman down. The guards had come down to watch the show and they were very impressed. He shared two cigarettes with them from his silver case, and they poured him a cup of their fiery brandy.

As she tried to recover, Violet looked over at her tormentor with hatred and dread. He had shown that he was capable of, and prepared to administer, ferocious pain to her body. She was ashamed that she had offered to fuck him and General Wang too. But who was she kidding? She would have fucked anybody. Her insides squirmed as the men gloated over her dismal, defeated form. She remained silent for fear that she would trigger a new round of abuse.

Violet was exhausted by her ordeal. When she was lowered from the gibbet, after her legs were freed, she collapsed to the floor. Li had the guards take hold of her arms and carry her back to her cell. There was no need to blindfold her, since the cell would shortly be as dark as a moonless night, and for safety reasons, in case she had to vomit, he left the gag out. He had the men hogtie her on her pallet. He left her to contemplate the costs of rebellion.

军阀 外家

CHAPTER SEVEN

Li came back about two hours later. Violet trembled as he untied her. He laid her on her belly, after freeing her hands, and applied a soothing salve to her wounds. He had her roll over when he was finished with her back and did her front. He gave her some water to drink. Violet cried quietly as his hands wandered her flesh. Never in her life had she ever imagined that she would have to go through something like the whipping she had just received. Never! It was unimaginable to her that someone could do that to another human being. For the first time, she began to truly understand the universe that she had come to inhabit.

The effect of the application of the salve to her body was calming as was the effect of being untied and being able to see. Her keeper's hands were soft and gentle, but firm. It was strange to her that she should so easily accept a man's hands on her naked body, especially one who had just whipped her like a fury out of hell. She realized that it was because she had come to accept the premise that she deserved to be whipped because of her infraction.

It was the hours and hours of lonely isolation that did it, she knew that. She longed so much for human contact, for the feel of someone's hand on her skin, to hear a human voice, to see a human face, that any contact was better than none. In her desperate hours, she had accepted the premise that somehow she deserved her deprivation of humanity and that she could only earn it back by playing by their arbitrary and heinous rules. Once she accepted that, when she sinned, of course she should be punished. Of course she would be whipped. Of course she should be returned to her cell and be condemned to hours and hours of misery.

What was happening to her? She should be outraged and repelled by the man! As his hands made her body feel warm and good, she could not bring herself to reject them.

When Li saw that the slut had calmed, he rose from the pallet and, picking up the whippy stick, tapped her on the thigh. "*Stand up,*" he ordered her.

Violet's eyes had been closed; she was so relaxed that she could easily sleep. But at the touch of the man's whip and the sound of his voice, her eyes flew open and, after looking up at him for a millisecond, she scrambled to her feet.

"*Turn around,*" Li instructed her. She did what she was told. Li brought her hands back behind her and tied them off. Then he tapped the stick on the floor where Violet had been bound before and said, "*Kneel.*"

Violet spun around and, with a sickening feeling in her stomach, brought herself to the floor. When she was on her knees, Li tapped the floor in front of her. He didn't need to say anything. Violet knew what he meant. She leaned over and lowered her head as far as she could.

A feeling of sorrow came over her as she felt her hands being tied back behind her and her ankles affixed to the irons in the floor. Her eyes filled with tears as the eunuch tied one end of a strap to her collar and ran it through the iron below her chin and then tied it off to the one about three feet away. He installed her gag and blindfold.

Violet trembled as she thought of the hours she would have to spend alone and immobilized. No matter how many times they did it to her, her feelings were always the same: loneliness and dread. She felt the man's hand run down her back and over her rear end. He was crouched down behind her to her left. The hand wandered over her skin. It was as if he were trying to comfort her for her upcoming ordeal.

In the darkness behind her blindfold, it seemed that the man's hands were some disembodied force teasing her skin.

They brought her back to that lazy state she had had when he had finished massaging her body with the salve.

When his hand descended between her legs, under her rear end, Violet gave a start. She felt his hand caress the smoothness of her pudendum. It was so strange to experience the reminder of the loss of her hair. His hand delicately stroked her denuded skin. She felt the familiar tingling she had felt when he caressed it before and her mind went immediately to the pleasures that she experienced then. She realized that he was going to excite her as she knelt there, all trussed up and helpless. "No!" she thought. "I won't give in this time, I won't! I'm not going to let them make me into a whore!" She was able to wriggle her ass just a little and she did it now in protest and she uttered a whine of disapproval. She knew that talking would cause the man to strike at her helpless body.

Li chuckled to himself at her response. She could fight it, he thought, but she had already crossed the line.

When Li dragged his finger the length of her sexual divide, Violet knew that she was defeated. It wasn't fair that yet another part of her body was betraying her. A wave of lust went through her. She tried to fight it nonetheless, but when he delved his finger inside her, after she had lubricated herself for him, she gave out a sigh and gave in.

Li took his time in caressing the helpless woman. He could hear her labored breath and her soft moans. When her breathing became heavy and her rear cheeks began to shudder, he ceased his manipulations and waited for the slut's reactions. She moaned her disappointment and need. "Good," he thought. He rose to his feet and took the lantern from the hook on the ceiling. "That will give her something to think about." He left the cell and locked the door.

Violet moaned in frustration. She hated herself for responding to him, hated herself for her need. What kind of person was she becoming, she thought anxiously. She should be outraged that he would touch her without her consent, outraged that the Chinaman had placed his hands on her at all. Her pussy ached with need and her body protested her truncated pleasure. She strained at her bonds in frustration and self recrimination. She had to get a hold of herself. She had to be strong. She couldn't let them do this to her. She couldn't!

A few hours later, he returned with some food for her. Violet did not want to eat it, since she had, during the dark, anguished hours alone, resolved to resist him. But when he gave her the order, "*Eat,*" she was too afraid not too.

It was a combination of sautéed duckling and rice. In spite of herself, she mouthed the bowl with relish. It contained that strange, not unpleasant spice that her breakfast has been flavored with. She could not place it. He had brought another serving girl with him and, after she ate, she gave Violet some juice to drink and wiped her face.

When the eunuch had her tied off and gagged again, leaving off her blindfold, he crouched down by her side, as he had done earlier, and began to stroke her skin. Although Violet's vision was forced downwards, she could still see the clogs on the feet and, up to her knees, the plain, white pegged pants of the maid. She gave out a whine of humiliation as she realized that the man was going to stroke her in front of the girl. She waved her ass in protest, but he paid it no mind. When she felt his hand glide across her love lips, and the sensations that it brought, she groaned in dismay.

As before, it was not long before she started to respond. When his fingers slid inside her she moaned. She closed her eyes to try and block out the presence of the young girl, but she kept seeing those slender legs and dainty feet in her mind.

She gasped when she felt the man spread her juices over her love button and began to massage it, delicately and expertly. She waved her ass again and struggled at her bonds. There was nothing she could do about it though. Her lusts kept rising higher and higher. She began to hope that he would stop as he had earlier, and, when she felt her passion approach its crest, she realized that he would not.

Dismay turned to joy as her pussy's first, powerful contractions struck her. Her body shook and she moaned. The throbbing of her electrified channel continued on and on. She was snorting through her nose. Her hands twisted behind her. She was astounded and chagrined when, after her orgasm subsided, he continued to stroke her puss. Within a few minutes, he had her panting and squirming again. When she came, she went, "Unnnnngh! Uuuuuuuuungh! Uuuuuuuuungh!" as the clamping of her canal drove her to unwanted pleasure.

After her pussy's convulsions had wound down, Li got up and, signaling the maid, exited the cell without ceremony. He left the lantern behind after turning it down.

The light was dimmed, but it still shone an ample light for Violet to experience the sensation of illumination all round her. When the door slammed shut, she began to cry. That had been one of the most humiliating moments of her life, worse than having to piss and shit on command. All women pissed and shat. There was no shame in it if the men had stripped away, by force, all of her right to privacy. Shaking and moaning in delirious pleasure at the behest of a strange man was something else entirely. Twice. Women with character, self pride and dignity didn't do that. But she had. The syllogism was clear. Since she did those things, she was without dignity, without pride, without character. She was lower than the commonest whore. She deserved what she got.

After the first hour or so, she decided that it was better when she was blindfolded. When in the dark, she could, at times, pretend that she was in her own little world. She overcame, intermittently, her grief for the loss of human contact. With the light on, she could not do that. She could see about three inches of the bottom of the door to her cell if she raised her head just a little. The floor underneath her was clear to her vision. The effect of having the light of the lantern all around her was to make her feel that a spotlight was being shined on her, that somewhere eyes were looking at her. It reminded her that she had climaxed twice before the eyes of the young maid. To do such a thing was anathema to her as a proper Englishwoman. Sex was enjoyable, but it was private, even secret. Humans were animals with animalistic needs, but it was better to have them dealt with behind closed doors to preserve dignity.

But that was the point, wasn't it. She had no dignity left. They had broken it down bit by bit starting with her confinement in the car after her kidnapping. The whole point of being so closely confined was to make her feel powerless, less than a person. Well, only a person needed privacy, dignity, self respect. An animal, like they were making out of her, needed none.

For the next five days, every morning, after she was fed, she was brought up to the living quarters to bathe and then to the bedroom to learn all about sex. She was brought up for the man's salacious purposes most days in the afternoon or evening as well. Sometimes both. Whenever he brought her food in her cell, he would stroke her until her passions were aflame. Sometimes he would let her come, sometimes not.

At first, he used either his hand or his mouth. In the bedroom to which he brought her three times on her second day at the fortress, she laid on her back, her legs spread, her knees raised, and he made her come again and again. Afterwards, she cursed herself for her licentiousness. It was like the man had cast a spell over her.

On the third day, in the afternoon, after he had made her come with his mouth for the first time in that session, he introduced something new and revealed about himself something that Violet would not have even suspected.

She was lying on her back on the bed, her legs splayed, as usual. She was trying to recover her breath from her orgasm. She was struggling to overcome her oxygen deficit thorough her nose, since her gag blocked off the other pathway. She pulled air in in little snorts. Li had left the bed and left the room, going into the closet. When he came out, he was completely nude but for a harness he was wearing around his waist and the flesh colored protrusion from his loins. Violet was astonished to see him that way, but also astonished to see that he had no scrotum. Beneath the prong extending from his loins was nothing! Then she realized that he was a eunuch. It set her aback. She had thought that he was assaulting her out of passion. But eunuchs don't experience sexual passion. He was just coldly, methodically molding her into a lust driven slattern!

She cringed when he got onto the bed. At first, she had been so surprised that she didn't realize that he intended to fuck her. "Oh, god, no!" she thought as she realized that the faux cock was not just for show. She whined with unhappiness as he approached her. Her quim was still dilated and juicy from his assault on it with his mouth.

The imitation penis that Li was wearing was an exact replica of his master's cock. He had had it made many years ago so that he could better prepare the general's sluts for him. He had several made and General Wang's wives liked to fuck his concubines and maids with them. One was kept in the concubines' chambers, not only so that he could fuck them there, but also, so they could fuck each other at his command. The general kept one in his bedroom for just such purposes.

Although the general wanted to be the first to fuck his new acquisitions, since Li was using his cock, essentially, it didn't count. Li would reserve the first penetration of the virgins for his master, but he would prepare their posteriors for his use, and their mouths. With the foreign sluts, who were very often not virgins, he prepared their pussies as well.

As Li approached her, Violet tried to retreat. She had no where to go. Her legs were fixed firmly in place. She kept staring at the long, thick protrusion. It was ribbed and sleek like an uncut penis. Its color approximated the slightly tawny skin of her assailant.

She looked at Li's naked body. Although he was lean, he was muscular as well. She could see the strength emanating from his chest. Since his level of testosterone was nil, Li had to take special efforts to build up his strength. But, like a woman, he could build it up if he worked hard enough at it.

When Li was fully between her outstretched thighs, he placed his hand on the faux penis and stroked it. He was watching the slut and he saw her eyes go to the instrument. They were wide with apprehension and horror.

"Cock of master," he told her in English, grinning.

Violet looked from the prong to Li's eyes and back again. Wang's cock! She was going to be fucked with Wang's cock even before he put a single hand on her. It was just too ironic! It was a strange world she was in, a horrifying, unsettling world where everything she had learned about human relations growing up in England was turned around. She was like that character from Mr. Carroll's book. She was Alice and she'd fallen down the rabbit hole.

She watched the eunuch approach her gate of pleasure. She felt the tip press against her labia and she pulled her hips back as far as they would go. She wanted to beg and plead with the man not to violate her. She was supposed to have the opportunity to refuse, hold her virtue dear. This was not the way it was supposed to happen.

Li let the head of the false prick slide along the line of Violet's divide. She flinched and moaned. Holding the instrument in one hand so to give it direction, he pressed it forward slowly. Violet uttered short, desperate exclamations of unhappiness, "Unnmpf! Unnmpf! Unnmpf!" through her gag. Her hands twisted and turned above her, tied resolutely to the headboard. Her eyes were wide, trying to communicate the words she was not permitted to say.

The tall, muscular eunuch now had purchase within her vaginal opening. The tip of the carved cock was just inside and would need no further assistance from his hand. He squared his hips with hers and, looking into her face for her reaction, slowly, ever slowly, let the piece slide in.

It had been years since anyone had pierced Violet's love lips and then maybe 9 or 10 times. The walls of her canal were tight. Violet felt them easing apart. He shook her head frantically, rocked her hips, struggled at her bonds, but nothing would stop the inevitable advance of the thing into her hole.

To Violet, it was bad enough to be raped, but worse yet to be forced to sex with an inanimate object. She could not get out of her mind the fact that it was a model of her owner's manhood. "This is what it will feel like," she thought. "It will be just like this."

As the wooden cock pressed homeward, Violet closed her eyes and prepared herself for the worst. When it had sunk in to its hilt, she looked up to see the grinning face of her assailant, inches away from her own.

"Nnnnnnnnn!" she moaned. "Nnnnnnnnn!"

At this, Li started his hip motions. He made sure that the pole rode along the upper part of the girl's pussy, dragging across both her hardened clit and the top of her cavern. He started with a slow, determined motion. He had all day and knew that his 'manhood' would never fail. The woman gave out a little grunt of unhappiness each time it descended within her.

After about forty strokes, Li began to see the signs of arousal on the slut's face. Her cheeks had become flush and her nostrils were dilating. Her eyelids were fluttering and her lips had parted and gained color and size.

He increased the pace of his thrusts. Violet opened her eyes widely as she felt her arousal building. "It's not fair!" she thought. "It's not fair! He shouldn't be able to do this to me!"

Her body said, "Give in, Violet! You know your going to anyway! Why fight it? Enjoy a good fuck!"

Her mind said, "It's wrong! Fight it! Fight it! You're not a whore! You're not a whore!

Whoever said that the flesh is weak was wrong. It is very strong and governs most of what we do. For Violet it was no less true. She felt the power of her lust overtaking her will. Her hips had started to involuntarily push back each time the wooden prong slid down her tunnel. Her toes had curled and her breasts were full. "Ahhhhhhh!" she moaned, "Ahhhhhh!" as her crisis came closer and closer. "Ahhhhhhhhhh!" she moaned louder. "Ahhhhhhhhhh!" And then it struck her. Her body jumped when her orgasm began. She tried desperately to close her thighs to force the fake cock deeper and deeper within her. She cursed herself even as wave after wave of pleasure flowed through her. If Li's cock had been real, he would have felt it clasping and unclasping his manhood.

He looked at her face with satisfaction. It was the picture of a woman in bliss. When her first orgasm faded, he continued his athletic pumping at her loins and it was followed by another. And then another. After the third, Violet tried to beg for no more, "Mmmmmmmmmpf!

Mmmmmmmmmpf!", but he kept going. Her arousal lagged only to be picked up again. Her back arched and her thighs shuddered. When her pussy exploded for the fourth time, he finally relented and slowed his thrusts.

He slid the false prick free. Sitting cross legged between her thighs, he gently stroked her belly and breasts. Her chest was heaving and her face was flushed with blood. A red patch had arisen across her chest. Her eyes looked at him wearily.

After a while, he got up from the bed and went back to his large, walk in closet. He took a cigarette from the pocket of his sheath and lit it. He came back into the bedroom. Violet had her eyes open, watching him. They were flooded with dismay. She had been violated, true and proper.

When he was finished with the smoke, he put it out and climbed back up on the bed. He set himself back between her thighs, the flesh-like prong still pointing out from his loins. He addressed its tip to her messy cunt and slid himself back in.

"Nnnnnnnnnnn," the woman moaned plaintively in fruitless protest.

This time he fucked her slow and leisurely, like a lover might do. He wanted her to come one more time.

Violet's body had trilled with post orgasmic satisfaction even as her mind was filled with remorse. When the cock reentered her, a wave of soft, comforting pleasure went through her. She closed her eyes and let the prick take her where it wanted to go. She was too weak to fight it. It was like a pleasant buzzing in her ear, just beyond reach of full consciousness. "Ooooooh, god!" she groaned laconically as she felt her lust growing. But it grew slowly and comfortably. It was a feeling that she could want to go on forever. When her orgasm came, after ten solid minutes of fucking, it was like an old friend come home, shaking hands.

Violet was still dazed when she was led back down to the dungeon. She complied listlessly with Li's order to get down on the floor so he could bind her. She barely noticed when he left, but fell into a deep sleep. When he brought her her dinner that night, Li fucked her again from behind as she knelt there, the little maid looking on jealously. He left the love object lodged in her pussy.

On the fourth day, it was time to learn all about ass fucking. Li didn't expect her to like it the first time. It would take some getting used to. And her philosophical objections would be stronger than having her pussy stuffed.

When she got on the bed, he tied her hands to the headboard and ordered her to turn to her belly and get up on her knees. He took a long strap and tied one end of it around her left ankle. He wound it around several times and then around the instep of her foot. It was wound twice more around her ankle and then tied off. The strap had formed a kind of stirrup. He took the other end of the strap and ran it through the same ring in the headboard to which her hands were tied. He brought it down to her right ankle and tied it off like he did on the left.

To insure that the sluttish foreigner did not try and move up towards the head of the bed to avoid her ass's impalement, he took two more straps and tied her ankles to the bottom corners of the bed. Once he had her ankles secured, he tied straps to the tops of her thighs and pulled them to the sides of the bed, about four feet behind her, where he affixed them to rings. Now, she could move neither her hips nor her legs.

She could protest all she wanted, she could struggle and cry out, but the master's cock was going up her ass.

Li started out rubbing her hairless pussy from behind. He had just shaved it a little while ago and it was soft and smooth. Violet's hips shifted as she prepared herself for another round of coital bliss. She had spent the night kneeling on the floor of her cell, all trussed up in the darkness deriding herself for her easy virtue. She was, nonetheless, ready for another round today.

Li waited until her pussy was good and loose. Her fluids were flowing, ready to ease the way of a cock. He had a little jar with him and he took out a dollop of jellied oil. With his two long fingers of his right hand, he pressed them against her little, brown star and began to grease it up.

Violet was horrified at what she felt. Now this was beyond the pale. Men fucked boys like this and each other. This was not an act any respectable woman would engage in, no matter how sinful her nature was. She mewed a protest. Li ignored it.

He worked his way into the rear portal with his two fingers. He spread them, turning them this way and that, slowly, so that the ring of flesh could expand. Violet kept moaning and whining, powerless to stop him. She tugged at her bound feet, trying to get down from her kneeling position, but could not loosen the ties. She tried to move forwards to the head of the bed, but the bonds around her thighs kept her in place. She moaned in frustration, but, all too aware of the consequences of talking, she did not dare beg to be spared this barbarous ordeal.

When Li thought that the hole had been prepared sufficiently, he dabbed a bit of the lubricant on the tip of the carved cock and knelt behind the frantically unhappy woman. He maneuvered the prick into position and began pressing it home slowly.

Despite his careful preparation, the brown ring began to tear as it expanded. This was inevitable until the slut learned to loosen herself properly.

Violet moaned in pain as the tissues stretched. She felt the man start to move inside her and she howled with unhappiness. But the worst was over. The faux prick slid easily back and forth over the tender ring. It just kept going and going and going.

After about twenty minutes, Li let the young woman rest. She had cried almost the entire time. He had some things to look to and so he left Violet perched on the bed, the imitation cock still solidly in her ass. He disconnected it from its harness and blindfolded her before he left.

Violet stayed there for about an hour. She tried to shake the disgusting thing from its lodgment, but it would just not move. She tried squeezing it out, but that didn't help. It was just a big, fat, invasive presence in her bowel. As she knelt there, waiting for her keeper to return, she could think of no other thing.

The bad thing was that she had experienced a tingle in her loins once the pain had subsided. She tried not to think about it. She was disgusted with herself for feeling anything but revulsion. It was just plain wrong. Only someone sick in their minds would enjoy such a practice.

When Li came back, he did not mount the wooden prong back on the belt. Instead, he sat down on the bed next to his master's impaled slave and began to caress her back and hind quarters much like he had done before. Violet despised the sensation of the cruel man's hands on her, at first. To her sorrow, the sensation of his soft hands gently rubbing her skin began to become pleasurable. Her pussy began to warm. His hand found her tender love lips as he snaked it under her belly. She tried to bring her knees together to prevent it, but he uttered a one word command and she ceased her opposition immediately. She whined as the fingers found her love button and began to rub it in soft, circular motions.

Li took his time, letting the subtle ministrations of his hand slowly draw the foreign devil deeper and deeper into her lust. He waited until she gave out her first, unhappy moan. He then took hold of the instrument in her smaller entrance and began to slowly move it back and forth over her dainty ring. It moved easily, and soon he noticed with satisfaction that the slut's hips were unconsciously moving with it.

Violet was beginning to experience a strange sensation. The abrasion of the cock against her anal ring started to accentuate the pleasure she felt in her quim from the eunuch's manipulations. She shook her ass and groaned in protest. Li had his pointer finger sliding up and down her labial divide, teasing her nubbin and then retreating. Violet emitted an impassioned, "Umnnnnpf" and shook her head. He began to move his finger faster and she gave out another, longer grunt. Her pussy had flooded and he had two fingers working it while he continued to slide the dildo back and forth. Violet felt her lusts rising and cursed herself. The tingling in her rear started to grow.

Faster and faster, Li manipulated her conch until she gave out a scream and came. Her hips rocked and her body shuddered. Her hands and legs pulled at their bindings. Her orgasm had entered a whole new dimension. The pleasure that flowed from her rear to her pussy accentuated and accelerated the pleasure from the man's fingers. It was like nothing she had ever experienced. "Oooooooouuu! Ohhhhhhhhh!" she cried out as she came. Her juices flowed and her heart raced. "Ohhhhhhhh! Ohhhhhhhh!" she cried again.

When Li brought her back to her cell in the dungeon, he left his master's replica cock in her dainty hole. She knelt with it there, bound into immobility for the rest of the day. He came down and, before he allowed her to eat her dinner, made her come again while plowing her little ring with it. Before he retired for the night, he went back and did it again.

All through the long, dark night, bound on her knees, the heinous instrument lodged within her smaller entrance, Violet rued her virtually bestial performance. How could she get pleasure from anything so perverse? What were these people doing to her? In a matter of a few short days, she had become a lustful slut, eager to perform for her keeper. She quailed at the thought of a real cock back there; she knew that she wasn't being prepared this way for nothing. She imagined the callous general kneeling behind her and sawing his prick in her most private place. Her body shivered with revulsion.

The eunuch had done it in the presence of the slender maid that time before dinner. When he came back the second time, he was alone. The aftereffects of having her ass plowed while he fingered her to climax lasted longer. The memories of the pleasure it brought her tormented her.

The times that Violet spent in her cell, alone and in the darkness throughout this period were worse than her time on the boat. On the boat, she had the horror of her capture and cruel isolation and confinements to torment her. That and the dismal projections she had about what was going to happen to her once she arrived at General Wang's fortress. But now was added to her mourning for her lost life and the cruelties of her present one, the fact of who she was discovering she was.

She had lived a long time without sex. Sure, she had thought about it from time to time, even experienced longing for sexual gratification now and again. She had engaged in self pleasure on a regular basis for a while, but discontinued it as being morally wrong and harmful to her psyche. She hadn't wanted to think about her lack of a companion. She liked her life as it was. If it were not for her father's death, she could have gone on happily for many years. To have so easily succumbed to the manipulations of the man made her morbidly ashamed. And by a eunuch as well!

From time to time, during the long hours she spent in darkness, condemned to immobility, she still cried and wailed for the wrongs being done to her. It was hateful to be so cruelly confined night after night after night. Why had she been chosen for this particular Calvary? Up stairs, high up above her, people were moving about at will, eating their meals from tables on refined plates and drinking from fine crystal glassware. They slept in beds, they disposed of their body's wastes in private, they had the benefit of light, even if it was the smallest, tiniest candle.

Where was the vicious, cruel General Wang while she suffered here, deep below his palace? Was he sleeping on fine, silk sheets? Did he have the comfort of a kind and willing companion? Was he clothed? The contrast of the evil warlord and herself could not have been, to her mind, more extreme. He was the highest of highs, she was the lowest of lows.

She enjoyed her baths with the diminutive, friendly maids every morning, but the rest of the day was hell. Yes, the eunuch had brought her physical pleasure, but at the price of self hatred and shame. He was demoralizing her day after day. Being under his control was almost second nature now, but it didn't make it any easier to accept. He still struck her viciously with his whippy stick whenever she hesitated in fulfilling one of his orders or misunderstood what he said. Her cruel lashing of her in the punishment room had driven all thoughts of resistance from her, but it didn't make her any more ready to accept what he wanted her to be.

And then was the ever present sword that hung over her. Sooner or later, she would be required to surrender herself directly to the cruel general, not just to his underling. She would be confronted with the author of all the cruel treatments imposed on her. What would her life with him be like? Would he beat her every day? Would he make her life a continual torment? When he got bored with abusing her would he sell her off to some one else and them to someone else and them to someone else until she ended her life as an abject whore in some dismal whorehouse? Or, once he had had his fill with her, would he devise some cruel way to end her days?

Crying had become second nature to the poor woman. At least several times every night, she broke into tears. They had made her into a thing to be used. When she was not being used, she was stored, like any other toy. Hour after hour, day after day of harsh confinement, beyond what any prisoner should have to bear, was taking away her humanity, bit by bit.

Sometimes, Violet thought of Robert. Was he trying to save her? It had been only a little over two weeks since she had been kidnapped. It seemed like years. Robert was her only hope. She had no family to pursue her rescue. She doubted that Uncle Neddie and Aunt Lillian had the wherewithal to come to Shanghai and press the local officials to mount an expedition to save her. Neddie was nearly seventy and Aunt Lillian not far behind him. Violet had had only distant relationships with her cousins. Would any of them uproot their lives to seek redemption for her? It was very doubtful. No, Robert was her only hope and she had rejected him. How foolish she was. If she had ignored his indiscretions they would have not even been out that night to encounter General Wang.

She had gambled her happiness by taking the trip to Shanghai and she had lost. Like most bettors, had she stood pat, she would have been much better off. Was her imprisonment a punishment for her hubris in believing that she could find happiness? Or if not happiness, at least contentment? For her pride in rejecting Robert? For the years she had remained aloof and disconnected with life? She saw now that she had been. She had subverted herself by pretending that the piano was her life when she had no life at all. And now even that was gone.

The fact that she would probably never play the piano again had been haunting her. She tried not to think about it, but it had been her only real pleasure. To hear those melodious chords arising from hammer and steel sometimes made her delirious with joy. She would almost certainly never experience it again. She doubted that the cruel warlord who, as Robert had said, had murdered hundreds of people, would find enjoyment in Chopin or Beethoven or Brahms. He pretended to have assimilated Western conventions. He called himself a general when he was just a bandit, a warlord. She remembered very well his well tailored, evening clothes on the fateful night that they met. To Violet, he was just a monkey in a suit. He was aping European refinement when all he had was a rapacious heart.

Was there any goodness in him? Tenderness? Empathy for others? Did he love? Did he experience true friendship? Did he know honesty and faithfulness and honor? How could he? Look at who he was and what he did. He was undoubtedly hip deep in the opium trade, a commercial evil almost as bad as the slave trade of the centuries before. Britain had eliminated much of the African slave trade. But it had subsidized and encouraged the drug trade. How could it be so moral on one hand and so immoral on the other? Couldn't people see what it did to people's lives? That it created and fostered monsters like General Wang?

There were times during her long hours of confinement, unable to move more than a finger or a toe, that Violet would feel an unhappiness so deep, so intense, that she thought that she would explode, wanted to explode, wanted just to end the horror that her life had become. Her predicament seemed so unreal that sometimes she could not believe that it was actually happening. Was her body really all pressed together and confined by ropes in a dungeon deep in a fortress, somewhere in the hinterlands of China? How could that be?

Was what she was feeling, the confinements of the ropes, the pressing of her flesh on her own flesh, the silence, the darkness, the loss of function and will, were they really real? Could she maybe wake up in her own bed back in England, her trip to Shanghai, Robert, General Wang all some horrible fantasy?

It was when she perceived of her predicament as unreal that she suffered the greatest mental torment. What was happening to her was so improbable that it was virtually impossible. That she, of all the women in the world, should have been selected for this hell was difficult to believe. She had to come all the way from England to meet at a particular spot at a particular time on a particular day, the particular person in the particular circumstances to produce this result. What were the odds? A billion to one? Probably more.

She had been kept naked for so long that she had almost forgotten that she was. What would she have thought just a little more than two weeks ago of parading around a strange fortress, all her intimacies exposed, for all the unknown, strange people to see, and not feeling shame and embarrassment every second that she did it? And her acceptance of her violations, what would she have thought of that? She would have laughed at anyone who had suggested that she would ever have given in without exhausting every ounce of strength that she had.

She had never thought that life was so fragile that she could lose it by a mere slip of the tongue. She lived in a safe world. She was a European, for god's sake. European women did not have to consider sexual slavery as one of the hazards of life. Maybe here in China women lived under that threat, maybe in Africa and in other places in Asia. For those women, her ill fate would have been seen as one of the risks of daily living.

Shanghai had a reputation as a city of sin and degeneracy. But that did not involve Europeans unless they chose it to be so. They lived in the International Settlement. They had big cars driven by faithful, subservient Chinese men. They had large houses, ate the finest foods, lived lives of relative leisure. They stood so high above the bulk of the native population that it was difficult to see that they were in the same world. They were two versions of reality living side by side. Well, she had been pulled into the alternative reality. It wasn't fair. She didn't deserve to be here. She hadn't sinned. It was all a terrible mistake.

Time was her immutable, implacable foe. Before her harrowing ordeal began, she thought of time as something to be used. You spent time with someone. You wiled it away. It flew, it dragged on. Now time never changed. It proceeded at its own inexorable pace. When the door to her cell slammed shut, she could immediately feel the heavy weight of it. She never knew when the door would open, how long her sentence of imprisonment would be, when would come her reprieve. She could count to a thousand, even a million, and nothing would change. There was not even the ticking of a clock to measure it by or to accompany her in her dark silence.

She had been denied all speech for two weeks. Barely a word of intelligible speech but for a single 'no', for which she paid a terrible price, and pleas for mercy uttered in desperation, had crossed her lips. And no one had spoken to her. You couldn't count the orders she received. Sure, they were words, but they were spoken at her, not to her. They asked for no information, implied no response other than immediate, complete and unquestioned obedience.

Could life be any harsher? She doubted it. Even a poor, starving man had some freedom. She had none. Not even, apparently the right of refusal. The eunuch had taken that away from her with his insidious seduction.

And, so, she waited, yet again, for the pleasure of her master.

Li came down early on the fifth day. There still much more to do with the slut and the general was due tomorrow. He had accomplished much of his goals. She had accepted her master's cock, had surrendered to her lusts. She had been introduced to sexual practices that were abhorrent to her. Today there would be a new one, one which did not involve her pleasure, just her obedience. But first, there was something to get out of the way.

Violet always waited with misery in her heart, the tingling of the keys which signified the opening of her door. It did not always bring respite from her ordeal. Many times, between and betwixt the arrivals of her keeper, the men who were the demons who ruled the hell in which she lived had come into her cell. Charged with her physical well being, they came in to give her water, to check on her welfare, to untie her bonds and let her shit in the pot they brought with them.

They always laughed and joked when they came in and they always came in together. Some of the time, her blindfold would be off. The light they shone in on her blinded her. If she was wearing it, they left it on. When she did have the chance to actually see them, the shifting light of their lanterns, they always brought in two, made them seem more like hellacious goblins than men. Unlike the men in the boat, they had no qualms about stroking her bare round cheeks, squeezing and abusing her breasts, rubbing their hands over her hairless sex. And, fucking her.

Once they had discovered the faux prick lodged in her cunt, she had become fair game. One of the men would watch while the other crept behind her and insinuated his cock into her slit. Whichever of them it was, they treated her the same. Her pussy would be rubbed by a rough, calloused hand. Once she reached lubrication, they would shove their thick meat inside her. They never waited for her pleasure. They were there for theirs only. The only saving grace was that it rarely took long.

They would pant and grunt as they fucked her, spilling their seed on her back rather than risking impregnating her. In the afternoon when her keeper had left the dildo in her rectum, they had been delighted that this path of pleasure had been opened.

Who was she going to tell? In the first place, she was not permitted speech. In the second, there was no knowing when she would be back as other than a special prisoner. If she complained, and she ever fell into their hands again, she could be sure of the most vicious, outrageous treatment that they could devise. Besides, there was no way she could know whether their abuse of her was part of her training dictated by her keeper or not.

There were other prisoners in the dungeon. Who they were, Violet never knew. The men were charged with their care, but took more amusement in their torture. On more than one occasion, perhaps they were instructed to do it, she didn't and couldn't know, they left her door open while bringing extreme pain and torment to one of their countrymen. Violet didn't need to know the words to know that they were pleading piteously for a desist to their torment, just as she had for hers. They would give out the most horrible, anguished screams. They would cry and blubber and screech and yell. Violet would quail and cry with them. To know first hand that such horror existed struck at her very soul.

The worst had been the time that their victim had been a woman. Violet cringed at the high pitched wails and screams.

As was undoubtedly intended, she saw herself out there, suffering whatever terrible torment that the goblins were inflicting on the woman. What could she have possibly done that merited the treatment she was receiving? Or had they simply pulled an unfortunate woman off of the street somewhere so that her torment could serve as a lesson to Violet? The screams were so awful, that Violet thought that they might drive her insane.

When they were done with their games, and their victim had been locked back in his or her cell, they would always come and fuck her.

As a result, although she welcomed the intrusion of even the slightest sound into her small, silent world, sometimes it presaged merely more abuse. The best that she could expect was that she would be allowed to rise for a few minutes while they sat her on her pot. They always, when she was done, after cleaning her with some filthy rag, restored her to her immobile pose.

This time, it was indeed the eunuch who had arrived. As usual, he was accompanied by one of the maids. She was holding the tray that contained her food and drink. Usually, she was allowed to eat and drink first before she was brought upstairs or, if she was to remain a bit longer in her cell, before the man would make her body perform for him.

He crouched down behind her and began his magic with his hands. He caressed her back, her thighs, her arms, her rear cheeks, until he had primed her for more intimate contact. When he took hold of her quim, she was already in a state of incipient passion. He rubbed and caressed her sex until she began to pant. Then she felt the replica of her master's cock coursing across her rear entrance.

Li sawed the instrument back and forth gently and slowly with his right hand while his left continued to build her lusts with the other. She began to huff and puff; she moaned a moan of pleasure. Just as she was ready to topple over the edge of bliss, he ceased the manipulation of her enflamed slit. The wooden prick, though, continued its abrasions across her tender anal ring.

He waited until her blood had cooled and resumed agitating her quim. This time her lusts built up higher and harder. She was straining at her bonds, rocking her hips, moaning loudly, and he stopped again. She groaned in frustration. But the teasing of her dainty star continued.

Li brought her to the edge of satisfaction four times. She was whining and crying, squirming in her confinements. Each time, the plowing of her anal opening went on and on.

On the fifth time, something happened, something that Li had known would. When the manipulations of her hairless pussy ceased, her rise to passion did not. It was his fucking of her ass that was now driving her to pleasure.

Violet was horrified that the prick in her private place was maintaining and building her excitement. It was, however, too late to stop. She kept thrusting back at the intruder, moaning and groaning as she came closer and closer to completion. She shook her head, pulled at her bonds, moaned loudly, and then it hit. "Uuuuuuumpf! Ummmmmmmmpf! Ummmmmmmmpf!" she yelled into her gag. Her pussy throbbed and pulsated. Waves of delight scoured her body. Her mind was lost in a haze of lust.

It was not until her passions had fully cooled that she reflected on what the man had done to her. Although he had stoked her flames of passion utilizing her puffy, soft quim, he had finished her off solely by using her ass. From now on, when she received a man's member in her bowels, there would be the possibility, and, eventually, maybe even the probability, that this moment would be relived.

Afterwards, all while she ate the porridge that they had brought her, Violet rued her body's continual betrayal of her.

Maybe she had been a slut all along, she thought. Maybe the general had spotted that in her and that's why he took her. Maybe it was better that she remain in her little cell than to face a world where her sluttishness would be on display day after day after day.

She was morose when the maids gave her her daily bath, and they could not cheer her. When Li escorted her again to the bedroom, she fully expected him to build on the success of the morning. That was not his plan. While she had been bathing, he had had the dildo vigorously washed.

"Kneel down!" he ordered her churlishly when they entered the room. She fell to her knees at once.

He stepped away from her for a few moments and then returned. He removed her gag and blindfold. He was standing there before her naked, the dildo proudly displayed from his loins. He sat on the bed and gave her a command. "*Suck cock!*"

At first, Violet did not now what his words meant. She had never heard him say them before. He leapt to his feet and scoured her back with his whippy stick. "Oooooooowwwwww!" she yelled. She cringed from the pain. "*Suck cock!*" he ordered as he sat down again. Then it dawned on her. He wanted her to put her mouth on the protuberation from his loins. He wanted her to pretend that she was sucking him off! While his meaning was clear to her now, the prospect of performing such an act was so disturbing that she paused in her obedience.

He rose to his feet and struck her three times. "Whack! Whack! Whack!" She cried out and fell to the floor. He struck her twice more until she rose again.

"*Suck cock!*" he yelled fiercely. Sobbing, Violet opened her mouth and put it on the ribbed, wooden prick. She groaned as she felt it fill her. Li took hold of her hair at the back of her head and started to move it back and forth. "*Suck cock!*" he yelled again.

She had always wondered what was actually involved in sucking a cock. Some of her girlfriends had done it, but they were somewhat reticent to discuss something that, if it got out, would ruin them socially. Only one of them claimed that she had actually liked it. So Violet had no idea what the act really entailed.

Assuming that a literal description of the act was involved, and pushing aside her disgust at the idea of the whole thing in light of the eunuch's lack of hesitancy in using his whip, she began to literally suck on it like she would a straw. Li could see immediately that she was doing it all wrong. He had hoped that she would be one of the ones that had done it once or twice, but she was clearly not. He pulled her face off of the cock and slapped it harshly.

"Oooooooh!" Violet screeched as her cheek erupted in pain. She looked up at the man unhappily. "What does he want?" she thought frantically. She would suffer untold pain until she discovered it.

Li decided that a direct demonstration would suffice the best. "*Stand up!*" he yelled. Violet jumped to her feet. "*Turn around!*" he ordered. She spun so her back was facing him. She felt him untying her hands. When they were free, he ordered her to turn around again and kneel. He put out his palm. "*Hand!*" he said.

Violet had never heard this order before either. She tried to think quickly what it could mean. "Whack!" he gave her a blow to her arm. She cried out in pain. He put out his palm and then put his other one in it. "*Hand!*" he said impatiently.

Tears flooding her eyes, Violet handed him her hand. She wondered what he was going to do with it and cringed. He took one of her fingers and put it in his mouth. He began to caress it with his lips, moving them up and down and stroking it with his tongue. He went on doing it for about thirty seconds. A light went on in Violet's head. She saw that the term was not really a misnomer, just an abbreviation for a much more involved act. There was sucking involved, but ever so much more as well.

"*Suck cock!*" the eunuch ordered again in Chinese, releasing her hand. Violet instantly subsumed the long, thick wooden object into her mouth. She pressed her lips tightly against it and began to move her head back and forth. She stroked it with her tongue as she had felt the eunuch do to her finger.

He made her suck the wooden prick for a good half hour. Her jaw began to ache. She wondered when he was ever going to let her stop. She choked when he forced it to the edge of her throat, fought for air when he kept it there. Li was enjoying the sight of the white slut on her knees to him, performing an act she almost certainly considered abhorrent. She didn't know that he was doing her a favor.

If she had ever started to suck the general's cock like she did initially his replica, he would have beaten her severely. All of this was for her benefit, although she didn't know it, wouldn't believe it. The general had no patience with reticent whores or whores who lay there like a fish while he pounded away at them. And she had intense competition in the seraglio. The Chinese sluts were finely skilled concubines, in grace and service. In his experience, the ones who pleased the master the most were the ones who suffered his torment the least.

When he felt that she had at least a modicum of training, he pushed her head back and ordered her up on the bed. He wanted her to experience coming with a cock in her mouth. It would be helpful to her to associate pleasure with giving oral gratification. It would give her greater enthusiasm and please her master or his guests more.

When Violet got up on to the bed, he had her lay down and he laid down next to her with his head going the other way. She looked at him expectantly. "*Suck cock!*" he told her. She leaned over him and went back to work. He grabbed her leg and pulled her over him until her smooth, soft, hairless quim was opposite his mouth. He started licking it slowly, letting her lusts build up gradually. He ran his tongue down the hairless divide and tickled the nubbin at its top. He drove his tongue into her crevasse deeply and stroked the roof of her cavern until she moaned.

In a short while, she was rotating her hips, trying to press her pussy against his tongue. He could hear her hard at work at the other end. He put his hand on her head and pressed it down until he heard her choke. He released her, allowed her to catch her breath and then pushed it down again. When he felt her thighs twitching against his ears, he flicked his tongue across her bud in a flutter. She groaned and her thighs began to shake. He pushed and pulled her head faster and faster to time it with her cresting wave of passion. "Gaaa! Gaaaa! Gaaaaaa!" she called out as she came.

He returned her to her cell for the afternoon. When he brought her up in the early evening, he had another lesson for her.

Waiting in the bed were the three maids who serviced her in her bath. When she came into the room, she was blindfolded. When he took the blindfold off, she eyed the three, young, naked women with alarm. She looked at him. He unfastened her hands, removed her gag and told her, "*On bed!*"

Violet had thought she was coming up for another lesson in cock sucking. All she had been able to think while she had had the wooden substitute in her mouth was that she would soon have the real thing. The act repelled her. But when the eunuch had licked her pussy while she gave service to the faux prick, she had found it exciting to have something between her lips. She began to wonder what the real one would taste like. And what would she do with his passion's product when he came? Was she expected to swallow it?

When she saw the young girls from the bathing room, a pit formed in her stomach. She had hoped and prayed that she wouldn't be expected to do this. It was contrary to God, contrary to nature. It was a sin of the first order. When she looked into the eyes of her keeper, she knew that she would do it anyway. She saw the fearsome command in his eyes.

Seeing her hesitation, he laid a solid blow of his whippy stick across her rear cheeks. She cried out and looked at him unhappily. "*On bed!*" he told her again. As she crawled up onto the mattress, he took a chair at the foot of the bed.

The girls were all smiling at her expectantly. One of them took her hand, led her to the middle of the bed and coaxed her to her belly. They pulled her arms over her head. She was trembling, ashamed at what the eunuch had ordered her to do, but too afraid of him not to do it.

When she was prone, the girls initiated a sensual massage of her body. Their soft, small hands felt good as they played them across her. One was doing her back, another the back of her legs and thighs and the other had hold of her arms and was massaging the muscles there.

In short order, all of Violet's qualms at contact with the other females passed. She became lost in the relaxing, gentle manipulation of her muscles. From time to time, one of the girls would plant a little kiss on her flesh. At first she recoiled at the oral contact with her body, but then it seemed to become a natural adjunct to their caresses. She was almost asleep, reveling in the feel of the soft mattress on her body, the freedom of her limbs, the comforting contact of the younger women's skin.

She awoke from her reverie when she felt the girls' hands urging her to turn onto her back. This was the part that she feared. When she rolled over, she saw the eunuch watching her carefully.

At first, the girls avoided contact with her sensitive parts. One of them had placed Violet's head in her lap and began to caress and stroke it. One of them caressed the fronts of her thighs while the other rubbed her hands across Violet's belly. Soon she had returned to that state of semi-consciousness that their massage of her back had bought her to. She had her eyes closed. Her hands were pressed in against her thighs.

When she felt lips slip over her nipple, she opened her eyes. This was the moment of truth. No matter how good their hands had made her feel, their caresses had now crossed over to actual sexual contact.

Instinctively, she raised her hand to push the lips away from her breast, but one of the girls gently took hold of it and restrained her. The girl at her breast flicked her tongue across the nipple and made Violet jump. She moved to the other breast, sucking, this time, long and hard on the stiffened tip, bringing a sigh to Violet's lips. A hand began to caress her inner thigh. The girl who had had her head on her lap, slid down next to her, on the opposite side of the one suckling her breast and began to plant little kisses on her face.

The girls all smelled of summer flowers. Their skin was soft and warm. Violet felt herself succumbing to their ministrations. A tongue and lips traced a line up her inner thigh to the edge of her sex. They flitted over it and descended the other one. Small hands were on her knees, spreading them. The girl who was kissing her breasts began to caress and massage them gently and lovingly. The girl who was kissing her face her put her lips on Violet's and she felt a tongue flit across them. Her arms were trapped between her sides and the flesh of the pretty, little maids who were assaulting her so tenderly.

Violet sighed languidly as the sweet hands and lips stoked her passion. When she felt a tongue slide up the divide between her labia, linger at the top and slide back down, she opened her eyes. A woman was kissing her sex! Before three days ago, no one had ever done that to her. Now she was having it serviced by a woman, and a woman who obviously knew what she was doing. Violet knew that she should stop her, stop them all, but she had not the power. It was her keeper's command and he was sitting not more than fifteen feet away.

When Violet released a groan of pleasure, the girls all giggled and increased the tempo of their attentions to her. A tongue was lapping at her pussy, a mouth was suckling her breasts and then she felt a hot mouth on hers. The girl's lips forced hers apart and a dainty tongue entered her mouth.

It was too much for Violet to take. She arched her back and squirmed her hips. Her thighs spread apart wider of their own accord. Little hands fluttered across her thighs as the girl's tongue worked magic on her burning crevasse.

When she started to come, she groaned into the mouth that had captured hers. The girl's tongue was dancing in her mouth, flitting against her tongue, scouring the insides of her lips. The girl at her breasts gave her nipple a long, hard suck as she firmly, but gently, squeezed her breasts. The girl at her loins had circled her hands around her thighs and was buried deeply in her quim.

Violet's body rocked with sensation as her pussy issued hard, pleasurable contraction after contraction. She felt like a hundred hands and mouths were pleasuring her all at one time. She groaned and sighed and screamed her passion. She had not known that Sapphic lust could be like this. It felt so natural, so good.

When her orgasm wound down, the girls all lay still against her body, hugging her and giving her little kisses. She was able to lift her hand and she stroked the body of one of them, she did not know who. The soft skin felt heavenly. Her fingers tingled wherever they roamed. The four women lay there peaceably for a long time.

Li was pleased. The foreign slut kept surprising him. He expected to have to beat her, but it did not look like she would ever shy at an order to pleasure with another female again. But there was one more test.

After the women had lain there awhile, they separated and brought Violet to her knees. She smiled at them gratefully. She hugged and kissed them one at a time and started to cry. It was the most heavenly moment she had experienced since her kidnapping. She felt warm and loved. The girls saw that she was crying and started to hug and caress her again. One of them pressed her torso and breasts against Violet's back. She started kissing Violet's shoulders and neck. The other two girls were kneeling in front of the happy Englishwoman and took turns kissing her mouth. They had their hands on her thighs and were rubbing them gently. As one of the girls slid her tongue in Violet's mouth, the other slipped her hand down between her thighs and began to caress her hairless slit.

Violet felt her lusts begin to burn anew. She had her hands around the waists of the girls who were kissing her, hugging them tightly. Their hot flesh enflamed her own. The girl on her right leaned back and, taking Violet's hand from around her waist, guided it to her pert, firm breast. Violet was being kissed passionately by the one on her left. The contact with the young woman's breast surprised her, but she obediently took hold of it and gave it a gentle squeeze. It felt surprisingly pleasurable. She felt her torso being guided forward. The girl on her right slid in front of her and lowered herself to her back. The other girls coaxed Violet between her thighs. The girl pulled Violet towards her, her hands on her arms and guided her lips to her breast.

Violet sighed as she put her lips around the stiffened peak. She suckled on it gently. A hand had slipped under her, between her thighs and was massaging her labia. The other girl was sliding her hand up and down her back, giving her her warmth.

The sensation of suckling another woman's breast was intoxicating to Violet. She shifted her attention to the other breast and seized it with her hand while she sucked and licked at the nipple. The girl beneath her moaned, sending a thrill to Violet's loins. Her thighs were rubbing against Violet's sides. Then, she felt the girl's hands on her shoulders. She exerted gentle pressure until Violet's lips slid across her belly. The other two pretty, shapely maids urged Violet's body back further and further until her mouth was hovering over the girl's beckoning slit.

Violet hesitated. Everything she had been taught told her that this was wrong, a perversion. She wanted to do it desperately, and didn't want it at the same time. She looked at the hairless slit anxiously. It was smooth as a baby's face. The girl's moisture glistened between the bare, soft, plump lips. Her legs were spread wide, expectantly. Violet wondered what it would taste like. She could smell the aroma of the girl's arousal. It was lust inspiring. She rubbed her hands along the course of the girl's lean, soft, enthralling thighs. She had never looked at another woman this way before. Was something wrong with her? Was what she was doing wrong?

The girls behind her were stroking her and caressing her. A hand was insistently pleasuring her divide and she could feel her need for completion arising. Seeing her hesitation, the girls behind her pulled her back. The girl to her right took her chin and turned her head. She kissed her passionately, swirling her delightful tongue in her mouth while caressing her breast. She felt the girl on the other side place her hand on her chin and Violet turned the other way to receive her lips and tongue. Her lusts took control of her.

She broke the kiss and leaned down. She brought her face close to the supine girl's pudendum and tentatively planted a kiss on it. She reveled in its warmth and softness. Daringly, she placed the tip of her tongue inside the girl's sexual divide and ran it the length of the slit. Emboldened, she slipped her tongue deeper inside, causing the girl under her to moan and dragged it upwards until she reached the button at the top. It was now or never. The taste had been fecund and rich. Casting everything she had believed about sex between women aside, she delved her head downwards, seized the hard nubbin of flesh and began to suckle it gently.

The girl below her moaned and her hips shifted. Violet's hands were holding the girl's thighs opened and she caressed them as she loved her button of pleasure. The smell, the taste, the feel of the girl's loins were driving Violet to ecstasy. The hand that was teasing her puss made her give a moan of her own. She began to lap at the girl's cunt eagerly. She pressed her lips hard down on her labia and extended her tongue as far inside the girl as she could go. She licked her way to the top and began to wash her clit again and again. The girl had her hands on Violet's head and was groaning with pleasure. Violet's dam was about to burst and the smell and taste of the loins she was servicing made her dizzy with desire.

The girl started coming before she did, but only by a few seconds. The sound of the girl's crisis launched her own. As she listened to the girl's cries of pleasure, she thought proudly, "I did that! I did that!" Then her mind emptied of all thought but of accepting the waves of pleasure that her throbbing quim was sending her.

When she was done, she collapsed on the girl's soft, pleasant belly.

军阀 外家

CHAPTER EIGHT

To top off Violet's introduction to performing cunnilingus, Li had had one of the maids adorn herself with the master's prick and fuck her until she screamed. He watched while she threw her arms around her assailant, kissing hard at her lips, her legs around the back of her thighs. She had clearly taken to female love. When Violet was too exhausted to produce yet another orgasm, he bound her hands behind her once again and blindfolded her. He did not install the gag, but rather made her prance through the fortress with the instrument of pleasure between her lips.

Violet had never been more conscious of the people scurrying back and forth around her than then. The faux cock stuck out from her mouth by several inches and was clearly visible to anyone who looked. Before, she had just been nude. This time, she was clearly advertised as the general's whore.

She walked with trepidation past the guard's station. She had never seen it, since all the times that she passed it she had been blinded. She did, however sense the presence of the men. Since they had started to abuse her, she had developed a second sense about their presence. She could smell them too, a distinct odor of sweat and malice.

As she passed them, she suddenly became aware of the significance to them of seeing one of her orifices plugged by the fake cock. It was a virtual signal that she had been 'broken in' at that hole and that it was now available for them. She realized that sometime during the night, they would come to her and take advantage of the announcement of the opening of this pathway.

She whined and cried as the eunuch tied her off in her cruel kneeling position. She wanted to beg the man, her keeper, not to leave her like this tonight. She wanted to tell him what the men had been doing to her. Then, it occurred to her that he probably already knew. It was either a planned or acceptable addition to her training to be the general's whore.

When the door to her cell slammed shut, Violet began a vigil for the arrival of the guards. Since her head was, more or less, pointed downwards by the cruel tie that led from the ring on her leather collar, she had to keep her lips purchased on the surface of the device so that it wouldn't fall out. It didn't take much to prevent it from sliding free; it wasn't heavy. It just took constant attention. She knew that if her keeper came down in the morning and saw it on the floor in front of her, she would suffer terribly.

It is said that those who are awaited are already present. It was true for Violet that night. The haunting shades of the men were all around her. She could feel their rough hands on her skin, hear their laughter at her predicament, the echo of their cocks where they had already pierced her several times. Her ears were poised for the sound of their keys in the lock to her cell. She spent the time waiting for their arrival on tenterhooks.

She did not have long to wait. She whined when she heard the keys jingling as the door was unlocked. Her keeper had removed her blindfold when he left and as it swung open, the eerie glow of the men's lanterns entered first. They were holding them in front of them, and Violet could only see the men as hulking forms. She had, during one of her tormented hours alone and in darkness, named them Scylla and Charybdis, the ancient monsters of Greek mythology. She had had only fleeting glances at their faces, but what she had seen was terrifying in its aspect. They seemed scarred and pockmarked and grotesque. They were demons of the under-world, presaging the torment one might find in hell.

One of their lanterns was hung from the hook above her and the other placed on the floor in front. Her body trembled as she felt the strap holding her head down loosened. She tried to keep her face pointed down, but one of the men placed his gnarled hand in her hair and pulled her head up. It was the one she had dubbed Scylla. He was taller and leaner than the other one. He took a long look at her. He was smiling repugnantly. The light shining from below him accentuated each vile aspect of his face. Violet could see that his teeth were ravaged from lack of care and the remnants were dyed a harsh red from use of the betel nut making him appear as if he had recently devoured someone. He placed his other hand on the end of the wooden prong that she had in her mouth and moved it back and forth slowly over her lips. Violet gave a groan of unhappiness which made him laugh.

The other man had gone behind her. He disconnected the strap that held her wrists extended behind her. His hands roamed her soft, plump rear cheeks. The calluses on his hands ran rough over her tender skin. The men exchanged words of sinister merriness between them.

The man in front of her, the one she called Scylla, stood up, and she could see him fumbling at his crotch. Both men wore a ragged, loose, brown tunic over tight, cotton pants. Scylla unbuttoned his fly and drew his cock from them. Violet could see that it was already hard. He rubbed his hand up and down it menacingly.

Charybdis had insinuated his hand under her and teased her conch into wetness. She felt the tip of his cock push aside her labia and, without ceremony, he entered her. As Scylla stroked his cock for Violet's benefit, Charybdis was applying slow steady strokes to her tight canal. Scylla removed the faux cock from between her lips. He tossed it onto the pallet in the corner and then pressed his prick forward so that Violet could accept it. Repelled by the thought of the man's prick in her mouth, she closed her lips tightly and shook her head away from him.

She received a vicious blow to her cheek. "Ahhhhhhh!" she cried. Her scream of pain resounded through the small room. He took hold of her cheeks and squeezed them harshly, forcing her lips apart. He leaned over to her and uttered something threatening to her in Chinese. She had heard the people crying out while the two guards had tortured them. She wanted no part of that. She gave out a great sob and opened her mouth. He shoved his steel hard prick right in.

Li, of course, knew what the men would do to Violet tonight. Violet was right. The presence of the faux cock in one of her holes was a signal to the men that, if they were careful and didn't mark her up, they could use her. The men hardly ever got a finely beautiful woman like the English slut to enjoy. In cell no. 3 was a middle aged peasant woman who had been arrested for peddling salt in a couple of the villages. Salt was a monopoly given out by the general to one of the local merchants in exchange for cash and other considerations. Scylla and Charybdis had been working her over for a couple of weeks. When the general got around to it, he would have her beheaded in the courtyard between the inner and outer walls of the fortress. Her head would be mounted on a post in the village where she was arrested. But fucking her was nothing like fucking the Englishwoman.

Like most servants, Li had his secrets from his master. He had a few irons in the fire. The guards were on his secret payroll and any information revealed by one of their 'customers' always came to him first. One hand washed the other. When he had a little treat, he gave it to them.

In any case, real experience at being used was good for the whore. Some night soon, she would be in her master's bed and she had better be ready for whatever he decided to do with her or she would pay the price.

Violet groaned with revulsion as the hot meat passed her lips. Scylla had taken hold of her hair at the back of her head and he was moving it back and forth while he plunged his cock in and out. The salty, hot taste of the cock shocked the proper English lady. That and the way it filled her mouth to capacity.

Charybdis was happily plowing away at Violet's quim. He wanted his turn at the whore's mouth and so he was being careful not to excite himself too much. Violet was revolted as she felt his thick rod coursing back and forth in her tunnel. The presence of this fiend's cock in her pussy made her want to wretch. Every part of her wanted to cast him out. It abhorred her to have her body possessed by the monster. It abhorred her that she had no say in who gained access to her inner self. Overwhelmed by the sensations of two unwanted, hostile, insistent cocks rabidly possessing her, Violet felt bile rising in her stomach.

The crisis of the grotesque man sawing at her mouth did not take long to arrive. He groaned his pleasure loudly as his cock began to spurt his essence. It took Violet fully by surprise. Her mouth was flooded with his cum. She had had no idea! It was disgusting! She yearned for him to finish with her. She struggled not to swallow any of the viscous fluid. She would spit it out as soon as she could.

When his cock's throbbing had waned, Scylla pulled himself from between Violet's lips. He quickly clasped his hand over her mouth, trapping his jism inside. Li had been specific on this point. He saw the dismay in the bound woman's face. He laughed and said something to her that he thought funny and laughed again.

Violet whined with dismay. "Oh, god!" she thought. The idea of having this man's seed in her belly, to mix with her food, to meld with her tissues, to become, even in any small way, a part of her, made her stomach roil. She tried to shake her mouth free of his hand, but he had it pressed firmly against her lips. Finally, seeing that she had no choice, she swallowed it, tears flowing from her eyes.

Charybdis saw that his partner was finished. He slid his piece from the young woman's tight fuck hole and got to his feet. Scylla stepped aside as the other man presented his cock to Violet. Her face contracted into a fierce grimace. She looked at the hardened cock unhappily. It had just been inside her leaking crevasse. Her fluids were all over it. This was too much! She would never suck it! Never!

Seeing the girl's resolution, Charybdis took hold of her nipples and gave them an agonizing twist. Violet screeched in pain. He did it again, harder this time, and her screech turned into a howl. He slapped her hard across the face, once this way and then the other.

Violet sobbed and cried. What had she ever done to deserve this, she asked God, the world, the universe. When would her torment end?

Seeing that she had no choice, knowing that the ogre standing before her with his cock in his hand would never give up his quest, Violet opened her mouth meekly. She felt the hot meet slip past her lips and she groaned in despair. Charybdis, like his predecessor, had no interest in advancing Violet's skills. He rode her mouth like a piston, seeking the entrance to her throat and then back again. Violet mewed and whined as the offensive, rigid rod did its work. Soon, his pot overboiled. Knowing what her assailant would require, this time she let the oozy discharge slide right down her throat.

When they were done with her, they tied her back down and reinserted the wooden prick into her mouth. Then they took their lanterns and left, slamming the cell door behind them.

Violet had learned what her master would expect her to do with his cum.

It didn't take long for Violet to realize that she could not keep the wooden cock in her mouth all night long if she didn't stay awake. Each time that she began to nod off, she could feel it slipping away from her. And each time it started to slip away, it was impossible to recover that part of the prong that had slipped out.

She struggled to remain conscious. Normally, she struggled to fall asleep, but tonight, for some reason, she was experiencing the exact opposite. Finally, hours after the guards had left her, she nodded off and the fake cock fell to the floor in front of her.

As soon as it happened, Violet sprung wide awake. Panic rushed through her. She couldn't see it in the absolute blackness that surrounded her. She tried to bend her head down further to see if she could troll for it with her mouth, but she could go down any more than several inches from the floor.

Violet spent the rest of the night in awful apprehension. Before, she couldn't stay awake, but now she couldn't go to sleep. She knew that the eunuch would strike her with his stick, but how many times? How severe a sin had she committed? There was no way for her to tell. Several times, at least, she figured. She was so fretful, that it was like she had already suffered the blows' impact.

When Li opened the door to her cell, he saw the fake cock lying on the floor. Violet was sobbing sorrowfully. He had known that she would drop it. It would have been impossible to hold it in. He wanted another opportunity to punish her. Time was growing short and she needed to be fully attuned to her obligation to obey before she became installed as one of the master's concubines.

He hooked his lantern up on the ceiling. While he went around behind her to release the bond holding her hands extended, the maid who had come with him stood by the door passively. She was holding the tray with Violet's breakfast on it and the little bowl that she would use to collect her water wastes.

Without further ado, Li let his whippy stick fly. Violet's mouth was open and she let out an anguished howl. He struck her again and the poor woman shrieked. A third blow resulted in yet another howl.

Li looked appreciatively at the results of his handiwork: three evenly spaced red lines on the Englishwoman's ass. That was enough for now.

Li retied her wrists to the iron bar embedded in the floor behind her. He stepped in front of her and retrieved the discarded faux cock. He proffered it to the still moaning woman's mouth. She took it unhappily. He bound her collar ring to the floor beneath her and then signaled the maid. After he retrieved his lantern, they exited the cell and he slammed the door shut.

Violet bemoaned the still burning damage to her rear cheeks but also the loss of the chance to eat and the opportunity to empty her bladder. It did not take long, after the long night, for the latter to reach a crisis. She tried and tried and tried to hold it back, but, ultimately, her water released itself.

She knew that she had earned another punishment. She moaned in the darkness. The smell of her urine rose all around her. She started to cry.

As expected, when Li returned, a few hours later, at almost 11 a.m., he smelled the released urine right away. Violet was looking at him, her lips trembling. He went behind her, released her wrists from the floor and gave her three more solid whacks on her ass. The young woman cried and sobbed dolefully when he was done. The prong in her mouth muffled most of her wails of pain.

He gave an instruction to the maid who had come down with him and she placed the tray on the floor and ran off. She came back in a few moments with a bucket of water and a scrub brush. Li released Violet from her bonds and had the maid hand the bucket and brush to her.

Violet spent the next fifteen minutes or so cleaning up her own spillage. She was crying the whole time. When she was done, Li retied her wrists behind her and had her stand by the side of the cell. He went out to the hallway and shouted something to the guards. He then came back in and waited for them.

A short while later, the guards wheeled in what was to Violet a strange contraption. An ache started to develop in her heart as she knew that whatever it was it portended no good for her.

The device the men were bringing in was known as the pony. It had a long board attached to a stanchion on both sides. The top of the board had been honed down so that it formed a sharply rounded 'v'. The guards, after giving Violet salacious looks, left the pony under the hook from which Li's lantern hung.

Li gave Violet a sharp command, "*Get on!*" Violet looked at him confusedly. She didn't understand what she was supposed to do. Li struck her with the whippy stick, producing a muffled wail from her. He pushed her towards the device and made a showing of lifting his leg over it. Finally understanding what he wanted, Violet lifted one leg and stepped over it so that the board was running between her thighs.

Her hands were still free from mopping the floor and Li tied them off in front of her. He took the end of the strap and attached it to the hook above her. Violet was raised so that she was standing on her toes, her heels lifted about four inches high.

There was a crank on the end of the pony and Li turned it now. It rose steadily until the edge of the board rested just between Violet's love lips, forcing them apart and pressing on her interior. Crouching down, he tied a strap to one of Violet's ankles, ran it through one of the iron bars in the floor and tied it off to her other ankle.

Seeing that the slut was mounted properly, Li retrieved his lantern and he and the maid left her cell, locking the door behind them, sealing Violet into silent darkness. He had left the faux penis in her mouth.

Violet was not quite sure what had been done to her. She knew that she could not stand on her toes for very long. When they started to ache, she carefully lowered herself on the board that ran through her legs. Her pussy settled firmly on it. It was uncomfortable but bearable.

After a few minutes, her pussy began to emit a dull throb from the pressure of her body on it. She shifted herself and stood back up on her toes. She could only do that for a few minutes and soon she was back with her pussy jammed down against the top of the board again. She pulled on her hands, lifting her body just a mite. That took the pressure off of her toes and her pussy. After a minute or two, her arms began to ache from holding her weight.

It was then that Violet realized the diabolical nature of the device. No matter how she configured herself, some part of her body would hurt, her arms, her toes or her pussy. At this realization, she panicked. She knew that it would not take long for the dull aches to turn into agonizing pain. "Oh my god!" she exclaimed to herself. And she began to whimper.

So when Wang's boat pulled in, she had been 'riding the pony' for three hours. The pain had turned excruciating. She wailed and moaned. Her face was awash with tears. The utter silence and darkness of her cell was closed around her oppressively. Casting aside any fear of punishment, she screamed muffled, distorted pleas to her jailors, to anyone who could hear her, to free her from the diabolic contraption. No one, of course, could.

Her teeth jammed down on the false cock that Li had left in her mouth. She prayed and prayed that the man would soon come back and release her from her torment. She tried to envision him walking up to her cell door and unlocking it with his keys as if her thoughts could reach out to him and make him do it. But it was not to be. Li was at the gate to the fortress, greeting the master.

* * * * * * * * * * * * *

General Wang smiled when he saw Li. He wanted a report on his new slut.

"*So, how is she progressing?*" he asked him.

"*She has progressed remarkably well, Lord,*" Li answered. "*She should be ready for you in two days. There is one final test.*"

This worked into Wang's plans fine. "*Prepare my other sluts for me,*" he ordered his eunuch. Li gave his master a bow and retreated.

* * * * * * * * * * * * *

It was close to three o'clock in the afternoon that Li came back down to the dungeon. When Violet heard the door opening, she started to sob. Her earlier cascade of tears had dried up after a while. She just morosely accepted the intense pain being suffered through her feet, her shoulders and her pussy. Her pussy was the worst. It felt like someone had kicked her there. It was an intense ache, profound even. She would lift herself a little on her toes and maybe twenty seconds later, when her tired feet could not take it any more, she would raise herself by her arms for another twenty seconds and then go back to her toes. When she could neither rest on her toes nor use her arms to support her without agonizing sensations, she lowered her pussy once more to the board, moaning with pain. She stayed in that position until she positively could not tolerate the intense throb on her pussy and the cycle started all over again. She shouted and yelled her frustration and pain into the small room. She pleaded and begged for someone to come and relieve her, her mouth trying to form the only words she had spoken in days. She would go through cycles of bearing up under the ordeal, crying silently, and then sobbing and calling out her misery.

When she heard and saw the door opening, she lost all control of herself. She begged and pleaded Li to release her. Hearing the words from her mouth, even though muffled by the prong that was jammed in there, Li lashed out with the whippy stick and struck her across her breasts. *"No talking!"* he shouted.

Violet broke out into a series of heart rendering sobs. She bit down on the dildo hard, trying to restrain her words of supplication. Her breasts were on fire. Li waited for a moment. He wanted her to get control of her self. Sluts are required to bear pain administered by their masters and, while they were allowed to cry out and moan, they needed to have the ability to rein themselves in.

Violet saw his impassive face and realized that he was waiting for her to calm down. She tried her hardest not to make a single sound. She could not help a high pitched, low volume whine emanating from her mouth. Try as she might, she could not suppress it.

Li was satisfied. That would have to do. She would learn later to be more stoical.

When Violet was released, she fell to her knees. The pounding of her feet, pussy and shoulders would not stop. Li removed the wooden shaft from between her lips and ordered the maid to give the poor woman something to drink. The diminutive maid advanced into the cell with trepidation. She placed the tray she was carrying on the floor and took up the small flask of juice and brought it to the sniffling woman's lips. Violet drank it down gratefully.

The callous eunuch ordered Violet to give him her hands. He untied them and then, ordering to rise up on her knees, tied them off again behind her back. He turned to the maid and said, "*Off with pants.*"

The maid, startled by the command, put the flask down on the tray and, after flipping off her wooden clogs, undid her pants and slid them down her legs. When she pulled them off, she stood dutifully awaiting his next order. Her hairless pussy beckoned.

Li tapped Violet on the shoulder with his stick and then the crux of the little maid's thighs. "*Suck pussy,*" he told her harshly.

Violet recorded the dismal order. She didn't know the words but understood their import. She looked up in the face of the pretty, young girl and edged herself closer. Her body was all wrung out from her experience on the pony and she was afraid that her keeper might put her back onto it. She gave out a little sob, curved her back, maneuvered her mouth to the trembling maid's loins and began to administer her tongue to her soft, smooth twat.

Li watched the English slut with satisfaction. Even after her terrible ordeal, she was able to follow his command. In spite of her earlier, initial reticence to engage in female to female sex, she was performing her duty.

Violet ran her tongue up between the girl's hairless love lips several times. She wriggled it between them, looking for her moisture. She lapped at the nubbin at the tip of her canal until the girl gave out a little moan of pleasure. Then she took it between her lips and suckled it until the girl's body swayed and she put her hands on Violet's head.

It took the tired, sore, miserable woman about fifteen minutes to have the girl writhing in the prefatory stage to her orgasm. Her hands gripped Violet's hair tightly. She was making little staccato moans, "Ah! Ah! Ah! Ah! Ah!"

Li appreciated the vignette he was viewing. Violet was resting flat on her thighs, her head was tilting upwards and he could see her head moving as she tongued the maid. Her bound hands hung behind her listlessly. It was a vision of subservience and obedience that thrilled him to watch. She was going to make a fine whore.

The maid began to rock her hips and thrust her pussy at Violet's mouth. Violet, sensing that the maid was near her crescendo of passion, increased her efforts. She lapped at the girl's long, hairless slit. She tickled her love button with her tongue. She grabbed it between her lips and suckled it, all like the eunuch had done to her.

When the maid's orgasm erupted, she shouted her joy into the little, dimly lit cell. She took hold of Violet's head and pulled it hard against her slit. Her eyes were rolled back in her head and her mouth was formed into a little 'o'. "Ohhhhhh! Ohhhhhhhh! Ohhhhhhhh!" she cried as the waves of pleasure washed over her, her voice pitched high and sweet. "Ohhhhhh! Ohhhhhhhhhh!"

As her pussy's throbs faded, the pretty maid pulled her loins back from Violet's mouth and leaned over and kissed her. Violet returned the kiss fervently. Despite her near exhaustion, the continued throbbing of her pussy, her feet and her shoulders, the scent of the girl's discharge had raised her lust.

Li tapped on Violet's shoulder and she withdrew her kiss. He ordered the maid to give Violet her food. The maid placed the bowl full of fish and rice with a tangy orange sauce on the floor. Violet looked back at her keeper before moving towards it. At his signal, she leaned over and began to eat it with gusto. She had not eaten for almost 20 hours.

When Violet was finished, Li had the maid wipe her face and then let her pee into the blue and white ceramic bowl. Once that was completed, the eunuch ordered Violet to her pallet. He tied her ankles together, but did not hogtie her, although he restored her gag. He ordered the maid to redon her white, pegged pants, picked up the lantern from the floor and she and he left the cell.

Violet fell asleep almost at once.

Li had told General Wang that there was one more test that the new slut would have to pass before she could graduate fully to the above ground world. About three hours after Violet passed out on her pallet, he came down to her cell to commence it.

Violet jarred to wakefulness when she heard the door to her cell opening. She saw the eunuch enter it holding the lantern up before him like some strange vision of Diogenes. He placed the lantern on the hook above him and untied Violet's ankles and hands. He tapped his whippy stick on the floor in front of him and Violet scurried into position kneeling before him. He tapped the hairless crux of her thighs and said roughly, "*Pleasure pussy!*"

Violet thought that she knew what he meant, but wasn't sure. She had never done this in front of anyone, ever! Did he really mean for her to...."

She didn't have the chance to get the thought complete in her mind. The whippy stick struck her against her left arm. It stung like the blazes.

"Owwwww!" she screeched. Her hand went to her injury.

Li gave the instruction again, louder now. "*Pleasure pussy!*" he ordered her. He gave her slit a not too gentle tap of his whip. Violet flinched as it struck her damaged flesh.

Not wanting to get into any more trouble, she took her right hand and applied it to her wounded crevasse. She delicately placed the two longest fingers over her slit and began to slowly rub her clit in tiny circles. She saw Li place a small sand clock on the floor in front of her. She saw the sand on the top quickly escaping to the bottom. It took her a moment to figure it out and then she realized that the eunuch expected her to come before the time was up. Panicked, she began to rub her pussy with more alacrity. She looked up and saw him looking at her sternly. His peering gaze put her off of her stroke. She couldn't do this in front of anyone! It was too private! She knew that if she did get off, she would put on a lascivious display before the man. That, she didn't want to do although she had come many times at his hand, or at the hands of others in front of him.

She managed to get her pussy lubricated and had begun the process of turning her body over to passion when the sand ran out. She looked at the eunuch and quailed. It wasn't fair! She couldn't just come at the drop of a hat! And her pussy was still sore too!

Li tapped his stick down at the spot where she had done so much kneeling and she quickly dragged herself to it. She was trembling in fear as he calmly tied her into her position. Before he tied her hands off to the iron bar behind her, he raised his whippy stick and hit her hard, three times in succession. "Whack! Whack! Whack!"

Violet screamed in pain. The strokes burned right through her. "It isn't fair!" she wanted to scream. "I just can't do it!" She remained silent, however, not wanting to exacerbate her punishment. Li bound her wrists to the bar in the floor and left.

She cried and moaned. He had set her an impossible task. He would be back and expect her to try it again. He was implacable. What was she going to do?

She listened in trepidation for the tell-tale sound of the key in the lock to her cell. Time passed at a glacial pace. He came back two hours later.

He loosened her neck and head and untied her hands. He ordered her to kneel up and then shouted at her, "*Pleasure pussy!*" He put the hourglass down on the floor in front of her.

Violet went to work right away. She was rubbing herself furiously. She moistened all right, but she just couldn't seem to trigger her lust. It was too stressful! How did he ever expect to do it! It wasn't fair! Time ran out just as it had before. It seemed to Violet that the timer was set to about three minutes. Three minutes to get herself off! It was impossible!

When the sand ran out, the eunuch gave her a harsh "whack!" across her breasts. She saw it coming, but he moved so fast that she did not have time to raise her hands to protect her vulnerable, soft, pale mounds. Violet doubled over and groaned from the pain. Li ordered her to again place her head between her knees.

She trembled as he tied her neck down again and her wrists together. "Whack! Whack! Whack!" He struck her ass three times again. She screeched and moaned her pain. Then, he left.

Kneeling in the dark, Violet despaired at ever being able to satisfy him. She thought of the board thing that he had put her on earlier that day and her body shook. "Please don't do that again! Please!" she moaned quietly. "I couldn't stand it!"

She thought desperately at how she was going to be able to accomplish her task. "Next time," she thought, "I'll pretend he isn't there. I'll close my eyes and pretend I'm at home in my bed, like I used to do it,"

When Li came back two hours later, he gave her another chance. She closed her eyes and thought of her warm bed back in England, the comfort of her little room. She had just started to feel her lusts rising when the hourglass ran out once more. She raised her hands automatically to protect her chest, but the eunuch brought the whippy stick down on the front of her thighs. She screeched with pain. Once she was tied down again, he gave her three more on her proffered rear cheeks. "Whack! Whack! Whack!"

Every two hours, Li returned. Each time she got a little bit closer, but to no avail. Each time she suffered a hard blow to her breasts, her back or her thighs. When he went to strike her breasts, she had put her hands in front of her defensively. "*Hands on head!*" he screamed at her. "*Hands on head!*"

Violet did not know what he meant her to do and he struck her across the thighs with a lightning fast blow.

"Ahhhhhhhh!" she cried out.

"*Hands on head! Hands on head!*" he yelled at her again, this time mimicking what he wanted her to do.

Sobbing, knowing what was coming, Violet complied.

"Whack!" The whip came down across her pale, lovely twins. She howled with unhappiness. And then, when she was tied down again, three hard blows to her hindquarters. Her rear cheeks were burning. She didn't know how much more she could take.

Finally, on the seventh try, fourteen hours after her travail began, something clicked. As she started to rub her pussy with her fingers, she thought of the beautiful, soft skin of the three maids who had pleasured her. She felt her hand as if it were one of their hands. She felt their heat on her body, their mouths suckling at her breasts. She became overwhelmed with desire for them. To her surprise, her pussy filled with blood, her breasts became taut, her breathing became heavy. She felt it coming.

She didn't dare look at the sand clock. What difference did it make? She just wanted desperately to reexperience the mind shattering pleasure she had enjoyed at the hands of the three, pretty, Chinese girls. She had her eyes jammed shut so that she could recapture every nuance of that experience. Suddenly, she was over the top. Her pussy clenched and reclenched savagely. She moaned and rubbed her pussy harder and harder, not in desperation, but in lust. "Ohhhhhhh! Ohhhhhhhh! Ohhhhhhh!" she called out.

Li was pleased. She had passed the test. It had taken longer than it had the Russian slut, but she had an advantage with her predisposed pussy. That whore came any time, any where. He would give the English slut her reward. Each time he had come down, he had brought one of the maids with him. He had permitted her to release her liquids and drink, but had gotten no food. Now, he let the maid service her and then place a bowl of food in front of her. Violet, after being signaled permission, ate it with relish, her hands on either side of the bowl her mouth buried in it. It was succulent. As she wolfed down the food, she thought of how used she had gotten to eating this way, how easily she had adapted to whatever conditions the man had imposed on her. But she didn't care. What was the use of fighting him? She was a whore and a slut and had just proven it without any shadow of a doubt. She could come virtually on command. How much more of a slut could she be?

When she was finished, the girl gave her something to drink and then washed her face as usual. The eunuch untied her ankles from the bars in the floor and ordered her to her pallet. Then, to her surprise, he ordered the maid to strip. The pretty girl doffed her light green top, her wooden clogs and her tight, white pants immediately. He then spoke to her in Chinese. She looked at Violet and nodded her understanding. She moved to Violet's little pallet and joined her on it. She took the woman's head in her hands and kissed her. Li took the lantern and left the room, plunging the women into darkness.

Violet was in seventh heaven. It was the first time she had been left without being bound since her abduction. She felt an untrammeled freedom. And she was not alone! For the first time she had been left in her cell and she was not alone!

The warm body of the Chinese maid comforted her. She hugged her close and nestled her face into her soft shoulder. She began to cry. All the horror and terror of the last two weeks came pouring out of her. She realized that her relative freedom, the benefit of warmth and companionship, had been won at the price of her soul. She had given in to the eunuch's campaign of degradation and had passed the course with flying colors. And her reward was the warmth of another female's body and the opportunity to take comfort from it.

The girl hugged her back tenderly. Her outpouring of sorrow was contagious and the girl began to cry too. The two women clutched to each other as if they were the last two persons on earth. Eventually, in the dark, their mouths found each others. Lust over came them both. Violet devoured the young girl's mouth as their bodies melded in an impassioned embrace.

Lips suckled breasts, hands stroked soft, hairless love lips, tongues explored each others' fecund, musky crevasses. Violet came violently once, twice, three times. She lost count. And she lost count of the number of times that the young girl squealed and moaned her pleasure in return.

Eventually, their passions lagged. Violet held the young girl's body close in the silent, entombed darkness that was her cell and fell asleep. When she awoke at the sound of her cell door opening hours later, she was still in her arms.

军阀 外家

CHAPTER NINE

When General Wang sat down for his breakfast that morning, he was feeling very good. He had had a wonderful session with his concubines the night before. His prick stirred at just the thought of it.

He had had all three brought into his room. He started out with Me Ling. She was a dainty creature, demure and desirable. She doffed her silken robe and crawled up onto his bed at his command. The other two knelt expectantly at its foot.

He took the slender, graceful creature in his arms and ran his hand over her breasts and belly. Her breasts were like two succulent peaches. He took one of them into his mouth. Her nipple turned to stiffness immediately and he suckled at it for a long time, his hand having captured its twin and begun to massage it gently. She moaned in passion. Her skin was as smooth as milk and just as pale. She was warm and smelled like fully blossomed orchids. He loosened his mouth from her breast and took her lips. They were plump and tasty. He let his tongue explore her hot interior. Her tongue danced happily with his.

The general's cock had grown stiff and needed a warm, wet place. He knew that his Whore Number One, he knew her former name was Me Ling, but she had lost that name when she became his concubine, at least as far as he was concerned, had a profound dislike for his cock in her mouth. Why, he didn't know. It was one of the finest cocks in China. It was long and thick and he could make it dance many times in a night. His cum was thick and creamy, a bright white. She should crave the taste of it, but there was no accounting for women. He could have had Li break her of this distaste very quickly. It would have, though, deprived him of the joy of watching her face darken when he ordered her to pleasure him.

They had been kneeling together on his bed. He was as naked as she. For a fifty year old man he was in supreme condition. He had not grown the ballooned waists of many of the other Chinese warlords who rested on their laurels and drank rice wine and fucked all day. His chest was strong and muscular, his hair still as black as the day he was born. He kept it cut short in the military style. He had a strong jaw and piercing eyes. Taller than most of his countrymen, he stood about 5'9".

His rigid cock was pressed up between them. He leaned back until he was flat on the soft, comfortable bed, taking her with him. When she was laying on top of him, he ordered her to "*Suck cock!*"

A shadow passed over her face but, to her credit, her impassioned demeanor immediately returned. She lowered herself until her mouth was level with his cock, dragging her tongue and lips over his belly and then subsumed his rock hard, tall manhood in her mouth. Her mouth was small, as was Pu Wei's, his number two whore, and unlike the Russian whore's, whose mouth could almost take all of him in. So Me Ling had to make up for it with skill. And as much as she disliked sucking cock, she was skilled at it.

She slavered her lips over the tip of his steel hard rod, dancing her tongue over the tip. Her tiny hand took hold of the shaft and worked it gently, but firmly. She covered his cock's end with the whole of her mouth and then descended his pole with her lips wrapped tightly around it as far as she could go. He felt his cock make contact with the back of her mouth and moaned his approval of her techniques. It was ironic that, while she abhorred having his dick in her mouth, she was, when it came right down to it, the best one at it.

She pleasured him for a full twenty minutes. Her long, black hair fell over his body as she suckled him. He could feel its light touch across his skin whenever she moved. She took his sac into her mouth and teased his stones with her tongue while fluttering her graceful fingers on his shaft. She pulled back his foreskin and gently, delicately caressed the sensitive skin within with her lips.

When he felt that his forces were ready to explode, he wrestled her to her back. This was the part she hated the most. He straddled her face with his knees and reinserted his cock into her mouth. Slowly, he lowered himself within her until his cock brushed up against the entry to her throat, and then he went past it. She gave a little cough as the head of his prick went into her esophagus. He held it there for a few moments, reveling in its tightness and the heat of her mouth along the length of his shaft. Then he slowly withdrew, giving the slut time to draw some air, and then he did it again. She moaned with distress as he paused longer this time at his furthest reach. He eased himself out slowly once more.

She may have been in distress, but she would have passed out from lack of oxygen before she did anything to disturb his reverie. He took his time, drilled his cock deep into her throat five or six times. Then he was ready. His hips started to move rapidly. His cock pumped in and out of her throat like the piston of an engine. He groaned with pleasure as his fires were set to high. When he came, he groaned. He held himself deep within her as his load passed down the length of his cock and spurted directly into her belly. Pleasure wafted over him. She made little mewing sounds, but made no effort to speed along his possession of her throat. Finally, he was finished and slowly withdrew from her.

The black haired beauty was straining for air when he exited her and took a long, deep breath when her mouth was free. He got off of her and, laying down beside her, kissed her lips and then her nipples in gratitude.

He decided she deserved a reward. He ordered Whore Number Three to come to the bed. He pushed Whore Number One to the foot of the huge, expansive mattress and told Number Three to "*Suck pussy!*" The blond haired Russian, her thick, bright yellow hair untied and flowing over her shoulders, nestled between Number One's thighs and, holding her them apart, buried her face in her quim. He watched as Number One's eyes glazed over. She placed her tiny hands on the head of the blond whore and shuddered in passion.

His cock had not fully softened. He was ready to do battle once more. He called out to Number Two. He remembered her original name as Pu, but why bother with names for sluts? "*Whore Number Two! On bed!*" he ordered curtly. She hopped from her kneeling position, shucked off her robe and joined him on the mattress.

Number Two's breasts were just a little larger than Number One's. If Number One's breasts were peaches, Number Two's were oranges. He licked and suckled at first one breast then the other while his hand wandered over her hip and took possession of her sexual mound. His cock had resumed its hardness. He reveled in the warm, soft skin of his property. All women should be owned, he thought. Why else did the gods put them on the earth but to give pleasure to men? Why would a man not take possession of a woman he desired and rule her like a lord, as he did. If he could, that is. Fate had played him a grand hand, he had to admit that. But it was his fate as it had been written and that was that. In the next life he could, heaven forbid, be a woman, and someone would, if he were enticing enough, put him in his seraglio.

His thoughts turned to the beautiful Miss Harris in his dungeon three floors below his sumptuous bedroom. Her accommodations were not so nice, he thought to himself, chuckling. What she needed to understand was that she had a role to play in this life. Fate had brought her thousands of miles to fulfill her destiny. He could no more resist taking her than she could resist the men he sent to take her. And as to the harshness of her treatment, well, he had to knock those stupid Western ideas out of her head somehow, didn't he? And, he had to admit, it pleased him that she suffered after the rudeness with which she had treated him when they met.

The warmth and softness of Whore Number Two's skin brought his thoughts back to her. He turned her so that she was on her knees facing his other two whores. He wanted to watch while the Russian one pleasured his first whore.

He reached down between Number Two's legs to make sure that she was ready for him. She was, as he'd known she would be. If she hadn't he would have beaten her. His finger slid inside her moist canal with ease. She clamped her pussy's walls down on it. Of the three, Number Two had the best pussy. She had well trained muscles that could hold a man unwillingly inside her. You would have to beat her to let you go.

He brought his steel hard prick to bear on her slice and pressed its head forward. She sighed as it entered her. She pushed back against him, encouraging it into her depths. Then she gave it a squeeze with her conch and it was his turn to sigh. He pleasured her slowly, leisurely. Number Three, the Russian wench, knew that it was her job to keep his other whore in pleasure for as long as possible. He might have rewarded Number One, but her primary duty was to please him. And he wouldn't be pleased if Number One came too quickly.

The one called Pu was moaning as she rocked back and forth on his cock. She would push back as far as she could go, her pussy, warm and welcoming. On the stroke back, she would clasp it tightly making him forcibly drag it back. His hands were on her hips and he was guiding her back and forth. His cock was hot and tremors of pleasure coursed through him. He pleasured her back long and slow. But fucking her steamy twat was only a precursor to the ultimate goal. When he had lingered long enough within her pussy, he slowly withdrew his hard pole. He pressed down on her hips, making her smaller, tighter entrance available to him. He heard her moan. He knew that she suffered with shame and embarrassment every time he plowed her ass. He didn't know why. It was the most natural thing in the world to take as much pleasure from a woman's body as a man could do. It was his duty in fact, since the gods detested wastage more than anything else.

That thought brought him back to Miss Harris. Didn't she know that she was tempting the wrath of the gods by not giving her beautiful body over to the pleasure of a man? She was well over 25 years old and unmarried. If she actually had been married, she would probably have been safe from him. He had honor. He never took another man's wife without killing him first. She should have married Robert Preston on the day that she got off of the boat. He wouldn't have killed Robert, he didn't think.

Wang pressed his tool against the second slut's dainty hole. It puckered reflexively. He pushed forward and the brown star eased open for him. This one might detest ass fucking, but she knew her duty to her lord. The tight ring brought a wave of pleasure to him as he descended into her bowel.

The bandit general sawed his cock back and forth. The slut beneath him moaned and sighed. She might find ass fucking distasteful, but she always reveled in it. Rarely did he come in her ass without her going into total rapture. So what was her problem? It didn't matter; her shame at being forced to perform the act made it all the more pleasurable to him. It accented his power over her and power was what his life was all about.

Whore Number One was reaching her crisis. She was panting and her hands gripped the hair of the blond slut tightly. Her dainty breasts were hard, her lips were puffy, her mouth hung open. He heard her start to mew her pleasure. It was the precursor to her explosion. He was ready to watch it, ready to time his and his subject's orgasms with hers.

Her chest started rising and falling rapidly, her eyes rolled back, her hips were thrusting up at the tongue that was pleasuring her. Suddenly her body seemed to contract and she screamed. "Oh! Oh! Oh! Oh!" She leaned her head back and howled.

Her rapture induced his. His cock exploded in the ass of Pu. In turn, his middle slut groaned with pleasure. Her ass was rocking back and forth seeking maximum abrasion against her tight, rear ring. He flooded her with his spewm; her ring grasped his cock tightly.

Wang drooped over the back of his whore and muttered his prayer to his ancestors and their gods. He must have been a saint in his prior life, he thought, to deserve so much pleasure. And deserve it he did. Everyone deserved what they got. If he had been visited with misfortune, he would know that somehow he deserved it. So when he was graced with success, money, power, women, all the fine things in life, how could he doubt that he deserved that too?

He withdrew his piece from the posterior of Number Two. She had her head down on the bed and was still panting after her explosive orgasm. It was time to take joy from the body of Number Three.

He ordered Number Two to clean him. She hopped off of the bed and returned with a small bowl of warm water, some soap and a washcloth. She dipped the cloth in the water, covered it with soap and washed his cock clean. When she had rinsed off all the soap, she took his softened rod in her mouth and drew her lips down its rubbery length. This was her signal to him that the job was complete.

He learned once from an American missionary doctor the importance of good hygiene when it came to ass fucking. He carefully explained the nature of germs and how they could be spread to the love nests of his sexual partners if he did not clean himself. The doctor was an intense devotee of the alternate path and Wang had just offered him the use of one of his whores for that purpose for the night. Ever since, Wang had been very careful.

The doctor received his reward. He didn't know how much the seven, young, pretty nurses who were traveling with him were worth. A quick deal was made and, in the morning, the nurses were stripped and thrown into his dungeon for conversion into whores. Wang tried them all out for several weeks before they were wholesaled to a buyer from Beijing. The doctor was well rewarded and, once he learned that he could live here like a king, using his share of the money Wang received for the whores and that which was to have gone to found his medical mission, bought one of the estates just south of the fortress. The doctor kept one of the pretty nurses for himself after Li Pao trained her for him.

His whores were all kneeling on the bed awaiting his pleasure. He needed something to put hardness back in his pecker. He got off of the bed and ordered Number Three to follow him. He could see the trembling of her lips as she complied.

A chain descended from the ceiling of his bedroom to about five feet above the floor. At its end were two leather bracelets. He captured the slut's right hand and closed it within the bracelet, and then the left, the other. The chain operated on a pulley attached to the wall and he went over to it and pulled it taut until the slut was standing on her toes. She was issuing a barely audible whine, her lips were closed tightly and her face was a mask of grief.

His cock had started to get hard just thinking about whipping the Russian concubine. Every time he saw her he was reminded what a score the capture of her family had been: 92 ounces of gold, once he had given three to Lieutenant Li. Her two sisters were worth another five ounces of gold each. The mother, he threw her in to sweeten the deal. And then there was the boat and all their other belongings. One of them was what looked like an ancient icon. He kept it in his treasure room. It was probably worth more than its weight in gold and so was good portable wealth.

He decided on the thin, leather encased whip. It would leave long lines wherever it landed. The blond slut grimaced when she saw it. She should.

One of her breasts was leaking milk. He smiled and stood next to her. He took the teat in his mouth and gave it a little suckle. A jet of warm, semi-sweet liquid came out. He swallowed it happily. He did not have the time or the inclination to milk her now. He would order one of the other sluts to do it later while he watched.

The whip would leave long, red lacerations. Not deep enough to bleed, but enough so that a wound would arise on the surface. They would heal within the week. Then he would put new ones on her. She looked so enticing with the marks of violence on her; he liked to have her always bear some sign of the whip.

He looked at her trembling body appreciatively. Her heavy breasts shimmered, her taut belly was moving in and out with her lungs as she drew one anxious breath after another. Her hairless puss was painted red. Each night before he fucked his sluts, an old, wizened witch of a woman from his native village examined them. She felt their bellies and their purses, sometimes manipulating them to climax. She had a wizard's sense of when they were fecund and, if they were found so, painted their pussies red to remind him not to discharge in them there. No one wanted to father a whelp on a mere concubine who was, after all, little more than a sex slave. The crony never failed. And if he fucked up, she had a potion that would take care of the problem within a couple of days. But it made the whores sick for about a week and he didn't like to be without them that long.

When he raised the whip, the blond whore whined in anticipation. He sliced it forward and landed it across her beautiful breasts. She stiffened and screamed, "Ahhhhhhhh! Ohhhhhhhhh!" He allowed them some demonstrations when he whipped them, but not too much. The slut, clamping her thin lips together tightly, wisely cut off her exclamation of pain as soon as she could.

He struck her again across her firm belly and she screamed again, this time a little louder. He stopped. "Maybe I should gag her," he thought. He decided that that would be best and took a gag from the cabinet on his wall. It had a long, leather prong and a shield that went across the lower face. She opened her mouth dutifully when he proffered it to her. Tears were already streaming down her face. He could tell that she was about to get out of hand and maybe start pleading for mercy or something. Then he would really have to punish her. He was doing her a favor.

He locked the gag behind her head and took a stance to resume his abuse of her body. He struck her again and again and again. Deep, miserable moans escaped from the gag, but little else. He ribboned her ass, her back and her thighs. And especially her breasts. Li thought that they were cow-like and maybe he was right. But it made her interesting, like horns on a horse. They were so pale, so delicate. The contrast between her snow white skin and the deep maroon of the lacerations was sweet to behold.

She was screaming and crying piteously when he finished with her. She looked like a white, ceramic statue marbled in red. He wanted to fuck her now.

He loosened her hands and she fell to the floor. "*Up! Stand up!*" he yelled at her. She struggled to her feet. "*On bed!*" he ordered and she stumbled over to it. The other whores had been watching and he could see the fear in their eyes. Some nights, whipping one whore was not enough. Sometimes he liked to see their gracious bodies dancing to a lash. They could never know when. Not tonight, he thought. Probably not. He would see.

He followed the blond whore to the bed. His cock was hard again and jutted from him proudly. He joined her and instructed the other whores to pleasure each other while he fucked her. She lay on her back waiting for him, her legs spread, her finger tickling her bud of pleasure, ensuring her readiness. He knelt and watched her for a moment. Less than a minute and her chest was heaving and her lips had become engorged. She was a wonderful whore. Just because she was number three, didn't make her the worst. In fact, in many ways, she was the best. But if he had elevated her over the Chinese whores, there would have been hell to pay. So he kept her at three.

The slut's slit had already parted and was glistening with moisture when he addressed it with his cock. He moaned with pleasure as her hot, tight sheath received him. That was another thing the crony was good for. She had a special salve that she claimed kept the whores' pussies nice and tight and she applied it to them once a month. As far as he could tell, it was working. She had another which stoked their sexual desire. He knew for a fact that that worked. The English slut had been getting dosed with it for the last week.

He needed no preliminaries with Whore Number Three and he started to pound his hips into hers right away. The girl moaned with pleasure. Her legs raised high and crossed the back of his thighs. Her arms gripped his shoulders tightly, her hands on his broad back. Each thrust produced a counterthrust of equal proportion. He could feel his lust building quickly. He circled his arms under her thighs and drew them back towards her head. He was pounding away and didn't want to make any mistakes. Higher, higher, higher, his lust built until he could bear it no more. The girl was screaming her orgasm from within her gagged mouth.

He yanked his cock free and, with practiced motion pierced her proffered rear hole in a continuous thrust. Her inner heat coated him, her slick discharge from her cunt eased his way. He groaned and his cock began to jump and throb within her. He had set off another powerful orgasm in the slut and she gripped her ankles above her tightly and pulled on them to improve his penetration. He collapsed in a heap on her. In the background, as he said his traditional prayer of thanks, he heard the excited sighs and moans of his other whores at work.

He sat back against the head of the bed and drew the Russian whore to him. She needed much comfort and it was wrong to be cruel to whores beyond what was necessary to obtain one's pleasure. He held her close to his body and she began to cry. These Russians were so moody. He had read Pushkin when he was a student at the British school in Shanghai. In fact, he had read all the classics and was an expert on Chinese poetry and history. He was a cultured man who happened to have large tastes.

He stroked the blonde's head softly while watching his number one and number two whores go at it. When they were done, he would have Number Two clean him again and then suck him off while he watched Number One milk the Russian whore's tits.

So, in the morning, he had good cause to feel optimistic about the day. He was drinking rich, black tea and eating some sweet cakes, his standard breakfast fare. That and the Russian whore's milk. She was kneeling beside him, her robe open so that her breasts were displayed for his enjoyment. They were suitably marked up by criss-crossing red lines and were as tight as drums, filled with her creamy production. He called her over to him and had her sit across his lap. He subsumed a fat nipple between his lips, gently suckling it until her milk flowed, and then contentedly let it fill him up.

The blonde moaned softly with pleasure as he drew the life giving sustenance from her. Her head lolled back and she closed her eyes. Her arms were draped lightly around his neck. When he had emptied one breast he began on the other. He had not had such a good milker since the German nun many years ago. He had lost her in a foolish game of dice.

When he was finished drawing the delicious, semi-sweet substance from the Russian girl, he saw that his eunuch and chief trainer of whores was standing there waiting for him.

"*Good morning, Li Pao,*" he said.

"*Good morning, Lord,*" he answered respectfully.

"*Have you anything to report to me on the Englishwoman?*"

"*Yes, Lord,*" he replied. "*In my opinion, she is ready to serve you. She still needs much work, but I think that her skills will develop quickly.*"

"*Fine, fine,*" Wang said. "*Let's have the ceremony tomorrow afternoon. Does that suit you?*"

"*As you command, Lord,*" Li said. "*I will have her ready and notify those who should attend.*"

Wang nodded his dismissal of the eunuch.

The taking of a concubine was a formal affair. One didn't just grab a slut and stick her in a bedroom to be stored for when needed. An actual whore living in the house would be an affront to his wives. And so, a formal ceremony was necessary to regularize the relationship. And to call them whores might be a little unfair. They certainly did not profit monetarily from the transaction. But the ideogram for concubine and for whore in Chinese in some contexts was very similar, 姨太太 and 娼妓, respectively. Although a concubine may add some culture and sophistication to the mix, and she was certainly not free to chose any other occupation for herself, her role was principally sexual, and the more wanton and lustful she was, the better, just like a whore. Certainly, in Western eyes, there was not much difference. Besides, this was not the 13th century and many Chinese institutions had undergone corruption and abuse over the years. No one expected a concubine these days to be more than a sexual instrument. They were technically outlawed, as was slavery, by the republican government of China. But Wang's writ ran in Junshan, not the Government's.

He had many things to do today. There was some discipline needed in the ranks of his little army, two men were due to be caned for infractions. There was the merchant Wu who had requested an audience. He was going to meet with the German engineer about the road to Gangkou, which would bring in considerable more trade to his port. They were also going to discuss the construction of his own coal fired, electric power station. If he built one, he could move his Shanghai factories here and get rid of those fucking communist agitators. It was a lot of money though and he would have to raise taxes.

He would deal with Miss Harris tomorrow. As he set the Russian slut down off of his lap, he wondered how the chemistry of his seraglio would change.

军阀 外家

CHAPTER TEN

When Li entered her cell that morning, Violet sensed that something had changed. He ordered her and the maid to their feet and told the maid to get dressed. Another maid was with them. For the first time, although she was required to get on her knees to do so, she fed her breakfast mush by the maid with a coarse, wooden spoon. Instead of feeding her directly from the bottle of juice, the maid poured it into a small, porcelain cup and brought it to Violet's lips. And she got to pee in the bucket all on her own. The maid wiped her afterwards.

Although some changes had occurred, not everything had changed. After she ate, Li ordered her to her knees and fastened her down as before. While the two maids watched, he stroked her to orgasm. Unable to resist the effects of his skillful manipulation of her sex, when she came, her body obediently shook and quivered in her confines and she shouted out her pleasure. Then, after Li installed her gag, the three of them left.

It was still dark, it was still lonely, she was still shamed and humiliated at the way that she was being treated, but she had reason to hope. Hours passed by at an interminable pace before Li returned. She was released from her cruel tie and allowed to eat by herself again. Li left the new maid behind together with a lantern. Violet's hands were tied off behind her back, and she was gagged, but she was otherwise free to stroll around her small cell. The maid brought her over to her pallet, laid her down and mouthed her to completion twice. Afterwards, they lay together, and the maid held her for a long time, occasionally gently stroking her hairless quim and kissing her breasts.

After serving her dinner, Li tied her down again. He had the replica of General Wang's cock with him and he used it to make her come. When he left, he left it inside her. As the door shut her into darkness, Violet whined at its offensive presence.

In the silent dark, Violet tried to take stock of her situation. Since the eunuch had left the replica penis in her quim, she had expected the guards to come into her cell and make use of her, like they had several days running, sometimes more than once. The fact that they did not was significant to her. There must have been some change in her status.

The eunuch's use of the dildo reminded her that she was being prepared for use by her owner, the general. She realized that she must be very close to the time that she would be presented to him. How would it happen and how would she act? The obedience she rendered to the eunuch, her keeper, and to the women who had pleasured her were, to Violet, on a wholly different plane than the surrender which would be required by Wang. The first were temporary measures forced on her by her keeper's whip, the awful confinement and the vulnerability she felt because of them. She didn't feel that all of a sudden she had become a lesbian. She needed love and comfort from somewhere. But surrender to Wang would be a confirmation of his ownership of her, that she was his slave, for life.

Would she have the courage to refuse him as she once had vowed? It was problematical. She had learned what it was to be whipped severely. She had heard the people screaming, pleading for mercy as the guards did god knows what to them. Did she have the courage to submit herself to that? And what would that prove? Was she the representative of the British Empire here and obliged to uphold the white man's standard? If it was learned later by friends and family that she had submitted to Wang, would her name join the group of social outcasts judged as 'not on'? Hundreds of miles from civilization, at least as she knew it, did that really matter?

There was just something deep inside her, though, that wanted to say 'no!' She would have to live the rest of her life with whatever decision she made, be it long or short. As the years went on, as Wang's slave, wouldn't she rue again and again the fact that she hadn't used all of her strength and courage to deny him her cooperation in her ravagement?

"Oh, Robert, Robert, Robert, where are you?" she thought miserably. He said that he knew Wang, that his company had business relations with him. Surely, that must have some weight in dealing with the bandit general. Maybe he was up there in the upper levels of the fortress right now, she thought hopefully. Maybe he's negotiating for her release at this very moment. It seemed to her that it was the kind of thing that certainly ought to be able to be settled with money. After all, Wang had proved his point and punished her, debased her. What more could he want? Didn't that make up for the 'face' that he lost as a result of her social blunders? Robert was a member of a family in England with a long, noble lineage. He was fabulously wealthy, at least his family was. Wouldn't they consider it as part of their moral obligation to save her? All Robert had to do was ask for the money, whatever amount Wang demanded, within reason, of course, and his family would give it.

She realized that all her hopes were on Robert. What if he learned that she had compromised herself by giving in to Wang's salacious demands? Would he consider himself honor bound then? Or would she be seen as a person with low moral character not worthy of redemption?

She struggled, momentarily, in her bonds, a symbolic gesture of defiance. Their implacable confinement of her made her stomach quail, as it often did. It reminded her just how abject a prisoner she was. The hard floor beneath her knees made them ache. Her shoulders strained with the harsh tie placed on her wrists, leading to the rod in the floor behind her. Her breasts were mashed against her thighs as her neck was pulled down tightly. Her curved back ached. Her ankles were secured tightly, incapable of movement. Robert wouldn't know how harrowing had been her treatment. He wouldn't know what is was like to spend hours and hours in the darkness, unable to move a muscle, blinded and silenced, praying for even a few moments of human contact. He would not have experienced the terror of a cruel whipping, or heard the pathetic screams of a helpless prisoner being tortured. He would just know, and Wang would certainly let him know, how she had surrendered her honor and her virtue.

The presence of the faux cock in her cunny was a ready reminder of what her future was. The callous and cruel general, the man who had all of this done to her, would undoubtedly possess that space for real very soon. The question would be whether it was with her surrender or without it. She could rationalize that she had been forced into it, just like she had been forced into the acts in which she had engaged since her capture at her keeper's insistence.

Surrender, to her, meant something different from being forced to do something. She had been forced to let herself be tied up, she had been forced to submit to the eunuch's use of her pussy and other orifices, forced, even to participate in woman on woman sex, at least at first. But she hadn't done it willingly, that was the point. Surrender was an act of will, a decision. After one surrendered, one cooperated with the victor, assumed his goals as your goals, confessed his superiority. She hadn't done that with her keeper, but that was certainly what General Wang would insist on. And though he might threaten her with all kinds of dire consequences, even death, he couldn't force her to surrender. That would be her choice.

As the seconds, and minutes and hours went by, Violet was certain that the morrow would bring her much closer to the ultimate moment. She wondered how it would occur.

When Li came in the next morning, he had two of the maids with him. One was carrying Violet's breakfast and the other was carrying a large, closed basket. Li let Violet, as he had the day before, be fed her meal with a spoon by the maid while kneeling on the floor. When she was done, he ordered her to stand and the second maid to open the basket.

Violet saw the maid draw out a long, blue, silk robe and a beautiful blue and green banner dress. There was even a pair of soft, cotton slippers in it. Violet started to cry. She had thought herself all cried out, but the prospect of wearing clothes after almost three weeks made the sorrow for what had been done to her well up. The brightness and color-fulness of the raiment contrasted starkly with the dull grey of her cell's dismal walls.

Li ordered the maids to help Violet adorn herself with the clothes. The sheath-like banner dress was pulled over her head, down over her hips and to just below her ankles. It was sleek and clung to her, accentuating her hips and her breasts. It was strange, after all this time, to feel the cool, smooth fabric against her body. The slippers came on next, petit, a little too small for Violet's feet. Next came the long, flowing robe which covered Violet's shoulders and arms down to her wrists and flowed down below her knees. Tears of joy in her eyes, Violet smiled happily at the two pretty, young maids. They executed a deferential bow to her and smiled back.

Ordering her to put her hands out in front of her, Li ran a leather belt around her waist, inside the robe, but over the dress. He then tied her hands together and affixed them to a ring in the belt in front of her. The robe was then tied closed around her waist with a silken cord, so that her bound hands were hidden. He placed a leather bracelet around each of her ankles and connected them with an 18" long, thin, steel chain. Because of the length of the dress, the bracelets and their connecting chain would not be seen by any observers.

The eunuch restored Violet's gag. He had her lower herself into a crouch while the maids adorned her with a yellow, opaque veil that covered her hair and disguised her leather covered mouth.

Violet was shaking with a mixture of trepidation and joy as Li led her from her cell. For the first time, she was not blindfolded. When they reached the guard's station, Scylla and Charybdis both bowed to her as she passed.

It was difficult to mount the long, curved staircase. Li had hold of her arm and patiently assisted her. His grip was firm but not harsh. When they reached the ground level, they were in the great hall of the fortress. It had a 30' high ceiling. The floor was covered by great blocks of multicolored, polished shale. The walls were covered by long, green, blue and red banners painted with slogans and representations of Chinese men in battle array. Men in uniform, men dressed as merchants and even one or two Western dressed businessmen were strewn about the hall, having business with General Wang, or one of his underlings, of one sort or another.

As she shuffled through the hall, the men all nodded their heads to her respectfully, a few of them actually bowing. She thought of all the times that she had been brought through this hall naked and blindfolded, once with the flesh-like, wooden penis distending from her mouth, and felt her cheeks go red. She had heard people around her, but hadn't known that there were so many.

The stairs to the upper levels was covered with a thick red and gold carpet. The stairway was broad, broad enough for people to pass them going down as they ascended them, two abreast each way. Violet's body was shaking. Was she being brought to the infamous general? Was her moment of truth going to happen now? Why were all the people bowing to her? Did being General Wang's sex slave devolve on her some kind of special status?

At the top of the stairs was an expansive landing. A 15' high window, with long, wide panes of glass separated by wooden frames sat opposite the top of the stairs. The windows in the room where the eunuch had conducted her sex lessons had been curtained, and it was Violet's first chance to get a glimpse of the outside of the fortress. She saw rough, tall mountains in the distance and a serpentine expanse of a broad, muddy river with wide, green covered banks. She only had a moment to look at it as she was pulled firmly and yet gently on.

They passed by the second floor and ascended to the third. The third floor was wood paneled and had finely carved marble and jade statuettes mounted on daises in neatly spaced alcoves down each side. Large, ancient prints on aged rice paper, depicting fabulous mountain scenes, flowered gardens, bucolic woods, with graceful, calligraphic Chinese ideograms were mounted on the walls in protective, glass covered frames. Here and there bunches of beautiful flowers, orchids, lilies, roses, were assembled in perfectly ornamented ceramic vases set on dark, polished, mahogany tables. The hallway was lit by ornate, over head, gold framed lanterns whose flickering light gave their traverse an unreal quality. The ceilings were high, about 15' to 20'.

As before, at the top of the stairs they turned left. The two maids turned right. People passing in the hallway, servants, maids, other staff members of the mansion portion of the fortress, all politely bowed, some deeply, some not so deeply. They came to a large, gate-like doorway with ornately carved figures of dragons, lions, tigers and other fierce animals arrayed on it. It was guarded by a young, uniformed soldier. He wore a smart cap and his uniform was neatly pressed. He had a large pistol in a leather holster that descended from his opposite shoulder like a Sam Browne belt. His body stiffened as they approached and he too gave her a polite bow. He then gave the eunuch a deferential nod and, using a key attached to a chain on his waist, unlocked the bolt and opened the door so that she and the eunuch could proceed.

When they crossed the threshold, Violet saw a vestibule area covered by a dark green carpet. The hallway extended to the right and left about 200 feet in each direction. Large windows sat at either end of the hall and doors lined each side. While the outside hallway had tall ceilings, this area was more cozy. It was darker, lit only by small lanterns about 20' apart on the walls. The ceiling was about 10' high and the passageway was somewhat narrower than the outside hallway, about 7 or 8 feet across. Here there were more flowers, but the prints depicted domestic scenes: gaily attired and coiffed Chinese women walking in gardens full of colorful flowers; people strolling through what looked like a park with cherry blossoms and geese gathered in a little group, their necks bent to the grass, much like Violet had seen in Conchou Park on that fateful day. In another, a man and a woman walked down a pathway, in a wooded area, the man in front, both dressed in colorful, silken robes. One scene showed what appeared to be a throne room with a man dressed in flowing robes and wearing an oddly shaped black hat sitting on a dais while a small crowd of people knelt and bowed to him.

They passed several maids along the way, but no men. They stopped at an ornate door and Li opened it. He guided Violet in.

It was the bathroom where Violet had frolicked on many occasions with the three maids who had introduced her to the joys of Sapphic sex. They were there in the room waiting for her. One, a short, child like young woman with a roundish face and dainty features was pouring oil from a small flask into the steaming bath water. The second, a taller, willowy girl was just lowering the vat where the water was heated into the tub, causing a great cloud of steam to arise. The third, more broad shouldered than the other two, with a long, almost regal face, was assembling an array of lotions and body care implements, brushes, scrapers, scissors, tweezers, next to the large, beautifully tiled tub. The all looked up at her at once and smiled. They were all naked, their raiment cast into a small pile on the side of the room.

Li untied Violet's hands and unfastened the belt from around her waist. He crouched down and freed her ankles from the leather bracelets he had applied in her cell. When he arose, he tapped his whippy stick on the edge of the tub and then pointed it to the assemblage of beautifying equipage. He looked sternly at Violet. She understood him completely.

When he left, the three maids, as one, assembled around her. They stripped her of the fine, silken attire and led her down into the tub.

Violet was all atremble. There was no question where all this was leading. Today was the day she had been fearing for all the time since she had been kidnapped. It was obvious that she was being pampered in preparation for the big moment. She thought of asserting a passive resistance, but the gay, loving faces of her three lovers, their warm, gracious smiles, gave her a feeling of peace.

They pulled her into the tub where they had bathed her several times before. This time, knowing that she had shared a special intimacy with them, kind of the turning point in her seduction by the eunuch, there was a whole different ambiance to their presence.

Their small, light hands gently urged her further into the three foot deep, hot, comforting water. She exchanged kisses with them all, tears rolling down her face. They rubbed their warm, soft bodies against her. A hand found her breast and lips settled on her mouth.

Violet sighed as an energetic, hot tongue excited her. She wrapped her arms around the adoring women. She accepted their apparent devotion to her happiness without question. The kiss broke, and her body was eased down into the water until it covered her shoulders. The women released her and Violet submerged her head, letting the hot water calm her anxiety.

The three girls washed Violet with loving care. They rasped the scraper all over her body, drawing off all the dead skin cells. It was like a new her was emerging from beneath them. It made her body seem raw and newborn. When she was cleaned and rinsed, they sat her on the edge of the tub and washed and rinsed her hair as before. After it was brushed and dried, it was pulled into a loose tie behind her head. One of the girls snipped away all the fugitive strands. Another shaved her legs and under her arms.

She was led to a soft, fluffy pallet near the tub and they helped her to lie down on it on her belly. She felt warm oil being poured onto her back and the hands of one of the girls begin to spread it all over her back and the back of her thighs and lower legs, her neck and shoulders. The hands were strong and yet gentle. The oil was soothing. Violet's mind began to drift away as they rubbed the perfumed substance into her flesh. She rolled over when urged and the oil was applied to her front. She sighed when the girl began to caress and massage her breasts. Lips brushed against hers and soft hands spread her thighs.

She issued a languid moan when a tongue drew itself along the length of her labial divide. Lips took gentle possession of her stiffened nubbin and a wave of soft, unfocused pleasure wafted through her.

Her whole body was settled into a luxurious, limp state. Hands softly caressed her belly and breasts, and soft, delicate kisses were planted on her lips and face. She was in heaven. The things that the women were doing to her were overtly sexual, but seemed to be taking place on a wholly different plane. A tongue lapped lazily at her clit and lips sucked gently at her thick, stiffened nipples.

Her orgasm approached her slowly. It was as if a soft, fluffy cloud had absorbed her body and she was floating in midair. She moaned softly when her pussy began to issue mesmerizing, lazy pulses. Her hands reached out dreamily to caress the flesh of her lovers. Her back arched and her thighs quivered.

Her orgasm had passed through her like a disembodied spirit. When it ended, her whole being seemed to be glowing. All worry had been drained from her. The three, young, pretty maids each gave her a pleasing kiss on her lips and she sank into a heavenly oblivion.

She did not know how long she slept. It could not have been too long. Gentle hands shook her and she eased into consciousness.

The women urged her to her feet and wrapped her body in an elegant, black, silk robe with a cascade of blue and yellow flowers descending from the right to left. She was led to a large, fluffy cushion and made to sit on it. While two of the women held her hands, the third used the tweezers to shape her eyebrows and to pluck small, stray hairs from her brow. A cottony puff was used to apply a white powder lightly to her face and neck, making her mien even paler than before. A bright red lipstick was applied to her lips. They trimmed and clipped her fingernails into rounded points and bright red lacquer was applied to them and the nails on her toes. One of the girls applied liner to her eyes and painted the lids a bluish green.

Violet knew that the purpose of all this was to make her more becoming to her lord and master. The young women were too happy and affectionate for her to offer any resistance.

When her toe and fingernails had dried, the women brought her back to her feet and escorted her to a door that led to a small room with turquoise wallpaper and a deep blue rug. There was another door to her left which Violet assumed led to the hallway. A large window gave view to the neighboring countryside. The sky was wonderful shade of blue and a few, small, puffy clouds wafted lazily across it. The sun was bright and poured into the room, making it seem friendly and gay. In the middle of the room was a 4' square lacquered table inlaid with pearl. The table sat about two feet off of the floor. Violet was led to a large cushion in front of it and she sat down on it, crossing her legs. One of the young women went to the wall and pulled a velvet chord that descended from the ceiling.

Violet gave a start when she felt her arms being drawn behind her. The broader, more voluptuous of the three, caressed her face and gave her a comforting, yet stern look, discouraging her resistance. A soft, silken cord was wrapped around her wrists, binding them behind her.

Violet was still in a dream like state. Somehow the binding of her arms behind her seemed natural and appropriate. A few moments later, the door to the hallway opened and a maid came in carrying a tray. On the tray was a variety of small, covered bowls and a ceramic tea pot, white, with dark blue flowers painted on it. There was a small, handleless tea cup of the same design next to it.

For the next twenty minutes Violet was fed the delicacies from the bowls by her three naked lovers. There was sautéed duck, a spicy pork dish, various crisp, fresh vegetables covered in a variety of sweet and sour sauces, a bowl of little crayfish covered with a light, fruity sauce, fluffy, white pieces of fish, carp, she thought, sprinkled with lemon juice. One bowl contained slices of peaches that had been soaked in a strong, clear liquor. There were cherries and slices of apples. And more.

The girls took turns using the chopsticks to feed bits and morsels of the feast to their pampered prisoner, careful to lift the food over her painted lips. They laughed and giggled as she opened her mouth to receive them and smiled as the delicate, refined flavors gave her cause to moan with pleasure. One of the girls was in charge of the strong, mint flavored, green tea, and she brought the small, handleless cup to Violet's lips to let her drink.

Although the elegant, appetizing luncheon had, to Violet, the aura of the prisoner's last meal, she put aside her concerns for the future and relished the varied flavors and textures of the food. Somehow, her stint as a debased, forlorn captive, deprived of all movement and light, seemed to momentarily recede from her memory.

When she had supped to her heart's content, they urged her to her feet and escorted her from the small room into the hallway. They brought her to another room, several doors down, and escorted her in. There, they made her kneel, crossed her ankles behind her and tied them with the same type of silken cord that they had affixed around her wrists. They connected the ties, not so harshly so that her shoulders were pulled back with discomfort, but enough so that she couldn't rise from her knees more than few inches. They all kissed her and caressed her face before they left.

The room was outfitted all in red. The rug was a deep, almost maroon red and the walls had been painted with a lighter shade. Small, red and gold pillows were strewn about it and there was a large vase with bright balls of flowers rising from it. There was no window.

She knelt there for about a half hour. All kinds of things ran through her head, but she was principally focused on her upcoming confrontation with the overlord of this fabulous palace. There was no other word for it. She didn't know what she had expected, but the sumptuousness and refinement of its appointments had impressed her. Wang must be, indeed, a wealthy and powerful man.

When Li came in, he was followed by two maids. One carried a tray with a large, covered, ceramic bowl that had steam leaking from its top. The other carried a basket similar to the one that the maid had brought to her cell earlier that day.

Li crouched down in front of her and pulled her robe off of her shoulders, exposing her breasts and belly. He placed his hands on her breasts seeming to weigh them and then ran his hands down her sides to her hips. He leaned forward and smelled her body, the fragrance of the oils that she had been adorned with wafting up to him. "*Legs apart!*" he commanded her, and she spread them at once. They were the first words anyone had spoken to her all day. The breaking of the silence was disturbing, as if a phase of her day's events had come to a close and a new one was about to begin. He placed his hand on her pudendum and cupped it, letting a finger softly caress the divide. His hand was hot and smooth. He continued until she had moistened and, when he was able to slide his finger easily inside, removed his hand as if satisfied.

He ordered the maids to loosen the ties around her ankles and wrists and then ordered her curtly to "*Lie down! Spread legs!*"

Violet obeyed. One of the maids slipped a pillow under her rear, elevating her hips. Her legs were spread widely, her knees raised. She had done this every day since the first with the man, her keeper. The other, presented the tray with the bowl to the eunuch. There was a small bar of scented soap on it, a brush and a razor.

Li plunged the brush in the hot water of the bowl and the brushed it against the soap, bringing up a light lather. He applied the scented lather to her loins and then slowly and carefully, scraped away all evidence of hair that had emerged over the last 24 hours. He pushed her labial lips this way and that, making sure that he addressed their soft sides. When he was done, he placed some cream in his hand and spread it all over her intimate place, rubbing it in gently.

Violet sighed, as she knew what came next. He placed his fingers above her smooth, soft labia and began a gentle, almost imperceptible massage of her sex bud with his thumb. He delved his thumb between her love lips and stroked the tender gap until he could run his thumb easily in and out of her.

Violet closed her eyes as the familiar feelings soon surged through her body. Her reactions to his caresses had become almost automatic, like he was pressing a button and turning on a machine. It did not take long before her breath started to become labored and her breasts became taut with blood. She sighed as the pleasurable sensations coursed through her. Soon, her thighs began to quiver. The two maids were kneeling up by her head and were holding her hands while caressing her face and breasts. One of them pinched a nipple sharply and Violet moaned.

As her orgasm mounted, she tightened her hands into fists, grasping at the small, soft hands that held them. Her hips began to rock as if they had a mind of their own. She pressed her lips together tightly. She called out when her crisis hit, "Ohhhhhh! Ohhhhhhh! Ohhhhhh!" Her body shuddered and tried to bring her knees together. The eunuch pressed his arms against them keeping them apart as he brought his task to conclusion. Violet gave out an exclamation of pleasure each time her enraptured pussy delivered an intense, throbbing contraction. Her toes had curled and she gripped even tighter to the hands that held her own.

When her pussy's spasms relented, the eunuch withdrew his hand from her quim. He gave her a few moments to collect herself, running his strong, but soft hands over her thighs and belly lightly. After she had regained her breath, he broke contact with her for a moment. One of the maids leaned over and softly kissed her lips.

Li picked up a small jar and a slim paint brush. He dipped the brush into the jar and began to apply a thin line of red over the edges of Violet's love lips, outlining the crevasse between them. When he was done, he ordered her to her knees and then painted the nipples and areola of both her breasts.

The maids helped her to her feet. There was a full length mirror on one wall and Li pulled her over to it so that she could see. Her nipples and sex lips stood out brazenly from her pale skin and were accentuated by the red of her toe and fingernails and her bright, red, full lips. Violet took a moment to recognize herself. Although she had been kept a destitute prisoner for almost three weeks, it looked to her as if she had put on a little weight. Her hips stood out just a little more pronounced and her belly had a slight, not unattractive bulge to it. She had dutifully eaten the large bowls of rice and fish or meat that had been given to her at every meal. Instead of the piteous waif she had expected to see, she saw a voluptuous, young woman. She could see that it was a body that any man would long to possess. She had never seen herself this way. It was as if she had been redesigned.

The maids, at Li's command, opened the basket and withdrew a red dress. It was bright red, with gold and silver threads and bright yellow, blue and green flowers on it. The dress was designed as a wrap. It overlapped, one edge being tucked against her left side and the other coming to the middle of her breasts. It was tied off with ribbons that ran down her breasts to her belly, just above the fulcrum of her thighs. Her shoulders and chest were bare but for two ribbons which came over her shoulders and were tied off to the bodice in little bows. A light shawl of red gauze was wrapped around her shoulders. Li wrapped a silk sash around Violet's waist and after tying it off in front, captured her wrists in it, affixing them in front of her with a bow. Red and gold slippers, bigger this time so that her feet fit in them perfectly, were applied to her feet.

Li ordered her to kneel. She was still wearing the brown, leather collar that he had adorned her with the first day. He reached behind her neck and unbuckled it. One of the maids handed him another one. This one was of polished, black leather and, like the first, had a golden ring in the middle. Several golden ideograms were embossed on it on either side of the ring. This band of leather had no buckle. Li placed the collar around her neck and ordered her to bend her neck down. One of the maids handed him a needle with a russet colored thread. The thread was made from very thin, but strong copper wire. As Violet knelt there with the back of her neck proffered to him servilely, he sewed the ends of the collar together through little holes that had been punched there. The holes were narrowly spaced together and it took him about twenty stitches to complete his task. When he was done, he tied the thread off tightly and covered the stitches and knots with a dollop of epoxy which would eventually harden like a rock. Anyone wanting to remove the collar would have to pick away at the epoxy with a sharp instrument and then cut through the threads with the tip of a very sharp pair of sheers. No hands would be able to remove it. It was intended, clearly, to be permanent.

The collar was snug, but not tight around her neck, so that it could be moved slightly up and down for cleaning purposes. It was not so loose so that it could be slipped up past her chin. Unless it was moved by fingers, it would stay firmly stationary around her neck.

When Violet had raised her head, the maids wove clumps of little violet, pink and yellow flowers into her hair. Then Li brought Violet to her feet and brought her again to the mirror. When she saw herself, she let out a little gasp. She was a paragon of beauty. The red gauze shawl made her appear ephemeral, the wrap revealed her now voluptuous curves, the fullness of her breasts. Her face was pale and fragile. The liner around her eyes made her gaze seem enticing, the color of the lids were like emeralds. She started to tremble. This was a person that she never knew existed. The red of her dress combined seductively with her full, dramatized lips. Her hands, bound before her seemed both fragile and inviting. The black collar around her neck advertised her subservience. This was how she was to be presented to her master. He would look at her lustfully. No amount of mere money would ever tempt him to free her.

Li attached the bracelets and chains to her ankles. He connected a golden chain to the ring in her collar and gave it a little tug. She followed him dolefully. Her stomach was turning over, her lips trembling. Her hands had become sweaty. An aching fear spread through her body. This was the moment she had been dreading.

She shuffled down the long hallway to a small door. Li opened it with a key. It led into a dimly lit corridor. The corridor snaked this way and that. They went down a set of stairs. At the end was another door. It had a solid lock on it and a little panel that slid open. Li peered out of it for a moment then turned to Violet. "*Kneel!*" he ordered her in a hushed voice. The chain around her ankles made kneeling difficult, but she slowly, obediently lowered herself. The eunuch turned back to the panel and peered out of it.

Violet's heart was beating hard in her chest. She was having difficulty catching her breath. She squirmed her bound hands. She knew that she could, unlike the harsh straps that had been used to confine her mercilessly over the past almost three weeks, easily pull her hands free. She didn't dare. The eunuch carried his whippy stick in his hand and she was deathly afraid of it. She could not imagine the torments he would subject her to if she were to disturb the beauteous vision he had assembled.

She could hear a Chinese orchestra at work in the other room. To her, the sounds were discordant and assaultive. Beneath the strange notes, she thought she detected the noise of a small crowd. They waited there for about fifteen minutes. Then the orchestra ceased their playing and silence reigned in the other room. The eunuch brought her to her feet. She could hear a strong, male voice speaking in Chinese. She thought that she recognized it. The voice stopped and, after a moment, the band began again, playing a soft, ceremonial, almost melodious tune. She heard the door un-locked from the other side. The eunuch put his hand on her head and pointed it down so that she was looking at the floor in front of her. Then, the door opened and he pulled her forward.

Taking tiny steps, Violet followed the eunuch's lead. The floor was made of a shiny, black and green swirled marble. People were sitting in chairs on either side of a wide aisle. The eunuch led her forward slowly. When they had traveled about a hundred feet he brought her to a stop. He removed the chain that led to her collar. She could see the first step of a platform in front of her. It was covered with a green, velvet cloth. A runner of red cloth ran up the middle. The music stopped.

"*Kneel!*" the eunuch ordered her sternly. She struggled to her knees, her head still pointed servilely downwards. Her body was shaking. Her mouth had gone dry. Her insides were churning and a deep ache permeated her. Her mind swirled with fear and dread. She could feel her lips quivering.

A deep, authoritative voice called out her name.

"Miss Harris, it's so good to see you again." It was the general.

Violet didn't know what to do. Should she reply? Should she ignore him? His conversational tone belied her status as his prisoner, his property. What should she do?

She felt the eunuch's whip under her chin and she dutifully followed it up.

The room was bright. The walls were made of the same marble as the floor. He was sitting about twenty feet away from her, three levels up, in a wide, high backed chair with ornately carved arm rests and a green sateen cover for the seat. He was dressed in a sharply tailored, well pressed, olive brown uniform. It had red epaulettes, gold buttons and a high collar. A broad, red stripe ran down each leg. He was wearing an officer's hat with a wide, black brim and gold braid. A braid of gold hung down from his left shoulder, and over his left chest were a series of sparkling gold and silver medals. His face was lean and forceful, his body trim. He sat with his hands on the armrests, his knees wide apart.

Violet's eyes had filled with tears. He looked all a blur to her. On his right and left, sitting on a level down from him on chairs made of light green wood and gilded around the edges, were two beautiful Chinese women. They wore ornate gowns and had shiny black hair that descended to their shoulders. There wore glittering jewels on their fingers and around their necks. They were smiling at her demonically. They were older than her, in their late thirties or early forties.

They had the look of self-satisfied, important, ladies of wealth. They wore banner dresses of green and gold.

On the left knelt three young women. They were dressed much like Violet, except their color themes were blue, green and lavender, respectively. Two of the women, the younger ones, were Chinese. They had dainty faces, slender hips. Their black hair fell down long behind them, almost to their waists. The third, to Violet's surprise had blond hair and was a westerner like her. She had big, blue eyes and a face as beautiful as a rococo angel. Her thick, golden blond hair was done up in a braid behind her. The other women kept their faces pointed downwards, but the blond girl, who looked to be in her early twenties, kept guiltily stealing looks at her. They all wore a black collar around their necks with a large gold ring and golden lettering, just like hers.

Sitting on either side of the platform lining the aisle up which Violet had been paraded, were men in military uniform, clearly officers, men and women dressed in traditional Chinese costume and some in Western clothes. Violet knew that they were all looking at her.

The general's eyes were peering down at her harshly, although there was a faint element of humor in them. He clearly was waiting for an answer.

"G,good afternoon," Violet was finally able to squeak out.

This seemed to amuse the general. "And good afternoon to you, Miss Harris. As you can see, I do have a uniform."

He was referring to her slight of him back in the casino a million years ago.

"Y,yes," Violet stuttered. "It's very nice."

Wang uttered a guttural laugh. He spoke in Chinese to the assembled crowd and there was a round of laughter from them.

"But we're not here to talk about my clothing, Miss Harris. We're here to talk about your future. As of today, you will be my concubine. This little ceremony makes it official. Although you were my slave from the moment my men seized you, you status will now be elevated. You will be an official member of my household."

Tears started to flow down Violet's face. Her body was visibly shaking. She tried to muster up her courage. She felt as if she would burst.

"Stand up, Miss Harris, so I can get a better look at you," the general ordered. "I saw you in the junk before you took your little journey here, but you were not in a position to readily display your charms."

"*Stand up!*" Li ordered her sharply. He poked her behind the back with his stick. Sobbing, Violet rose to her feet. The memory of her confinement, the man who had stood over her, examining her before the boat had sailed her off to her imprisonment, the long, lonely days of tortuous, forced immobility, all came rushing back to her. This was the man who had dictated the cruelties imposed on her. This was the man who held the power of life or death over her.

When she reached her feet, standing unsteadily before her master, he spoke again.

"You are a very beautiful woman, Miss Harris," he said. "I will be pleased to have you serve me."

The vision of herself in his bed, him pumping away at her sex, invading her with his long, thick cock, a cock that she was already familiar with, jumped into her head. She shuddered as she considered it. A hole had formed in her stomach.

"Cast away your shawl and turn around, please, Miss Harris, so that I can see the rest of you."

Li stepped forward and pulled the bow free that had confined her hands. Slowly, obediently, Violet drew the red shaded, gauze shawl from her shoulders and let it fall to the floor around her feet. She turned her body so that her ass was presented. She had to move slowly, in little steps to avoid

tripping on the chain between her ankles. She saw the
expectant faces of the small crowd. She knew that she should
refuse the cruel man's orders, but she had not the courage.
Needless to say, there had never been a moment like this
before in her life.

When she was back to her original position, the general
smiled at her. "You have a very enticing form, Miss. Harris. I
am delighted at everything I see so far. But I need to see
more if I am to properly appreciate your charms," he said
politely. He gave a stern order in Chinese.

Li stepped behind her and reached to her front. One by
one, going from top to bottom, he pulled loose the bows of
her dress. Its sides pulled apart and when he stepped back,
the beautiful, red and gold flowered dress slipped to her feet,
revealing her naked body to all.

Violet experienced the almost overwhelming urge to
shield her intimate parts with her hands. It really didn't make
much difference, did it? And Li would certainly whip her if
she did.

"Ahhhhhh!" General Wang exclaimed. "A beauteous
sight! You are truly a delight! Please turn around once
more."

Sniffling, her body shaking, humiliated and shamed, she
turned slowly around, exposing her heavy breasts and denuded
loins to the audience. She couldn't help but think about how
the eunuch had adorned them in red to make them more
prominent. There was a murmur of approval as she brought
herself into view. She quailed when her rear cheeks were
brought into the sight of her enslaver, knowing that he would
covet the small, dainty hole between them. She stopped when
her breasts and belly were again presented to him.

"Yes, yes, the promise of the delights which I observed
when we first met have all proved true. I am happy to make
you my whore," he said.

Violet's sobs became louder. She made a mewing sound when she heard those fateful words. Her hands were visibly shaking, her lips trembling. She looked up at the man with hatred.

"I'm not a whore!" she yelled out at him suddenly as loud as her tremulous voice could go. "I'm a subject of the British Empire! You can't do this to me!" She was surprised at her own courage. It had all welled up in her. All of the resistance she had put aside during the eunuch's abuse of her had finally arisen. All of the humiliation and pain she had suffered on her journey up river, all of the terrible, dark and lonely times dreading this very moment, terrified as to what the cruel warlord would do to her, welled up, energizing her. She knew that there would be terrible consequences for her effrontery, but she didn't care. Something had snapped inside her. She would not surrender!

Out of the corner of her eye she saw the eunuch lifting his whippy stick. The general raised his hand and stopped him.

Wang laughed. He said something to the crowd, mockingly and was rewarded with another round of merriment. It was good to have his subjects see him defy the mighty British Empire, to know that from here on in, he would be taking nightly revenge against its insults to the Chinese nation.

"I can't do this?" Wang asked her defiantly. "And who says that I can't. Your glorious British Empire is powerless to save you here, Miss Harris." He said her name with contempt. "And you are no longer one of its subjects anyway. You are a slave now. A slave is not a subject or a citizen of anywhere. You have no rights. No one is going to come and save you. You will do as I command. You will give me the pleasure of your body with all your heart and devotion or you will suffer terribly. In a few moments, after we are done speaking, you will crawl to me and take my cock in your mouth and caress me until I spill my essence into you. You will swallow and absorb it and then you will enter my seraglio, never to leave it again until I tire of you. I will never speak English to you again. You will learn to obey my commands in Chinese or you will suffer. After today, you will no longer have a name. You will be called Whore Number Four. Do you understand that?"

His voice rose as he spoke. At the end, it was heavy with authority, insistent, demanding, broaching no opposition, the kind of voice that made strong men quail, not to mention a defenseless, young woman.

"No!" she yelled back, her voice tremulous with her fear. "I won't do it! I won't!" Her heavy breasts shook as she shouted at him. Her face was a mask of anger and defiance.

"You'll do it, Miss Harris, or you will go back to where you came from today and you will suffer terribly!" he returned. "Then I will bring you back in two weeks and demand the same task of you as today! If you refuse again, you will go back into my dungeon. And on and on until your body will no longer be worth possessing. Then I will have you strangled in your cell, your body burned and scattered to the winds. Is that clear?"

It was perfectly clear, and the prospect of a return to the dungeon for treatment even worse than that she had already received appalled her. She thought of the violent, horrifying screams of pain she had heard. She thought of the whip, the endless hours of loneliness and isolation, the violation of her body by the two guards. She felt like her body was about to enter into convulsions. She drew out one final vestige of courage. "You are wrong! Robert will save me! Unlike you, he is a man of honor and a gentleman! He will do whatever it takes to free me! An expedition will be formed and they will blow you little fortress to pieces with you in it!"

Wang laughed. "There will be no expedition, Miss Harris. No one even knows that you are here!"

"That's wrong," Violet replied. "Robert knows. He was there the night we met. He'll tell the Governor General of the Settlement and an expedition will be formed!"

"Ha! Ha! Ha! Ha!" the brutal bandit laughed. "Yes, you're right. Robert knows. But he will do nothing. You are laboring under a huge misconception, Miss Harris. I did not kidnap you because of the insults you gave me that night in the casino. I was angry when you gave me bad luck, but in the very next place I went, I won a considerable amount of money. I had forgotten all about you. Robert came to see me about four in the morning. He was looking for me frantically since he dropped you off at your hotel. He asked me to take you, begged me even. He said that you wouldn't marry him, that you would make him the laughingstock of the international community, threaten his relations with his father. You were a piece that needed to be taken off of the board.

"He was to give you one last chance to change your mind and you, stupidly, refused. Where is your pride now, my English whore?"

His statement shook her to her core. It couldn't be true! "You're lying!" she shouted back at him. Her nakedness seemed to give her the aura of a goddess. The audience stared at her, mesmerized. They could hear and see the battle of wills between their overlord and his minion. It was like watching a mouse challenge a lion.

Wang laughed again. "I'm not lying," he returned. "He wrote you a letter. I brought it back with my on my boat. Here, I'll read it to you."

He made a motion and one of the servants brought him an envelope on a silver tray. He picked it up and opened it.

"'Dearest Violet,' it begins," he said. "You English are so contemptible," he interrupted himself, "with your pretensions of civility and your hypocritical codes and customs," he told her. He grimaced and went back to the paper. "Here is what your Robert says,

'My Dearest Violet:

When you read this, you will have been taken in concubinage by General Wang. I am very sorry that this had to happen. There was really no other way.

You have no idea what scandal would have rocked the international community here if you had rejected me because of Qua Li, my Chinese mistress. I would have been a laughingstock. It would have effected my position at the firm, damaged my relations in the Chinese community, made it hard for me all the way round. My father would have changed his will to make my brother, Lawrence, Earl. I couldn't let that happen.

I'm sorry that you had to meet Qua Li in such terrible circumstances, but you will meet again when we come up to see General Wang in a few weeks. I think that you will be in a position to better appreciate her charms then than you were when you first met her. She is certainly interested in seeing you again. I'm sorry to say that she bears you a considerable grudge for kicking her out of the house and I fear she will ask General Wang to let her punish you severely. Under the circumstances, I can't say that I blame her.

When we ran into General Wang, that night, I was at a loss about what I was going to do. I was determined that you would not go back to England and make me look ridiculous. I never did buy you a ticket to the boat. I told the hotel concierge to have your luggage brought to my house. I had no plan, really. I thought that somehow I would keep you confined at my mansion until you changed your mind. It was insane, I know. It would never have worked and I would have been in worse trouble than before.

But when we met Wang and you insulted him, I had a brainstorm. It came to me after I dropped you off at the hotel. What if he were to kidnap you? No one in Shanghai or anywhere else knew that you had rejected me. Once you were kidnapped, I would have the sympathy of the entire community. You would have vanished onto the black heart of China never to be seen or heard from again. There would be no connection to the general. You would simply disappear. I scrambled around half the night looking for him and when I finally found him, he agreed readily. He was greatly impressed with your charms.

You have to admit that I gave you every chance that I could, right up to almost the last moment. I told General Wang that if you refused me for the last time, I would bring you to the park and leave you alone for a few moments by the pavilions where we, in fact, parted. I knew his men would be able to accomplish your abduction there with ease. There would not be a single soul who would be willing to give a description of your abductors to the police out of fear of retribution. I, of course, as your forlorn fiancé, reported it at once, as a good fiancé should. I knew that it would come to nothing. I had no descriptions of the car or the men to give them. By the time any kind of investigation started you would be well on your way to Hunan Province and General Wang's fortress.

I must say that it has worked rather well. Antonia, Lord Hoover's lovely 21 year old daughter, has made me her special project. We go out every night dancing or whatnot, to "help me forget." I plan to propose to her once a respectable amount of time has gone by. I have to thank you, after all, since she is much younger and prettier than you. And she is not quite as smart, so my little infidelities will be easier to disguise. The rumor is that Lord Hoover is prepared to settle an income of 5,000 pounds a year on the man who can make his daughter happy.

I'm sure you will remember our last chat in your hotel room, when I told you that I thought someday we would look back at that moment and wonder how different things could have been. I guess that moment has come quicker than you would ever have believed.

The only advice I can give you is to bear up as a good Englishwoman should. Wang has a cruel streak, but he treats his whores rather well.

I will see you soon.

> Regards,
> Robert G. Preston, Esq.'

As Violet listened to the letter, her blood grew colder and colder. What she was hearing stupefied her. She wanted to shout out to Wang that it was a forgery, a lie, but that last bit about what Robert said to her in the hotel room, only Robert would know. How could he have done this to her? "Oh my god! Oh my god!" she thought to herself in panic. The proof of her betrayal drove an ice pick through her heart. An ache so profound arose in her that she felt as if someone had stolen her soul. "How could he do it?" she screamed inwardly. Had he known the torture and hardship he was delivering her to? How could anyone be so cruel?

Suddenly, Violet felt more alone and helpless than she had ever felt in the boat coming up river or even in her dark, silent cell deep in the fortress's dungeon. Then, she had hope, hope that someone would save her, hope that someone who had some small amount of affection for her would lead the charge that saved her. The room spun around her. Everything she had supposed about honor, justice, human decency had been overthrown and smashed down on the floor right in front of her. There was no one to save her! And to make it worse, the man who had betrayed her, delivered her into the hands of her oppressor, her enslaver, was going to come and see her in her shame and disgrace.

Would Wang let that Chinese girl whip her? She realized with a shudder that he probably would. Would he make her fuck Robert as well? The thought of it made her stomach churn. She fell to her knees, covered her face with her hands and started to sob uncontrollably.

For several minutes, it was the only sound in the room.

"So you see, Miss Harris, there will be no expedition," Wang told her after pausing to let the impression of the defeated Englishwoman pervade the room. "As if the British Government would risk electrifying opposition all over China for one foolish woman. You are my whore now and will be until I say you are not and then, you will be somebody else's whore. If I were you, I would do everything in my power to avoid that eventuality as long as I could. Who knows where you could end up?

"When Robert comes, he is my partner after all, I will ask him not to be too severe with you. You didn't know that he was my partner? Well, the British government has outlawed the opium trade. Robert has been busily arranging alternative sources of supply ever since. There will be no interruption in the flow of Opium to China. Robert will probably become one of the richest men in the Far East. And you threw that all away because he was fucking a Chinese woman. It's too bad for you."

Wang sat back in his chair. The little play he had put on for his subjects had to come to a close. He spoke to Violet sternly, harshly, "You will now crawl to me on your hands and knees. You will take me in your mouth and make me come. If you do not do so now, I will have you taken away back into my dungeon. What do you say, Miss Harris?"

Violet was having trouble bringing herself under control. Her whole body was wrought with grief. She felt like she had to throw up. The floor was hard and cold. She was all alone. There would be no redemption, not in this lifetime. She knew that eventually she would give in. What did her pride matter now? It was her pride that had destroyed her. She thought of the three wonderful Chinese girls who had made love to her. She yearned for their arms now. If she became Wang's whore, there would be ways to assuage her grief. She would still have some small ways to enjoy life, wouldn't she? But in the dungeon was only pain and misery.

She saw the faces of her oppressors down there, their scarred and grotesque miens, remembered the implacable ropes that held her confined so cruelly hour after hour, day after day, the beatings, the despicable humiliations. The idea of one of the men placing his hands around her neck and strangling her made her sick with fear. And then to be scattered to the winds as if she had never existed? She couldn't bear the thought of it.

She remembered the deference she had been given as the warlord's concubine, the nods and bows, the fine clothes, the delectable food, the comforts that the luxurious appointments of the fortress promised her, the soft, accommodating bodies of the three Chinese maids. There was no choice really. The eunuch had proved that she was a whore anyway. Somehow, she believed, God would not abandon her. He will leave her enough to live on with. Fate will decide what her future holds.

Violet was suddenly filled with a certain calm. It was the serenity of someone who has lost all and knows that she must meet her fate. She rose from her supine pose and looked up at her master. He would rule every aspect of her life and her body from now on and far into the future. He would be like a god unto her. Slowly, she began to creep forward, as if her body were struggling not to obey her. Her ankle chain dragged along the cold, marble floor. She was conscious of all the eyes upon her naked form, her swaying breasts, the glimpse of her denuded love lips that peaked out under her as she mounted the steps. Her sole articles of clothing were the black band advertising General Wang's ownership of her flesh, her entire being, and the confining bracelets on her ankles, designating her as one who had been deprived of all rights. She was almost grateful now that Scylla and Charybdis had shown her what cock sucking was really all about. She did not want to displease her lord.

When she reached the callous general, he had taken his cock out from his pants and was proffering it to her. She recognized it. It had been in her mouth before. What a simple task it was really to take it in once again.

Trembling with emotion, she opened her mouth and slowly moved her head forward so that the stiff, thick meat would cross over her lips. She felt its heat as it passed over them. She closed her mouth and pressed her lips firmly around the stiff cylinder. Slowly, she began to move her head back and forth, washing it with her tongue, sucking ever so gently on it.

Tears were flowing down her face. They were tears of sorrow for what had been done to her, for the naïve, young Englishwoman that she had been, but also tears of relief as she realized that the worst part of her ordeal was over: the ordeal of waiting, wondering what would be her fate. Well, her fate was decided now.

Violet began to pleasure the hard rod with more purpose. She let her soft lips slide along its ribbed surface, she let her tongue caress it. She could feel the eyes of the audience upon her naked form, caressing her proffered rear cheeks, ogling the bare sex that was displayed beneath. The whole world had become reduced to the drama enfolding before the assemblage and the soft textured, but steel hard meat in her mouth.

Wang put his hand on her head and she heard him moan softly. She sensed that the end was near, the dividing line between what she was before and what she would be, drawn. His hips started to rock back and forth. His hand found purchase in her hair. She looked up and saw his almost anguished face. His eyes were closed. His cheeks had turned a light pink.

When his cock began to throb, she was ready for it. It pulsed and jumped as his hot cum was spurted into the back of her mouth. She knew what to do and began to swallow it, resigned to accepting it as a part of her. The general moaned. His grasp on her hair had become tight and he pressed her face hard down upon his pulsing cock. "Arrrrrrgh! Arrrrrrrgh!" he exclaimed as the pleasure that his new whore had given him passed through his body.

When his cock's dance finally ceased, he released the slut's head, letting her slip his meat from her mouth, and said a little prayer to his ancestors.

* * * * * * * * * * * * * *

In the gallery, Lieutenant Cheng, who had been her caretaker on the boat from Shanghai, clasped his hands into fists of rage. He saw the woman he had become obsessed with degrade herself at General Wang's command. His heart ached for her. Now, she would go into his seraglio and disappear forever but for those public occasions the general deigned to bring her out. She would have to submit to his degradations time after time, lie down with his friends and cronies, the Western visitors who came by to visit, representatives of the national government, bankers, money lenders. It made him want to strike out at the general. Why did he deserve her beauty? He knew he had to bide his time, but somehow, he swore, he would free her from her enslavement and claim her for his own.

军阀 外家

CHAPTER ELEVEN

Violet dressed herself sullenly before the crowd. The eunuch tied her hands behind her back, reattached the chain to her collar and marched her off. She was taken from the council chamber to General Wang's bedroom.

When they got to the bedroom, she was made to strip and was allowed to pee in a little chamber pot. The room was much larger than the eunuch's. As soon as Violet saw it, she was aware of her mistake. The bed was bigger about by half, the room much larger. It was well decorated while the other bedroom, the eunuch's own room, she supposed, was stark. White, lacy linens hung drooped from the tops of the four bedposts, the bed was covered with a red, satin sheet. The pillows were large and fluffy. Ornate, polished furniture populated the room. The walls were papered in a cream color with designs in bright white embossed on it. The rug was a deep shade of blue.

Li ordered the English slut up onto the bed. She had done well. His master could not have asked for a better demonstration of his victory over the fucking British than today. He had been appalled at first when she began her rebellion. He should have known that his master, the cleverest man he had ever served, was ready for her.

She crawled up onto the luxurious mattress. She would wait here for her master's pleasure. He bound her hands behind her with a white silken cord and then bound them to her ankles. He left about a foot between her wrist and ankle ties. This was not a binding to degrade and embarrass her; it was just so that she would not move.

He applied a blindfold to her but left off the gag. There was no need for it now.

Violet lay there afraid and helpless for a long time. After several hours, the eunuch came back, fed her, allowed her to void again and then placed her back on the bed.

The sheets were cool, the bed soft and comfortable. It was far better than the dungeon. Her bindings left her legs bent back towards her head, but not so that it hurt her shoulders like before. She had the sensation that she was merely a bound package awaiting her recipient.

She dreaded what the warlord would do to her. She had sucked him off and would undoubtedly do so again. But he would also fuck her, her pussy and her ass. That's why they had been prepared.

Before she was brought to the master's bedroom, they stopped at another room on the way. In it had been a little, old, Chinese lady. She was dressed simply in a plain, light blue, sheath dress. Her hair was all grey and her face was wizened.

Despite her somewhat harrowing appearance, Violet felt calm before her. The old lady's smile revealed red teeth ruined by betel juice, but it was friendly and warm. She had Violet strip down once again and kneel in front of her. She ran her hands over Violet's body, assessing her breasts, stroking her belly. She even caressed her hairless slit until Violet gave out a moan of pleasure. She gently drove two fingers deep inside her while she closed her eyes like she was feeling for something. When she was done she smiled again at Violet and kissed her on the lips.

Before she allowed her to dress, she used a small brush and painted her love mound red. She gave her a cup of some concoction to drink.

Lying on the bed, Violet found her sexual desires rising. She pressed her knees together in frustration. Her nipples were taut and hard. Her pussy burned. She tried to decipher why. It wasn't because she knew that she was going to be fucked; she had no desire for the evil general. Maybe, she thought, it was the result of all the times that the eunuch or one of the pretty little maids had made her come. But she had gone hours and hours just yesterday without sex as she knelt bound in her cell and it hadn't bothered her. Was there something in the drink the old lady gave her, she wondered. There was something about it reminiscent of the spice that had been in her food.

General Wang had decided to make an early night of it. After all, his new English slut was waiting. After a light supper, he walked down to his bedroom. It had three entrances. The first was from the main hallway so that he could enter it directly after his day was done or during it if he had need or if he wanted to fuck one of his whores.

Another entrance led to a passageway that in turn led to the bedrooms of his wives. Thus, he could enter them without anyone seeing him, most particularly his other wife, or he could take her by surprise, maybe fucking a maid or one of the sluts. If so, he would make her continue and work it into his own plans.

The third door led to another corridor that led to the concubine's quarters. He could go there without interference or have one of them brought here without need of using the hallways.

When he entered the room, he saw the slut on his bed. She was naked, as he had expected, and bound, as was the custom. He saw the red paint over her pudendum and was disappointed that he wouldn't be able to discharge himself there tonight. "Well," he thought, "there will be other nights."

He decided that he wanted to take a better look at his new property. He stripped himself down and crawled onto the bed. She flinched when she felt the bed depress and it humored him. She would get over that quickly enough once she got used to her status as a sex slave.

She was lying facing him, her arms and feet behind her. She was blinded by a black cloth across her eyes. He left the blindfold on for now, but released her ankles from her wrists and guided her legs until they were straightened out. He pushed her back until she was leaning on her bound hands. Her wonderful breasts were exposed to his view. He took hold of one. It was soft and firm all at the same time. The nipple was lovely, a nice, wide aureole, smooth with little bumps and fat, long nipples. Li Pao had mentioned his intention of putting her in milk, but had had instructed the eunuch to wait until the poor wench got settled. She didn't need to experience all the varieties in which she would be used all at once.

He leaned over, took one of her nipples in his mouth and suckled on it gently. It was heaven to have between his lips. He muttered a prayer to the gods in his mind for their munificence in putting beautiful women in the world and for allowing him to have so many of them. He captured her other breast in his hand and squeezed it softly, appreciating its heft and resilience. He had developed an appreciation of the breasts of the foreign demons although esthetically he agreed with Li Pao that small breasts made a woman appear more dainty and feminine. He lifted his head from her breast and ran his hand down her side to her hip and over her right flank. Her body was hot and she gave a little sigh as he traversed her tight skin. Her little love lips were tightly closed as a result of her bindings and he decided to loosen them so that he could caress the soft, plump object of men's desire.

Violet had heard the man enter the room. There was no mistaking who it was from the authority of his footsteps. She heard him undressing and she suppressed a moan of fear. When the bed depressed as he got on it, she jumped reflexively.

His lips were hot on her breast and it excited her, far more than she would have expected. His tongue flitted over her nipple and she fought off a sigh of desire. His powerful hand took hold of her other breast and her mind rolled over at the sensations brought by his knowledgeable massage. When his hand ran down her thigh, she thought that she was going to break out into a moan and she stifled her urge to squirm.

But when he spread her legs and took hold of her burning purse, she could no longer hold herself back and gave out a long, languid moan. She heard him laugh and say something in Chinese.

Wang rubbed the soft, hairless pussy until he saw a glistening between the slut's lower lips. He dragged his finger along her labial divide and she moaned again, this time squirming her hips. She was a hot slut. He was going to have to give Robert a special thanks for encouraging him to acquire her. Of course, he would be allowed to fuck her as much as he wanted during his two week stay. That was only fair. And the little Chinese girl, it would be amusing to watch her put stripes on the Englishwoman, but not too much.

He looked at the plump lips of his new concubine. She had done well this afternoon in using them. He knew, of course, what went on in his own dungeon and that the men had used her there. There was little that went on in his duchy that he didn't know about. It was all for the better so that she could perform well in her ceremonial induction into his household. It wouldn't have done to have had her choking and squealing or trying to spit out his seed. As it was, his audience saw an English slut tamed before their very eyes. She had been better than expected. He had had to goad her with the letter from Robert in order to defeat her. It was exquisite to watch her break down and dissolve right in front of him.

His finger had now found easy entrance into her flush canal. He was stroking her gently but firmly and her breath was becoming labored. He wanted to fuck her, but there was something that needed to be done first.

Wang stepped off the bed, dragging Violet along with him. His finger had hold of the gold ring in her collar. The ideograms spelled out "General Wang's Concubine", not that anyone who came into contact with her from here on out wouldn't know that in advance. He just liked to see it written on them. Li Pao had suggested once that he get the words tattooed on their bodies, but he didn't want to mar their flesh that way. When he thought of it though, it might not be a bad idea for the French whore and the young women he put to work for her. Theirs would say "General Wang's Whore" and be tattooed on their bellies just above their slits and again on their lower backs. This way, anyone who fucked them fore or aft would see it before they brought their cocks home.

When he had the former Englishwoman on her feet, he dragged her over to the chain that led down from the ceiling. He loosened her hands from behind her back and then fastened them in the bracelets that dangled from the end of the chain. The woman had begun to whine and sniffle. She was very bright, he thought. She knew exactly what was about to happen.

He went to his closet and retrieved a whip. He chose the one with the solid, black, wooden handle and seven thick, leather cords. It would not mark her flesh beyond turning it a bright red from abuse. It would sting horribly and was designed to bring out the cries for mercy that he wanted to extract tonight.

Violet stood shuddering in the middle of the general's bedroom. She knew that she was going to be whipped. This, she assumed, would be the first of many. She promised herself that she would not shout and scream for mercy. Her theory was, the less she screamed and pleaded for surcease, the less enjoyment the cruel man would get out of it. She could feel the sweat already running down her armpits. Her mouth was dry and her stomach quailed. When she heard the general's footsteps return, she let out a small sob.

Wang wondered for a moment whether it would be better to leave the blindfold on or to take it off. It would be an exquisite experience for her to be assailed by invisible tongues of fire while she danced for him. On the other hand, with the blindfold off, he would get a better look at her face and be able to witness her expressions of horror as the whip came at her again and again. She could also dance and try to avoid it, which would be an educational experience for her. She would never be able to avoid it.

When Wang removed her blindfold, Violet stared at the man in horror. She saw in his hand a heinous instrument. He looked demonic in his naked form. She could see his mighty erection protruding from his loins. Tears were already flooding her eyes. Her heart was beating fast. "Oh, god!" she thought. "Please don't let him do this!"

He enjoyed the look on her face. Her tears were heart rendering. Westerners might not understand it, but there was an esthetics of suffering. Every human emotion, fear, anger, anguish, pleasure, had its own beauty. If one only saw happiness, one was missing half of life. He knew that she would suffer and that she certainly would not think that his enjoyment of her pain was sufficient consideration for the act of torturing her. But that was her fate. He did not dictate that it would be she, out of all the English women in China, who would fall into his hands. It was her destiny. The gods must have decided that she needed to suffer more before her soul progressed. If that was the case, he was doing her a favor.

When the first blow crossed her belly, Violet gave out a deep moan of pain. She tried to remain silent, but couldn't help herself. The leather cords felt like a hundred bee stings across her flesh. She looked at her assailant and saw that he had a pleased look in his eyes. The second blow landed across her pale, white rear globes. Her spine stiffened and she gave out an anguished groan. He did her back, her thighs, her belly again and her rear end twice more. Each blow was worse than the first, and yet, still, Violet held back her pleas for mercy, her cries and sobs. Wang was impressed. This English whore was tough. She had a strong personality and fire within. She probably didn't know she had it in her until this afternoon when she stood up to him. That had been an admirable act of courage. But he knew how to get her off the mark.

Violet watched as once more the evil instrument was raised above the general's head. She steeled herself for yet another rush of agonizing pain. She was praying, hoping that he would stop soon, for she didn't know how much more she could take. Already her moans had gotten louder and longer and her tears were cascading down her face. Her hands were balled into hard fists. When she saw the blow heading for her breasts, she could hold it in no longer. "Ahhhhhhhh!" Ohhhhhhhh!" she cried out as her breasts were scoured by the evil instrument. "It hurts! It hurts! Oh, god, please stop! Please!" she called out miserably.

Satisfied that he had broken the dam of her resistance, Wang continued her ordeal. He hit her twice more across her breasts making her squeal and beg and plead for desistance. Her feet danced on the floor and her body twisted this way and that. It was covered with a sheen of sweat. The pale, untouched parts of her flesh were like little islands amidst a sea of red. He struck her back, her thighs, her rear and her breasts again. Her knees had buckled and she was swaying on the chains that held her hands aloft. Her skin was turning a bright red. She begged and pleaded for him to subsist. It was what was nice about this whip. You could just keep going as long as you wanted and the only result was the shade of red that you produced.

Violet's breasts were a bright red when he finished. As was her ass, her belly, her thighs and her back. Wang stepped back to admire his handiwork. The woman's screams and pleas had gotten louder and louder until she could scream no more. She hung listlessly in her bonds. It was enough.

He released her hands from the chain and she tumbled onto the floor. He left her there moaning while he put the whip away. When he came back, she had curled up into a little ball and was crying. "*Stand up!*" he shouted at her. She looked at him piteously and tried to rise. It took her three times to get on her feet.

"*On bed!*" he ordered. She stumbled over to the mattress and climbed aboard. He followed her. She was kneeling, waiting for him, fire in her eyes. He crossed his hands in front of him, showing her what he wanted her to do and she complied at once. He tied her wrists together and then, forcing her on to her back, tied them off to the headboard.

He knelt between her outstretched thighs. Her red painted love lips matched well the shade of the rest of her. She thought that she had had it bad tonight. "Wait until I decide to whip her pussy, then we'll see how long she lasts," he thought.

He brought himself up over her torso and began to kiss her breasts. He licked them and suckled them, teased them with his tongue, shifting back and forth from one to the other. No other part of his body was touching her. It took a while, but eventually, she gave out a sigh of tell-tale arousal. He had to thank the old woman again, he thought. He raised himself further up and placed his lips upon hers. She recoiled at first, but thinking better of it, allowed him to enter her mouth. He closed his lips on hers and intertwined their tongues.

Violet had been fraught with remorse over her failure to keep her pledge not to beg and plead for mercy. The man was too cruel, too determined to make her suffer and abase herself for her to win that fight. When he tied her hands off on the top of the bed, she steeled herself for his penetration. She was surprised that he leaned over her, not touching any part of her abused body and started to suckle her breasts.

At first, it felt like a leach had hold of her. She was so repelled by the man who had abused her that she would rather die than show him any lust. How could she feel lust when her body burned as if it had been lowered into a toaster? Inside she despaired at the thought that this torment would now be part of her life on a regular basis. How could she survive it?

After a while, she began to feel a familiar tingle in her loins. The mouth at her teats began to bring a sense of longing to her. She was trying to withhold evidence of her growing arousal. She held her breath, tried to keep her body still. But then she had to take a deep breath to compensate. It was followed by a sigh of pleasure. Just a small one, but evidently picked up by her assailant.

His lips pressed against hers and she dutifully allowed him to enter her mouth. She felt a surge of desire as their tongues intertwined. His hand drifted down her belly, careful to pass lightly over her bruised skin. She felt the hand capture her sex and a finger trace a line from the edge of her perineum to the top of her slit. It passed gently, but firmly. Her body shuddered. It passed back down and up again and she gave out an almost stifled moan. It lingered on her stiffened love button and her hips involuntarily shifted. It plunged within her and her eyes rolled back and she sighed.

Wang was pleased at the slut's response. He let himself slowly drift down her belly, dragging his tongue along her tortured skin until he reached her center of desire. He lapped his tongue along the path that his finger had taken once, twice, three times and she moaned again.

He took his time pleasuring her dilated pussy. He sucked gently on her little nubbin, dragged his broad tongue up and down her sex, plunged his tongue deeply within it. When he began to flick his tongue at her clit repeatedly, fluttering over it lightly, she groaned and began to pant. He let her rise to her heights and then he slowed his efforts, bringing her back down. He let her rise again, virtually to the point of explosion and then brought her back down once more. Now she was squirming and twisting her torso, her breath was heavy and she was moaning her delight. He licked the length of her slice once more in an upwards direction and then took hold of her rigid love button and sucked on it hard, flitting his tongue back and forth. Her wave of lust crested and broke. She cried out, "Oh! Oh! Oh! Yes! Yes!" as her hips bucked and her legs tried to draw him into her center.

He brought her over the top once more with his mouth and then, pushing her legs aside, mounted her. He held himself over her with his hands so as not to touch her scoured skin, their only point of contact his cock and her pussy. He plowed back and forth, his desires rising to the breaking point. She came again as his lips found her mouth. She sucked at his tongue hungrily. He felt himself approaching the point of no return. He placed his hands under her thighs and lifted them upwards. Like he had the Russian girl the night before, he slid from his concubine's hot crevasse and pushed his cock against her dainty ring, pressing himself forward. He was slower this time though, knowing that the girl was not yet accustomed to pleasure there. She moaned with pain as his thick cock strained the little ring to the breaking point.

General Wang waited until his slut had adjusted to the presence in her bowel. Her liquids on his cock had at least eased his path. Once he could slowly draw his cock back and forth without any sign of pain from her, he began to saw himself within her with relish. He looked down at her. Her eyes were wide and she was staring back at him. "There's a whole world in there," he thought. "She has a deep soul. Maybe I should learn more about her."

The thought passed quickly as his crisis loomed. His hand was on the slut's flush, soft pussy and he continued to agitate it as he fucked her ass. He groaned and his cock began to pulse and jerk. He could feel his throbbing prick jetting his cum deep within her. He increased his pace of fondling her clit and she too burst into orgasm. Their shouts of pleasure mingled and filled the room. Wang gave out one last, "Arrrrrrrrgh!" and he had exhausted his forces for the time being.

He saw the woman's chest rising and falling rapidly as she tried to recover from her bout of passion. Her beautiful face was flush, her nostrils flaring. She gave him a look that was both grateful and hostile. He was beginning to like her a lot.

Leaving the slut tied on the bed, Wang went to the bathroom and cleaned himself off. He returned to the bedroom and poured himself a glass of scotch. He enjoyed the British whiskey, a little more so since it was made by Scotsmen and not by Englishmen. It gave him a pleasant burning sensation as it descended his esophagus. He looked at the whore on the bed as he stroked his softened tool. He would be hard again in a few minutes if past experience were any indicator. He thought that maybe he would use her mouth again. He wondered how much better she would be with a hand on her pussy.

* * * * * * * * * * * * * *

Three months later, four women stood at a window of the concubines' quarters watching the general's steamboat work its way down river. Two of them, the Chinese girls, had thoughts of relief as they watched it go. The other two, the Russian and the Englishwoman, had feelings that were a little more complex.

Wang had used Violet every night for five days after her induction as his concubine. And sometimes during the day too. She had wondered why he had not discharged himself in her pussy until the day when the little old lady did not paint her love lips red. Then he emptied himself in there three times.

After the initial week, his use of her tapered off a little. He often had her pleasure one of the other women while he fucked another, or lick at Me Ling's pussy while she sucked him off. Or get licked by Pu Wei while he fucked the unhappy Chinese girl in the ass. He had beaten her badly a few more times, but the Russian girl, Tatiana, remained his preferred victim.

She fit into the routine of the concubine's quarters easily. The Chinese girls were of good nature and she had taught them how to play gin rummy. Her three maids took care of her daily and it was rare when they did not bring her pleasure. She usually insisted on responding in kind.

When Robert came, her life was hell for a week. He abused her savagely. He fucked her until she was raw and he had the Chinese slut whip her every night. After the week was out, he and the general went up to the mountain lake the general liked to visit to escape the June heat, and brought the two Chinese concubines with them.

A few days after they left, one of the maids, who spoke a smattering of English, brightened her day when she told her gleefully, "Qua Li in dungeon," pointing to the floor. The maids hadn't cared for her either. Clearly, Robert didn't want the tramp to interfere with his campaign to woo Antonia Hoover.

She was glad to see Robert go, but unhappy when he told her, as she was tearfully giving his cock a goodbye suck at his command, that he would be back in the fall.

Life was generally bearable when she wasn't getting fucked or whipped. Li Pao, she had learned his name, shaved her pussy every morning and brought her a delightful morning orgasm every time. Her puss would start watering when she leaned back and spread her legs. When she wasn't being used, he brought her and the other women off three times a day.

She romped with the other concubines often as well. The Chinese girls, using sign language, their hands and the faux cock of their master, began to teach her a few tricks that would help her better please him and avoid his whip.

Her special favorite was Tatiana. She had watched the girl moping around for about a month. While Violet was doing her best to learn Chinese, Tatiana had no interest in it. One day, she laid down her gin hand to the dismay of the Chinese girls and said "Voila!" She saw Tatiana turn her head. Then Violet asked, looking at her, "Parle vous Francais?"

The girl's face lit up like a candle. She had, it turns out, studied French in her conservatory before they fled Moscow and was virtually fluent in it. Violet had studied it at Cambridge and was not so much fluent, but she was learning fast. After that they became lovers. They spent every day side by side that they could. Violet loved to suckle her breasts. Li, seeing this, gave her the job of milking the pretty, young Russian girl at least once a day. While she was drinking her fill of the delicious nectar, she would caress Tatiana's delicate, plump love lips and make the girl produce shattering orgasms. Violet mourned for her when it was Tatiana's turn to service the general. With a foursome, she could now teach the others bridge.

Another daily ritual was a cup of the old Chinese lady's potent elixir. Its effect was to keep the concubines randy all day and into the night.

Only twice, so far, had Violet been forced to serve any of the general's guests. They were both following dinner parties. One was not too bad, a local merchant who Wang was trying to impress. The other, though was not so good.

He was a German major. He was there for the purpose of selling the general some weapons, a French 75 and the new German light machine gun. They had conversed in English, their only common language. Wang had her expose her breasts to the major all during dinner. Naturally, the major, who was staying several days, took her to bed with him. It turned out that the major lost two brothers in the trenches during the Great War, one at the Second Battle of the Somme and one in the final months of the war, shot by a sniper in his trench near Ypres. He detested everything English. Knowing this, Wang thought that he would enjoy abusing an Englishwoman for a few days. He did. He beat her with a riding crop unmercifully and he plunged himself into all of her orifices with rage and abandon. For his convenience, Wang had her kept naked in a little cage in his room so that he could retire there anytime he wanted to renew his campaign against her and all things British. Presumably, Wang got the best price available for the weapons.

About a week ago, Li Pao had started his attentions to her breasts designed to bring about her production of milk. Five times a day, she knelt in the middle of the communal room in the concubines' quarters, while Li massaged, stroked and suckled at her breasts. The idea was that she would be producing regularly when Wang returned.

The concubines were allowed to give each other pleasure almost any time they wished and they did so often. The rule was, though, that it had to be done in the communal room in front of everyone. In addition to the concubines, normally, there were two or three older women to act as caretakers and chaperones, as well as a bevy of maids. Each of them had three. What happened in their rooms between them and their maids was their business. One of the chaperones was teaching Violet mahjong.

The food was exquisite. The clothing was all silk, colorful, finely tailored. It was a proverbial gilded cage.

Both Tatiana and Violet were glad to see the abusive warlord go on his trip, although their back sides still burned from his obligatory, goodbye caning. Now there would be only his number one wife to deal with. This time, Wang had taken his number two wife on the trip and his number one was madder than a Tasmanian devil.

But sadness enveloped them as well. Violet thought about her English home and the things that might have been, the things she lost, how cruel Robert had been and how he had betrayed her. All of her heart wanted to be on that boat. The seraglio was so well guarded and the journey to Shanghai and freedom so long that she knew it was virtually impossible that she would ever escape. She thought about it though, from time to time, and had vowed that if she ever got the chance she would take it in an instant, regardless of the consequences.

So, Violet stood at the window, holding her blond lover's hand as she watched the steamboat round the bend that would take it out of her sight. She could not help but cry.

The End.